SOLITUDE

A SEAN COLBETH MYSTERY

SEAN COLBETH INVESTIGATES

BOOK SEVEN

CHRISTOPHER H. JANSMANN

Ephram Cotte
& Company
PUBLISHING

ISBN: 979-8-9858668-9-6 (Kindle Edition)
ISBN: 978-1-960914-17-0 (Paperback)
ISBN: 978-1-960914-18-7 (Hardcover)

Library of Congress Control Number: 2024913418

Printed in the United States of America

For Paula:
Your support through all of the endless hours spent staring at the screen mean more to me than you can ever know.

For Rocket:
May heaven allow you to finally catch that rabbit you've been chasing in your dreams. I miss you, my friend.

Books by this Author

Chronological Order

Blindsided

Pariah

Outsider

Peril

Ditched

Bygones

Downhill

Duality

Focus

Bewitched

Requiem

Vengeance

Mirage

Solitude

Masks

Sean Colbeth Investigates

Blindsided

Outsider

Downhill

Duality

Bewitched

Contents

ONE

I never tired of watching the stunning sunrises from the back porch of my bungalow. Its seaside location and nearly due East orientation ensured that I'd always have a front row seat to the best show Mother Nature could provide; while I tended to be at swim practice most mornings long before dawn, on the rare occasions I was home at that hour, I never missed a chance to grab a fresh cup of coffee and wander outside to marvel at the long tendrils of golden light as they crept above the horizon and slowly — ever so slowly — brought meaning to the world. Sunsets were no less enjoyable save for the fact they were more or less by inference only; the sky would subtly shift from that familiar ocean-infused cerulean into darker hues that allowed the tapestry of the stars above to sparkle into existence. Every now and again, the magic hour would become a breathtaking explosion in reds and periwinkle, a byproduct of pollution carried up from the larger cities further down the East coast. While many had tried — me included — no photo taken had ever done the experience justice.

Having spent time on the West coast visiting my best friend Vasily Korsokovach, I'd had my share of the unique sunsets only the Pacific Ocean could provide; nothing, perhaps, could top the evening we'd been in the hot tub at that cottage in Saint Lucie, watching the sun shift from gold to red as a pod of dolphins frolicked in the swells below. Those moments of transition — from night to day and vice versa — always heightened my sense of the relentlessness of the passage of time, something that had felt all the more acute to me as I closed in on my fortieth birthday. As much as it was just a number (and not a significant one, honestly), a small part of me had nonetheless begun to evaluate all I had done up to that point in my life, sorting everything into three buckets: accomplishments, desires and regrets. I imagined I was like anyone else facing the beginning of my middle-aged years and saw the level of accomplishments far below where I would have wanted — and regrets, in a similar fashion, overflowing.

Desires, on the other hand, seemed to be something of a black hole for me. Having spent most of my formative years as a competitive swimmer, I'd not been exposed to pop culture and its attendant materialism; there was very little I wanted in the way of treasure save for making that singular connection with another that would last to my dying breath. My first attempt at such a thing with my ex-fiancé Deidre Thibodeau was atop my sizable heap of regrets and had nearly been accompanied by my friendship with Vasily about a year earlier; the past two years hadn't seen me at the top of my game, relationship wise, and as the calendar turned to August, I was beginning to think the current year might well make it a trifecta.

That's what led me to be standing on a rocky outcropping hugging the shoreline of Carpenter's Island, sipping from a lukewarm Samuel Adams beer as I watched the sun slowly set behind Windeport village. It wasn't the first time I'd been to the largest island in Windeport Harbor, but most of my trips had been in my official capacity as Police Chief and had never involved an overnight stay. After losing my job with the Village — as well as being in somewhat ambiguous territory with my current girlfriend, Suzanne Kellerman — I'd been in the right frame of mind when an old friend from high school living on the island had come calling. Taking care of her dog while she dealt with an out-of-state family emergency had provided a reasonable excuse for me to escape what had become the claustrophobic confines of Windeport for a week or two, one that allowed me to ignore the real reason I wanted to get away from the Village.

Sipping from the beer, my eyes drifted from the periwinkle display on the horizon to the brown coated dog pleasantly lying on the rock beside my feet. Despite only having met Rocket a few days ago, he'd already adopted me as a member of his pack and had quickly become my constant companion during my wanderings around the small island. His wrinkled face and floppy ears spoke to some sort of Shar-Pei in his heritage, but the nose made me think of a Labrador Retriever my cousin had once owned. Sipping my beer again, I lamented the crazy hours of my chosen profession and my subsequent inability to care for a pet; I wasn't quite sure how Vasily had pulled off adopting a cat back in July other than the fact he could share the duties with his partner, Alejandro.

Thinking of the duo made me frown, for I'd thought I'd been on the same track with Suzanne right up until it was clear I wasn't. In fairness, the weird detente we were going through at the moment was mostly my fault; Suzanne had been telegraphing that while she cared for me deeply, her last relationship had left her with deep scars and a wounded heart that would take far longer to heal than I'd anticipated. My making what I thought was an innocuous suggestion we combine into a single household had blown apart our relationship; while we continued to talk, whatever connection we'd had appeared to have thinned enough that I'd dejectedly buried the engagement ring I'd bought deep in the sock drawer of my dresser, unsure of when I might retrieve it. If ever.

The lights from the homes along the shoreline of Windeport began to twinkle in the distance, my cue that I'd need to pick my way back to the path I'd taken to my vantage point before it became too dark to do so. Rocket seemed to sense my shift and slowly pushed himself off the smooth surface of the rock, then turned to follow me as I hopped from boulder to boulder, easily matching my moves with practiced ease from years of doing the same with his pet parent. In fact, Rocket had been the one to lead me to that particular spot; we'd been circumnavigating the eight-mile trail that hugged the perimeter of the island when he'd stopped, sniffed and then bolted into the brush. Alarmed that I'd lose my ward just a few days into my stay, I'd bounded through the branches only to find Rocket sitting expectantly on the other side, tail-wagging, with the setting sun just behind him.

Pressing back the branches, I heard the twigs snap beneath my sneakers and smelled the strange scent of the forest, that earthy mix of decay and rebirth that always felt so quintessentially Maine. Coming out to the trail, I needn't have bothered trying to get my bearings for Rocket swiftly turned left and headed back toward the more built-up portion of the island. Less than half a mile later, the path widened into something closer to a country lane, though it was barely big enough for the golf carts that appeared to be the primary mode of transportation on the island. The lights from the small fishing village that had grown up from the wharf where the mail boat had dropped me off a few days earlier lent a cheery ambiance to the warm evening, though the swarm of mosquitos that had descended upon me as soon as I'd entered the forest took a bit away from the experience.

The trail began and ended at a paved road that was oddly serpentine, given the rather level geography on that portion of the island; I knew the four-star private resort on the northern edge was on somewhat higher ground from the runs I'd taken around the island loop, but the difference in altitude could only have been on the order of a hundred feet, if that. My high school geology teacher had taught that most of the islands in Windeport harbor had been scraped away from the mainland by glaciers millions of years earlier; the idea that sheets of ice had so radically reshaped the shoreline had always fascinated me. Rocket kept pace as I headed back into the village, his head bobbing as he scanned the route for any potential threats. I smiled to think that I had been so thoroughly adopted, and smiled wider at just how unconditional the love radiating from my new canine friend was. There were many reasons why I was not looking forward to returning to the mainland in a few weeks; leaving Rocket behind was swiftly rising to the top of my list.

Village was a bit of a euphemism for the short block of businesses that faced the water and the modest marina arrayed around the single pier jutting out into the harbor. Slots for six vessels housed only two, a sign that fishing was no better a vocation on the island than back in Windeport. I walked past the waterfront and then stepped onto the raised concrete sidewalk that ran along the small commercial district; the two-story municipal building appeared to be holding some sort of meeting in the council chambers on the second floor, given the foot traffic and the lights from the windows above. The front doors for Bert's Cantina had been thrown open, allowing notes from some sort of jazz set to waft out into the night air to mingle with the heavy aroma of fried fish. A small grocery store that made my parent's pharmacy seem like it had been the size of a Walmart had already closed for the evening, and beside that was the satellite office for the Maine State Police. As a courtesy, I'd swung through and introduced myself to the young officer who was currently on rotation; he'd gone bug eyed at my appearance and had only relaxed — slightly — when I'd explained I was on vacation.

Rocket turned at the end of the sidewalk and guided me into the quaint residential portion of the area just outside of the village; nearly all of the homes were of the stereotypical island variety, that being small, white clapboard-sheathed single-story affairs crammed full of windows facing the ocean. My friend lived nearly at the very end of the row in a slightly larger A-framed version protected by an ornamental white picket fence. An effort had been made to maintain what little yard there was, though as I opened the gate, it appeared to my eye that the patch of green that was supposed to be grass had seen better days. I paused outside the screen door and reached down for the garden hose that was coiled beside it; part of my duties while taking care of Rocket included ensuring the picturesque window boxes under the windows were watered nightly. Gardening wasn't exactly my thing, but I'd been assured that it was hard to kill the petunias and snapdragons that were currently in bloom; that hadn't stopped me from inquiring as to whether replacements could be shipped in from the mainland just in case.

Twisting the handle to the spigot on, I wafted the shower-like gizmo on the end of the hose across the flowers, watching as carefully as I could under the dying light of the day to ensure I didn't drown anything. Rocket sniffed at an edge of the fence before circling back to me and settling down into his prone state, his eyes darting between my hand and the flowers I was watering. The overwhelming peace of the moment wrapped itself around me, emphasized by a quiet trickle of the water over the petals of the flowers; crickets in the forest beyond were barely louder than the whisper of the swells as they lapped up against the rocks just a few hundred feet from the gate. Turning my head, I could just see the edge of Windeport; squinting slightly, I thought I could make out the dark form of the cruise ship that was currently anchored between the island and village. I smiled slightly at the idea that I didn't have to deal with that particular form of hell any longer, though it was tinged with understanding that I did, in a way, miss it, too.

Movement at the edge of the fence caught my attention, and I shifted my gaze to the tall figure in typical jogging attire as it appeared out of the gathering darkness. I didn't need to glance at my smartwatch to know it was probably close to eight for my neighbor tended to leave around that time each evening like clockwork. The head lamp he wore for his nightly constitutional (his word, not mine) flashed in my direction, and I heard him clear his throat as he prepared to speak.

Deciding to beat him to the punch, I smiled and called out. "Evening, Charlie. Out for your walk, I see."

"Ayuh," was the dry reply. The sound of his walking stick as it tapped along the pavement in front of the cottage slowed as he approached the gate. "Weather looks to be turning," he added as he stopped and then rested his hands against the top of the gate. "Storms tomorrow."

I glanced upward at the dark sky. "I've not been following the forecasts," I said before reaching down to turn off the water. Crossing the short distance to the gate, I smiled. "Not that it matters, I suppose. Things tend to change on a dime in Maine."

"Ayuh," he nodded.

Charlie Kampert looked every bit of his seventy-six years, a result of having spent his life pulling lobster pots from the bay. I knew from our earlier conversations that he was a recent widower and had no immediate family on the island. The walks were something he and his wife, Annie, had done each night; it was perhaps a homage to his departed spouse that he'd kept up the pattern.

"Big doings up to the hotel," he continued.

"Oh?" I asked. Charlie, despite appearances, was also an incurable gossip. My friend had warned me the septuagenarian liked to talk; given my profession, I was predisposed to listen, so as far as Charlie had been concerned, he'd found a new friend with whom he could bend an ear.

"Ayuh," he nodded, the fading light picking up his white whiskers. "Tessa's kid is tying the knot with a girl from Boston."

I nodded, for the upcoming wedding had been all anyone on the island had been talking about. It was apparently bad enough that the young man had fallen in love with someone from out-of-state; that she was from Massachusetts had made it something of a scandal. "Is that *this* week?"

"Everyone arrives tomorrow," he nodded sagely. "Wedding is Saturday afternoon."

Blinking, it took me a moment to realize it was Wednesday; living in the timelessness that was the island had interrupted the internal clock I'd come to rely on rather badly. "What the hell are they going to do for two days?" I asked. "Don't take this the wrong way, Charlie, but there's hardly anything to do around here."

The older man laughed, a deep thing that made me concerned he might devolve into coughing. "That's why people stay up to the hotel," he reminded me. "To get away from everything."

"I suppose," I replied. "How big is the wedding party?"

"As big a crowd as the mail boat can carry," he answered.

Thinking back to the cramped compartment I'd shared with bags of letters and packages on my run out to the island, I nodded. "Not many, then."

"Nope. And if they miss the boat tomorrow, they'll miss the wedding."

"I find it hard to believe the boat only runs twice a week in this day and age," I said.

"There aren't many of us out here these days," Charlie replied. "Not counting the tourists, I think there are maybe fifty full-time residents; about that many summer on the island."

"But back in your heyday?"

"Oh," Charlie whistled. "Those weren't so long ago, honestly. Twenty years ago, it was two-hundred, two-fifty. Enough we had to build that school."

I nodded, for my runs had taken me past the now derelict building that had in better times housed the K-8 school. "I remember," I said. "The high school-aged kids had to come across to join us at Windeport Regional. The mail boat must have been far more frequent then."

"That it was." Charlie paused. "It's Prince Spaghetti Day tomorrow at the hotel," he continued. "I'm going to head there for a late lunch if you want to join me."

"Absolutely," I smiled slightly. "Though I didn't think anyone still referred to Wednesdays like that."

"The old ways die hard here," he laughed. "I'll pick you up at one."

"Sounds good," I replied. "Enjoy your walk."

"Ayuh," he nodded as he turned and then slowly disappeared into the darkness.

It had become dark enough that light from the small lamp I'd left on inside the A-frame had begun to spill out onto the small porch in front of the screen door. Returning to the hose, I coiled it up and then stepped to the door; the jingle of the license at Rocket's collar told me my companion was right behind me. Pulling open the screen door, I stepped aside to allow my canine friend to enter ahead of me; as he had the last few evenings, he paused just inside the door and scanned the great room for any changes since our departure. Not finding any, he traipsed across the hardwood floor to his wide dog bed lying just beside the hearth, climbed on top of it then proceeded to spin around three times before coming to rest facing me. The comfortable familiarity of his pattern was endearing, but I also knew I had a part to play at that point; smiling, I crossed to the open kitchen on the other side of the space and opened the ceramic container holding the dog treats Rocket favored. Pulling out two (despite knowing he was to only get one), I broke them up into smaller bits before carrying them back to my waiting companion and placing them just below his cushion. I'd barely made it back to the fridge to search for my own adult treat before Rocket had devoured the entire pile; I decided not to turn and verify that, for that was how we'd gone from one treat to two in the first place. His literal hang dog expression had been impossible to ignore.

The kitchen wasn't much more than a galley, really, and sported appliances from the 1970s. Julie had inherited the place from her folks when they'd moved to South Carolina about a decade earlier; much like my father, they'd left Maine in search of fairer weather and a more favorable tax situation. Pulling at the handle of the jade-colored fridge to pop the door open, I marveled a bit at the time capsule I was currently living in; while the burnt orange sectional in the living room was an appropriate match to the green-and-white shag carpeting in the bedroom on the loft above, the paisley wallpaper in the bathroom made me queasy each time I used the facilities. My bungalow had been a similar homage, albeit to the 1950s; with Suzanne's help, I'd spent the last year and half giving it a more contemporary feel.

Thinking of Suzanne made me frown slightly, and I shifted my focus back to the mission at hand. Scanning the shelves of the fridge, I pulled out the last of my Sam Adams and closed the door; I'd already planned on hitting the grocery store after my run in the morning, and mentally added beer to the bottom of my shopping list. Popping the top from the bottle, I turned and smiled to see that Rocket had already begun to snooze; if the pattern held, he'd awaken about the time I went up the steps to the loft to retire myself and would quickly relocate to his secondary dog bed beneath the window in the bedroom. Glancing at my watch, I knew I wasn't ready to turn in quite yet but was also at loose ends as to what to do until I *was*. I'd brought a laptop with me, but the internet was sketchy at best on the island; similarly, other than the rooms at the resort, cable television wasn't an option, either. Fortunately, there was a large console radio on the fireplace mantel, already tuned to the station out of Bangor that carried the Red Sox broadcasts. Knowing there could be worse ways to spend the evening, I flipped the unit on and then took up a corner of the couch I'd claimed as my own and sipped at my beer.

Between the dulcet tones of Joe Castiglione, the slight buzz from the beer and Rocket's gentle snoring, something inside me let go and I dozed off; I awoke with a start at the sound of a massive crash out in front of the cottage. Fully awake and completely in law enforcement mode, I pushed myself up from the couch and crossed to the screen door; there was a small flashlight on the table beside it which I grabbed before quickly exiting the cottage. Snapping on the light, I crossed the small front yard and pushed through the gate, headed in the general direction of a loud series of curses issuing from somewhere further up the road, curses that were hurled in tandem with random *clunks* of something heavy being dropped.

Waving the flashlight ahead of me, it didn't take long for me to find the cause of the commotion just in front of the last cottage on the lane. A significant amount of firewood in various shapes and sizes was strewn across the path; it wasn't hard to deduce they'd been thrown from the metal cart that a figure was hurriedly trying to refill with the debris strewn about them. *How* they'd been thrown was a bit of a mystery, though given the uneven grading on the lane, it was probable a tire on the cart had hit a rock or one of the many exposed roots I'd seen during my travels and had subsequently tipped over.

Pausing at the outer edge of the debris field, I held my light up in a non-threatening manner and called out. "Do you need a hand?"

The figure's head snapped in my direction, making it clear I had approached them unawares. "I wouldn't say no," was the reply after a considered moment. The voice was masculine and deep. "I hit a rock back there and lost my load."

"Bad luck," I said as I carefully approached. "Especially in the dark. Isn't it kind of early in the season to stock up on firewood?"

He chuckled. "I have an old-fashioned wood-fired brick oven at my place," he replied. "I make all of the bread for the hotel."

My eyebrows went up. "I ate there yesterday," I said. "Those rolls were yours?"

"Yes," came the reply.

"Take it from a guy who tries to avoid carbs... they were amazing. I couldn't get enough."

"Thank you," he laughed. "Though that has to be the strangest compliment I've ever received."

I shrugged. "Take it as high praise; swimmers always have a weakness for that sort of food."

My mysterious companion was close enough that I could see his eyes widen. "You're Chief Colbeth, aren't you?"

"Former Chief, yes," I said, holding out my free hand. "And you would be?"

"Régis," he replied as we shook. "Régis Delannoy. Everyone calls me Reggie, though."

"Nice to meet you, Reggie." I cocked my head at the way he pronounced his name. "That accent...?"

Reggie smiled. "French," he laughed. "Or what is left of it. I've been in the states longer than I lived outside of Paris, but I suppose some things never really leave you."

"That they don't," I replied as I balanced the flashlight on the edge of cart and began to gather up the wood.

"Are you here for the wedding?" he asked.

"No," I answered as I dropped my load into the cart and went to retrieve more. "I'm watching Julie Crabtree's place for a few weeks while she deals with some family issues down in South Carolina."

"I'd heard about that," Reggie said. "Her mother is getting a stint?"

"Yes," I replied. "Normally not a big deal, but there are other health issues at play."

"How do you know Julie?"

"We went to high school together," I said. "She swam with me on our club team for a few years, but basketball was more her thing."

"All-American at UMaine, right?"

"That she was," I nodded. "How long have you lived on the island?"

"A while," he replied easily.

I felt my eyebrows go up at the vague answer but decided to let it go. "Well, that seems to be about it," I continued as I placed one last piece of wood atop the impressive stack we'd piled into the cart. "Do you want help getting this back to your place?"

"No," he answered quickly. "I've got it from here. But thanks for the offer."

"At least take my flashlight," I said as I picked it up from where I'd balanced it on the edge of the cart and handed it to him. "You can return it tomorrow."

Reggie clearly dithered before taking it from me. "Thank you. I don't know when I'll get back down — are you sure you won't need this?"

"I think I saw another in the cottage, so I'm good."

"All right." He paused. "Thank you for your help."

"My pleasure."

I waited for a moment and watched as Reggie lifted the end of the cart and then began to push it down the lane; I had no idea how far he had to go and was tempted to follow him just in case, but I'd gotten the clear impression he didn't want the company. Of course, that had only piqued my curiosity, so I decided on the spot to adjust the route of my morning run to see if I could determine just where Reggie had his place.

It was a small island, after all; the odds that I'd literally run across him again were pretty good. I wondered a bit at why my investigative instincts had been triggered; while it was easy to assume I was simply looking for an excuse to slip back into my law enforcement persona, I'd been a detective long enough to trust my instincts and follow them where they led.

Wherever that might be.

Two

Rocket woke me with his cold nose just a hair before five-thirty the following morning; used to getting up far earlier for swim practice, it felt rather indulgent to have slept in. Not having ready access to a pool on the island helped assuage my guilt for missing several weeks of workouts; my open-water friends would have scoffed at that and handed me a wetsuit, but I'd never been one to enjoy doing laps amongst the seagulls and ocean swells. Besides, it was always hell getting the salt out of my goggles whenever I'd made the mistake of wearing them into the sea.

Rocket watched as I rolled out of the twin bed that barely held my six-foot-plus frame, then patiently waited while I changed into running tights and a muscle t-shirt. He trundled down the steps to the kitchen with me but betrayed his impatience by continuing to the screen door while I diverted to the fridge for my water bottle. Tail wagging, his expressive eyes followed my movements until I finally joined him at the door, whereupon he did a one-eighty and pressed his nose to the screen.

"I take it you're ready?" I asked with a chuckle as I pushed the door open.

Almost as if he'd understood me, he turned his face up to mine and hung his tongue out for a moment, then dashed through the open door. I grabbed a few poop bags from the bone-shaped cylinder sitting on the table by the door, slid them into the small pocket in my tights normally occupied by my iPhone and followed Rocket out into the dawning day. For early August, it was exceptionally mild; as I started the running workout on my smart watch, the air was thick with the salinity of the ocean. Pushing through the gate, I watched with no small amount of mirth as Rocket bounded out ahead of me on the lane, then paused to see if I would follow. Laughing, I nodded at him then dropped into an easy jog that I slowly began to ramp up in intensity. Julie had warned me that Rocket would expect to join me on my runs; he'd been accompanying her nearly from the day she'd adopted him. I'd been pleasantly surprised that he was able to keep up with me — at least, until I came across the medal Julie had won for taking second place in her age division at the Boston Marathon. My ego had thus been properly chopped down to size.

Heading up the lane was not the path I'd taken the past few days, but that didn't seem to matter to my canine companion. I followed him as the barely golf-cart-wide lane shrunk to something closer to a bike path as it entered a thick portion of the forest covering that end of the island. Pine straw littered the dirt path, deadening my footfalls and bringing a cathedral-like silence to the area; other than robins bobbing for worms and a random rabbit that darted across the trail, Rocket and I had the forest to ourselves. The quiet solitude was all-encompassing; while Windeport wasn't exactly a metropolis, it *did* have a certain rhythm and pace that was far faster than island life appeared to be. It was hard not to deny just how intoxicating it was, too.

The trail twisted a bit and then came out into a wide, grassy glen; after the semi-darkness of the forest, the vibrant dawning sunshine made me squint for a moment while I reached for my sunglasses. Slowing my pace slightly, I watched as Rocket paused to sniff a cluster of rocks on one side of the trail, then stopped altogether when he circled around behind them to do his business. Sighing, I pulled one of the bags from my pocket and then leaned down to clean up; while I wasn't thrilled to have to carry an extra load on my run, I knew from prior runs there were trash cans further up the path where I could make a deposit (as it were). Tying off the bag, I started to jog again, following both Rocket and the trail as it dove back into the shade of another portion of the forest.

As I ran deeper into the forest, I began to wonder if I had made an incorrect assumption as to the location of Reggie's home; it became more of a certainty when the forest thinned out to reveal the sparkling swells of the ocean. Barely a hundred feet later, I found myself back on the perimeter trail, heading toward the northern tip of the island. Pausing at the spot where my pathway through the forest had merged into the groomed trail, I didn't *think* I'd been so focused on my thoughts that I had missed any signs of habitation; looking at Rocket as he waited for me a few yards up the trail, I realized if I *had* missed something, my canine companion wouldn't have. Folding my arms against my chest, I felt myself frowning; I'd watched Reggie head down the lane with his load of firewood. I'd assumed his home wouldn't have been much further from where I'd met him, but it was clear that hadn't been the case.

I didn't dream the encounter, did I? I wondered to myself. *No... I didn't. The flashlight wasn't on the table this morning.*

Tapping a finger along my arm, I reset my assumptions and then started to jog once more. The ocean looked a little darker that morning, something I had learned long ago meant a storm was brewing somewhere in the distance. Squinting against the bright sun glinting off the water, I could just make out the white tinged waves at the edge of the horizon that portended a shift in the wind; I expected within a few hours, we'd have photo-worthy surf pounding the rocky outcropping I'd discovered with Rocket the night before. A slight incline in the trail brought my attention back to the path; as I passed the third mile of my run, the first of many trash cans appeared, and beside it, a small drinking fountain with spigots at both human and canine heights. Pausing my workout, I dropped the bag into a bin, then pressed the button to fill the small bowl Rocket had taken up position beside. In moments he was merrily lapping up the liquid, deftly working around pine needles I'd failed to clean from the dish before filling it. I remained amazed that such a small island had provided for pets in that way; in my travels, I'd often seen such accommodations in far more massive metropolitan areas like Los Angeles or Boston. Knowing the infrastructure alone had to have cost a pretty penny made me wonder how the island had managed to afford it in the first place.

At length, Rocket turned his damp face in my direction, a clear indicator he was ready for the next leg of our workout. Starting up my watch again, we both took off; it wasn't long before the trail exited the forest once more, though this time it was at the edge of a perfectly green fairway from the golf course at the hotel. Two golf carts were parked side-by-side at what looked like the tee for the hole in question; a trio of well-dressed players were patiently waiting for a fourth who was posed just above his ball. With a massive metallic *twang*, the player whacked at the ball, sending the small smidge of white up into the deep blue sky. From my vantage point, it was hard to tell where the ball came back down; judging from how the player angrily jammed his club back into the bag at the rear of one of the carts, it was somewhat clear the results were not as desired.

Such a fickle game, I thought. *Why anyone plays it is beyond me.*

Mile four found me passing along the edge of the shoreline in front of the four-star hotel. I wasn't entirely sure if the strange scoop of a lagoon just below the three-story building had been carved from the rocky coastline by the hotel or was naturally occurring. Given the dearth of white sandy beaches in Maine, I presumed the former; either way, it was an impressive spot that likely gave Kennebunkport a run for its money. Workers from the hotel were already out on the beach, raking the sand in spots or raising umbrellas over the pairs of lounge chairs facing the waves slowly rolling along the edge of the shore. A lifeguard appeared to be opening up the stand that stood watch over the area; his deep tan accentuated the red of his board shorts, indicating perhaps that he'd been on duty the entire summer. I had to slow to a stop where the paved path from the hotel intersected with the running trail so two more lifeguards could lug a sizable case of white-and-blue striped towels out to the sand; another set was right behind them wheeling a cart topped with multiple wide-bodied insulated water jugs of a sort we had used at the pool. Rocket seemed to be on a first name basis with one of the guards, of course, and insisted on saying hello to each and every one of them as they passed.

While he did his thing, I looked back up the slight hill to the hotel. I knew it wasn't as big as the Colonial on the mainland, but it still felt impressive; it was clear the white-clapboard exterior had been carefully looked after, as had the vibrant green of the lawn and the perfectly planted flower gardens along the path. I could see the wide patio that was just outside the restaurant; it had been a pleasurable experience dining out there the first night I'd been on the island, and I looked forward to having lunch with Charlie later that day in the same spot. Double doors beside that led to the main reception lobby, which was housed in a unique single-story structure sandwiched between the two multistory wings that appeared to contain the guest rooms. I'd not explored much of the hotel beyond that, given I wasn't a guest staying there, but knew from the brochure I'd snagged from the concierge that in addition to the pool and nine-hole golf course, there were also outdoor tennis courts and a perfectly manicured croquet court. Like everything else on the island, the resort felt like it was from a particular moment in time, perfectly preserved and yet paradoxically still fully functional.

Rocket nudged me along my thigh, and I reached down to scratch between his ears; the traffic (such as it was) had cleared, so I started to jog once more with my companion close by. The trail began to curve back toward the south, bringing me along the edge of a wide grassy area that hugged one wing of the hotel. I slowed slightly, for a large white canopy that had been erected a few yards from the building caught my attention; more workers appeared to be setting up large, round tables in the area beneath, surrounded by white plastic chairs that looked supremely uncomfortable. I didn't need to see the raised platform at one end to know I'd found the spot where the wedding would be taking place; twisting slightly, I could see why that spot had been chosen for it had a nearly unobstructed view of the ocean behind it.

"This is a rather picturesque spot for a wedding," I said to Rocket. "The only thing missing would be a flock of white doves."

He looked at me as though he'd understood, then hurried down the path, his tail held high in the air; it was a not-so-subtle reminder that he knew his breakfast was on the horizon — assuming, of course, his human remembered. I smiled and took off after him, increasing my pace so I could finish the last four miles at something closer to a workout than the just-barely-faster-than-a-walk we'd done for the first four. Rocket seemed able to keep up, though I kept a close eye on him, ready to slow down should he begin to look as though his energy was flagging. Aside from one additional water break, we made good time and arrived at my cottage just a bit before seven.

It took a few minutes for me to rustle up the items on Rocket's menu, but in short order he was happily snarfing down the ungodly concoction from a bowl that was labelled *Spoiled by Design*. I started a pot of coffee — Julie didn't believe in the benefits of a Keurig, apparently — then set about making my own breakfast. As the cottage also didn't have a microwave (seriously?), I'd been forced to make my oatmeal on the gas stovetop, old-school; toast was a similar adventure using the strange device that fit over a burner. *That* had been quite a challenge; my first morning trying to use the gizmo had resulted in a severely blackened piece of sourdough that even the seagulls had rejected. Consequently, I kept a close eye on the bread and turned it regularly. I'd picked up the loaf at the small grocer by the wharf as part of my initial supplies; unfortunately, they'd also had pints of beautiful local blueberries on sale that were impossible to resist. I'd bought two and stashed them in the fridge with the intention of using them with my oatmeal.

I'd just poured the oatmeal into a wonderfully sized ceramic bowl I'd found in the cupboard and was on my way to retrieve the blueberries when there was a knock at the screen door. Looking up from the counter, I wasn't entirely surprised to see Reggie standing there, shaded slightly by the fabric of the screen. Ignoring my cooling oatmeal for a moment, I went to the door and pushed it open.

"Good morning," I said with a smile.

"I hope I'm not interrupting," Reggie said. He was wearing a t-shirt bearing the logo for what looked like a rock band, and cutoff jeans; the shirt was tight enough that it was clear he worked out.

"No, not at all," I lied. "I've just made a pot of coffee. Could I offer you a cup?"

"Thanks, but no," he said, smiling. Reggie's teeth were perfectly perfect in the way that meant they had been adjusted; what was more striking were his gray eyes, an unusual color I'd rarely come across. They were a complementary match to his dark brown hair and fair complexion. "I just wanted to drop off the flashlight you'd loaned me."

I took the small device from him. "There was no need to return it so soon."

Reggie shrugged. "I was going right past your place this morning. It made sense to do it on the way."

I nodded. "You work down in the village?"

"No," he shook his head. "Like I told you last night, I do the baking for the hotel."

"Oh, right," I nodded again. "So, you did."

"I've got a batch in the oven at the moment, which meant I had time to get to the grocer for more flour."

"You must go through quite a bit of that."

"That I do," he smiled. He stared at me for a moment. "Well, thanks again."

"Anytime." As he turned to go, I impulsively spoke up. "Reggie?"

His tall form paused at the edge of the porch and turned back. "Yeah?"

"Would you mind if I checked out your oven?" I asked. "I've never seen one in action."

"There's not much to see," he said uncertainly.

I shrugged. "Still, it sounds fascinating."

Reggie looked at me for another long moment. "All right," he said. "Today isn't good — I have a ton of work to do still."

"Tomorrow, then?"

"That works," he nodded. "I'll be coming back down for more supplies in the afternoon and can take you back."

"I look forward to it," I smiled. "Thanks."

Reggie nodded again and then fled as though he'd been a wild animal I'd accidentally cornered in the front yard.

THREE

By the time Charlie picked me up in his golf cart for lunch, the storm I thought was coming had darkened the skies considerably and brought with it wind gusts that made eating on the outdoor patio at the hotel next to impossible. To my great disappointment, we were shunted instead to the quaint main dining room of the restaurant, which, while elegant in its own weirdly period-specific way, was not quite the same as having a front row seat as the tide turned. I wasn't all that surprised to see the space packed with patrons — after all, there were only two restaurants on the island in the first place — but that made the ambient noise loud enough it successfully drowned out my casual conversation with Charlie. I was therefore somewhat relieved when the dessert dishes were finally removed and my companion stood, clearly ready to return to his cottage. I similarly rose and followed him back out into the main lobby of the hotel, then spied the signs for the restrooms; having had one too many cups of coffee with my sumptuous meal, it seemed wise to make a pit stop before we made the journey back to the southern tip of the island, especially since the top speed of my dining companion's golf cart appeared to be about two miles an hour.

The thought of enduring another trip with Charlie motivated me to call an audible. Pulling him aside at the doors that led to the wide curved driveway at the front of the hotel, I smiled. "Lunch was amazing. Thank you for inviting me."

"Glad you enjoyed it," he replied.

"I enjoyed it a bit *too* much," I sighed, rubbing my stomach. "If it's all right with you, I think I'll walk back to my cottage. I need to work off that slice of cheesecake you talked me into."

Charlie grinned. "You didn't need much convincing, Mister Man," he replied.

"I suppose I didn't," I laughed. "If you are free later this week, I'd like to do it again."

"Sure," he smiled. "Just flag me down when you see me."

"Will do," I replied.

I watched him exit and begin to head over to where he'd parked his golf cart before I circled back to the men's restroom; re-emerging a few minutes later feeling a bit more comfortable, I took my bearings before heading toward the doors leading to the beach. The reception desk appeared to be dealing with an influx of guests, a clear indicator that the mail boat had likely delivered another round of wedding guests to the island; getting around them forced me into the small seating area for the lobby bar, which like the restaurant, seemed to be doing a brisk business. I'd quite nearly tacked around the worst of the mess before I realized someone was calling my name.

"Sean?"

Pausing at the edge of the carpet that delineated where the bar ended and the lobby began, I turned and scanned the bar patrons, uncertain if I'd been hearing things. My eyebrows went up when I caught sight of a familiar face standing at one end of the polished bar; the short woman with long, naturally blond hair was wearing a half-surprised expression that quickly turned into a full smile. Reversing course, I worked my way back through the crowd and took up a spot beside her at the bar.

"Corinne? Corinne *Wallace*? What the hell are you doing here?"

"Attending a wedding, it seems," she sighed as she put her drink down and pulled me into a hug. "Damn," she said after releasing me, "it's been a while."

"It has," I nodded. "How long has it been? Was it, what, five years ago I consulted on that case for you?"

"Seven, actually, but who's counting," she laughed.

I felt my face flush slightly. "Time flies, clearly," I replied. "Are you still working in Riverside?"

Corinne nodded. "I've moved up to Deputy Chief, actually. My mentor retired two years ago; my penance for past transgressions is, apparently, being forced into management."

"That is always the way," I laughed. "I had a friend tell me once that all great teachers wind up being promoted out of the profession they love; I've long felt that was true for law enforcement as well."

"Case in point," she smiled as she tapped her chest. "Are you still in Windeport?"

"Not exactly," I replied, which caused her to raise her sculpted eyebrows. "I had a bit of a kerfuffle with the Village Council, and they cancelled my contract back in July as a result."

Corrine's eyes went wide. "Shit."

"It gets better: they fired all of my staff, too, and outsourced all Public Safety functions to the County."

"That sounds like a bad decision."

"It was," I nodded. "I'm out of the loop, of course, but my spies tell me the County overtime tab is larger than my fiscal budget *ever* was."

"Serves them right," she laughed, then looked at me. "You can't possibly have retired."

"I didn't," I shook my head. "As it happens, I'm going to work for the State next month rebuilding their Major Crimes unit. I've already hired back all of my people, but I have a few spots open still if you're looking for a change of scene."

"It snows here," she frowned. "And I don't think Marco would enjoy the cold."

I had to search my memory for a moment. "Your boyfriend was playing for the Major League Soccer team based in LA when I was there, wasn't he?"

"You have a good memory," she smiled. "Marco is still with them, but this is his last year; his mother is pulling him back into the family business whether he wants to go or not."

"I presume the two of you are still together...?"

She held up her ring hand and angled it so I could see her diamond. "You could say that."

"Nice!" I laughed. "And congratulations. When are you tying the knot?"

"Next April," she replied. "Marco has a ton of family in Mexico City; finding a date that they can all get to the States together was difficult."

"I can imagine." I leaned closer and lowered my voice. "It might be easier to elope, though."

"Don't think we've not considered it," she chuckled. "Save for the fact that Marco's mother would personally kill us, then dig us back out of our graves and kill us *again*."

"Sounds like a woman not to be trifled with."

"Exactly." Corinne looked around the lobby. "Are you here for this madness, too?"

"Me?" I asked. "No. I'm actually watching a friend's dog for a few weeks; I had no idea until yesterday that this watershed event was taking place."

"Lucky you," Corinne sighed.

"You know the family?" I asked.

Sipping dark liquid from her tumbler, she nodded. "I'm the fucking Maid of Honor. The bride was my roommate at UCLA."

"You sound excited," I deadpanned.

Corinne smiled slightly. "I hate weddings. Always have. And while Dot and I were good friends in college, we haven't exactly kept in close contact since." She sipped from the tumbler again. "As you are well aware, careers in law enforcement generally make it hard to get away; I think I've been to Boston twice since we graduated, and she visited me out in California once. To say I was shocked when I got the invitation would be a bit of an understatement."

"I think you might be underselling what you mean to your friend," I observed.

"Maybe," she replied. "Don't get me wrong: I still consider myself her friend, just not one good enough to have been tapped to be the Maid of Honor."

There was something in her expression that told me it was a subject she didn't necessarily want to continue with; smiling, I changed directions. "What do you know about the groom?"

"Only that he helps runs this hotel for his mother," Corinne replied. "I'm not entirely sure, but I think his father passed away when he was a teenager, so he's more-or-less been part of the family business since then."

I searched my memories and frowned. "I remember that, actually. I'd not been running Windeport P.D. all that long when the call came in for us to wake old Dr. Phillbert and get the Harbormaster to run him out to the island."

"They must have had a doctor on the island," Corinne said.

"Physicians are few and far between in this part of the state," I said. *Just ask my girlfriend.*

"I'll keep that in mind," Corinne laughed. "Anyway, he met Dot last year at some sort of hospitality conference they were both attending in Atlanta; she's a regional sales manager for one of those firms that provides towels and other sundries to hotels." Corinne rolled her eyes. "Not that she needs to work."

My eyebrows went up. "Don't tell me: Dot's part of the Beacon Hill set?"

"Exactly," Corinne sighed. "Old money, too, dating all the way back to the Revolution."

I glanced at the crowd still checking in at the hotel. "They can't be all that thrilled she's marrying an innkeeper, then."

"Not in the slightest," Corinne confirmed before waving at the line for reception. "This is just a fraction of the society set down there; in some ways, it was a stroke of genius to hold the wedding in a location that had a hard capacity cap."

I thought again of how crowded the mail boat had to have been. "Indeed. Even with this reduced attendance, I'm going to need a bingo card to keep people straight."

"I can help with that," Corinne said, then began pointing at members of the crowd. "That older couple there, the one with the woman who looked like she's been sucking a lemon?"

"I see her."

"Those are Dot's grandparents. They apparently interrupted their endless summer on Cape Cod to be here."

"Guess they didn't like swapping one beach for another," I observed dryly.

"Agreed." Corinne nodded at a slightly younger couple behind them. "Those two are her parents. Her mom is a full-time socialite."

"I didn't know that was still a thing," I replied. "At least, not in this day and age. Makes me think of women in layered dresses sitting around dishing on each other over tea in the drawing room."

"These days, it would be a side table at an upscale Starbucks," Corinne laughed. "But the concept is still the same."

"The more things change," I sighed.

"Indeed." Corinne nodded to the man beside Dot's mother. "Her father manages the family's money, which is to say he drops by the bank every now and then to verify the number of zeroes on the statements."

I glanced sidelong at Corinne. "You don't seem to like Dot's family very much."

"Save for her, they're all pretentious pricks," Corinne replied. "When Dot expressed interest in going to college, they threatened to cut her off from everything. She was supposed to marry one of the many trust fund babies that attended her cotillion and have a flotilla of babies, not get an education and do something in the world.”

“Heavens,” I chuckled. “A heretic.”

“In more ways than one,” Corinne smiled. “My friend somehow managed to get out of that life unscathed and has been quite successful. She deserves a little happiness after all of that.”

The wistfulness in her voice wasn’t hard to hear. “Everything all right between you and Marco?” I asked.

Corrine’s face flamed slightly. “Oh, we’re going through a bit of rough patch,” she replied. “What couple doesn’t?”

The tone of her response told me it wasn’t a line of inquiry to pursue, so I let it go. “Who are those women waiting beside Dot’s mother?”

“Ah,” Corinne smiled. “One is the spinster aunt who lives with the family at the mansion in Boston. The other is the lady’s maid for Dot’s mother.”

“Lady’s maid? *Seriously*?” I asked.

“Yep,” Corinne nodded. “I suspect the husband’s valet is unloading the luggage from the golf cart out front.”

“Why do I feel like we’ve stepped through some sort of time warp and landed back in the nineteenth century?”

“I did say they were from old money.”

“No kidding.”

I started to make another dry observation about how times had changed when the elegant woman identified as the aunt happened to turn her gaze in my direction; I didn’t think the look of distaste in her expression was especially tied to me, but rather the general circumstances she apparently found herself in. It was clear she had standards, and that we were all well below them. The amount of privilege and, frankly, sanctimoniousness in the look was a little breathtaking, even for someone who found himself frequently disdained for being in law enforcement. I wasn’t sure the island was big enough to ensure we didn't cross paths, but even so, I made a mental note to avoid her at all costs.

"This appears to be quite the family," I finally said.

"Imagine being born into it," Corinne said as she smiled at me. "I'm glad I ran into you; besides Dot and her immediate family, I don't really know anyone attending the wedding. It's nice to have a friendly face in the crowd."

"I remind you I'm not on the guest list," I said.

"I can fix that. I'm allowed a plus one, and as it happens, my plus one is back in California."

"I don't have anything to wear," I objected. "And before you tell me I can run home to get one, the mail boat won't be back until the weekend."

"Well, it was worth a shot," she sighed. "Are you still swimming?"

"Normally twice each day," I nodded, "though I'm taking a bit of a hiatus since the island doesn't have a pool I can use. I'm running instead."

"There's a one here at the hotel," Corinne replied.

"True. It's probably not long enough," I smiled. "And I'm not a guest."

She looked at me. "Are you honestly going to tell me you didn't pack a Speedo?"

I smiled sheepishly. "I cannot tell a lie," I replied.

Downing the last of her drink, Corinne waved to the bartender to get her bill. "Come with me, then," she said as she handed him her credit card. "If it's long enough — I recall you were rather picky on the yardage out in Riverside — you can have my spare room key and use the pool."

"Corinne—"

"I won't take 'no' for an answer," she smiled as she signed the receipt and then stood.

Against my better judgement, I followed Corinne from the bar and out into the still busy lobby area; she paused to take her bearings, then crossed the short axis of the lobby to a corridor I'd not caught on my first walk through the space. Judging by ornate doors and small numbered placards beside them, it appeared we were passing through the first floor of the south wing of the hotel; at the first intersection we encountered, Corinne paused, then turned left, leading me past a small elevator alcove and to a double glass door that clearly exited the building. Pushing the door open revealed a short stone walkway that ended in front of an ornate metal gate; even under gray overcast skies, the water in the pool just beyond looked like a sparkling oasis. Digging her room key out from a pocket of her jeans, Corinne pressed it to the reader beside the gate, allowing it to open with a metallic *clunk*; pulling at the handle, she held it open and waved me in.

I passed through and then paused on the strange lime-green tile of the pool deck to survey the facility. The view of the ocean from the deck was nearly stunning despite the glowering clouds; it was easy to see how guests could while away their day on one of the many lounge chairs facing the crashing waves, watching as people waded into the surf or walked along the island path that hugged the curve of the cove. Given the weather, both the beach and the path were not as busy as I suspected they ordinarily might have been; a slight gust of rawness from the sea reminded me why I'd not eaten on the patio with Charlie. It took more effort than I'd expected to return my attention to the pool; to my surprise, half of it appeared to have been partitioned off for lap swimming, with space for four generously sized lanes. The other side was wide open, possibly to accommodate anyone wishing to simply frolic in the water. Three lanes were currently in use with people slowly churning through various strokes, while the fourth sat empty. Having spent a fair amount of my life around pools, I quickly determined this particular one was around twenty-five yards — just about perfect for many of the workouts I had committed to memory. I started to smile as I turned to Corinne.

"You'll take the key," she observed before I could speak.

"I will," I laughed. "Don't get me wrong: the running paths on this island are amazing, but I'd far prefer to be in the water."

"I hesitate to point out we are *surrounded* by water," Corinne observed. "Which I would think would suit you, since you're part fish and all."

"I'm not a fan of open water swimming," I replied. "There's something about not being able to see the bottom that always freaks me out. That and needing a wetsuit for water so cold."

Corinne arched an eyebrow. "I thought you surfed?"

"I do," I nodded. "That's different."

That eyebrow arched higher. "I would love to hear your tortured explanation of why, but I'm afraid I need to get ready for the bachelorette party."

I smiled. "Maybe another time. I'm sure I'll be back here for lunch again tomorrow."

"I might have a better idea," Corinne said as she looked at me thoughtfully. "If I bought lobster, would you host me for lunch at your cottage?"

"Detective, are you trying to escape from your duties as Maid of Honor?"

"Most definitely," she replied with a smile. "Shall we say noon?"

"I'll be honest, it's been a while since I've cooked lobster," I hedged. "You might be safer having one of the lobster rolls at the restaurant here."

"I'm willing to take the chance," she laughed.

"Won't you spoil your rehearsal dinner?"

Corinne rolled her eyes. "The outfits I have to wear for both that *and* the wedding are so form fitting, I'll be lucky to be able to sip a little wine. This might be the last real meal I get before the festivities get underway. Indulge me. Please."

"All right," I nodded with a smile. "I'll have to go to the grocer for supplies; how about I meet you there? Say, around 11:30? Then we can walk up to the cottage together."

"Deal," she replied before handing me the keycard she was still holding. "Not that this is a *quid pro quo*, but here you go."

"Thanks." I glanced toward the beach as I slid the plastic card into the pocket of my shorts and felt my eyebrows go up as I caught sight of a familiar figure. "I guess the show must go on," I murmured.

Corinne caught my glance and looked in the same direction. "Someone you know?"

I shrugged slightly. "That's Reggie," I said as we watched the young man push his cart along the walking path. Based on how he appeared bent to his task, I assumed the cart was fully loaded with that day's bread delivery for the hotel. "I met him by accident last night when his cart accidentally overturned in front of the cottage. He's a baker and provides fresh bread to the hotel." I frowned slightly. "I'm surprised he's making a delivery at this hour, though. I'd have assumed it would arrive earlier in the day."

"With the wedding and the increased number of guests staying here because of it, I wouldn't be surprised if they have him doing double duty," she laughed. "Kind of a cute hunk, isn't he?"

"That's more Vasily's department than mine," I deadpanned, knowing that Corinne had worked with him a time or two as well.

Corinne laughed. "I suppose so," she replied. "Funny you should mention him; I ran into Vasily at one of those stupid tri-county Public Safety meetings the week before last. I had no idea he was engaged."

"It's a fairly recent development," I smiled. "I've been helping his fiancé plan the wedding, but we've not made much progress."

"Encourage him to hold it someplace warmer than Maine," Corinne replied as she wrapped her arms around her blouse. "The beach is just as beautiful in Southern California, honestly."

"I don't think that will be a problem," I laughed before looking at my watch. "I'd better get going; Rocket will be looking for his afternoon walk."

"Then I won't delay you any further." Corinne looked at me for a moment, then surprised me by leaning up and quickly kissing my cheek. "It is *really* good to see you, Sean."

I thought I saw something in her eyes that made me immediately uncomfortable — despite whatever was going wrong between Suzanne and myself, the last thing I was looking for was someone else to help me drown my sorrows. It was painfully clear that Corinne was searching for *exactly* that, and thought she'd found a likely candidate. I smiled as gently as I could before replying.

"I hope you can work out whatever is wrong between the you and Marco," I said quietly.

Corinne got a wry look, then nodded at what had remained unspoken. "Hope springs eternal."

"Do you want to talk about it?" I asked. "I'm not exactly an expert on broken hearts, but I can promise an empathetic ear."

"Maybe," she sighed, then looked at me again. "I'd appreciate that, actually."

"Then I look forward to seeing you tomorrow."

Four

I found Rocket was indeed waiting patiently for me on his dog bed when I returned to the small cottage; by then, a light drizzle had begun, so I dug through my bags to retrieve my waterproof anorak before heading back out. Seeming to sense that a deluge was imminent, Rocket made short work of our walk and managed to get us back to the cozy confines of the A-frame just as the rain began in earnest. The temperature plunged as the front moved over the island, dropping low enough that I decided to start a fire in the hearth to drive away the worst of the rawness. Rocket seemed to appreciate my efforts, for after I got the small blaze underway, he settled in with his nose facing the dancing flames, let out a huge sigh then quickly nodded off once more.

For my part, I spent the rest of the afternoon with my laptop balanced upon my lap, working through the long list of things that needed to be completed before I took over as Commander for the statewide Major Crimes unit. As questionable as the internet connection was, I could do little more than review the documents Captain James Roberts had sent over and then type up my action items in the word processor; it seemed fortunate I wasn't on duty, for my only connection to the mainland was the fully functional retro Trimline phone sitting on the table beside the couch. I wondered if the satellite office for the Maine State Police had more solid broadband; at that point, tin cans connected via string would have been better than the sketchy data plan my wireless carrier had assured me worked "everywhere in Maine." Since I was going to be down in the village in the morning, I figured it couldn't hurt to pop my head in and chat with the young officer running the operation and see what my options might be — even though I wasn't actually working. Yet.

Who am I kidding? I thought with a snort. *I've been on the clock from the moment I accepted the offer from Jimmy…*

I took a break to make a BLT sandwich with the amazing sourdough bread I'd picked up from the grocer for dinner, then fed Rocket before returning to my list; when my back began to ache from being hunched over the laptop, I decided it might be best to call it a day. Setting the laptop onto the small coffee table, I stood and stretched my arms upward as though I were prepping for a racing dive and smiled with satisfaction as the tension eased slightly in my back. The fire had burned down to glowing red embers; Rocket raised his head questioningly as I raked them to oblivion, then leisurely rose to follow me up the steps to the loft.

The roofline allowed for a strange skylight just over the bed; for the first few nights, I'd been treated to watching shooting stars as I drifted off to sleep, but with thick storm clouds overhead and rivulets of rain drifting down the glass, it appeared I wouldn't see anything that particular evening. Not that it mattered; I dropped into a deep slumber the moment my head hit the soft pillow, only to be startled awake by a massive clap of thunder around two the next morning. Brilliant bursts of lightning filled the space, bright enough that I actually found myself squinting each time it happened. Between the screams from the wind as it whistled around the eaves of the house and the percussive blasts of thunder, it was nearly impossible to get back to sleep. I gave up a bit after three and grumpily went back down into the kitchen to make some coffee so I could ride out the rest of the storm; settling into the couch, I was slightly surprised when Rocket jumped up beside me, then more surprised when he tentatively put his chin on my thigh. Scratching behind his ears, I realized his eyes had gone wide and he was panting; ignoring the drool as it dribbled down my leg, I patted him on the head and whispered into one of his floppy ears that all would be well in a few hours. He seemed to understand and at length allowed himself to drift back into whatever dreams canines had; I suspected more than one might involve chasing the rabbits he'd been keenly aware of during our last morning outing.

Somewhere along the line, I managed to nod off myself; the brilliant mid-morning sun streaming through the windows facing the ocean ultimately woke me once more. Blinking the sleep from my eyes, I frowned when I realized I'd slept through both my morning run and breakfast; looking down at Rocket, he was still solidly snoozing and therefore oblivious to the fact that we had yet to go for his walk. Doing some mental calculations, I decided if I planned properly, Rocket and I could still do the island circuit before meeting Corinne in the village; I took a quick shower, shaved, then woke up the poor, tired pooch to give him the chance to eat his breakfast before we left. I wasn't surprised at how quickly he snarfed down what was in his dish; by the way he eagerly joined me at the front door, I knew he was more than ready for the main event.

The clear day showed no traces of the storm that had ravaged overnight, though we did have to step around more than a few tree limbs that had dropped across the island trail. Just before we emerged into the clearing by the hotel, we came across a large pine tree that had not been able to withstand the pounding from the gale force winds; falling parallel to the trail, it created an unusual wall that Rocket insisted on investigating thoroughly. Despite that, we made good time and still managed to arrive at the edge of the small fishing village with twenty minutes to spare.

The rumble that issued forth from my stomach was a loud reminder that I'd skipped my own breakfast; the delicious smells coming from the small café nearly tempted me through the open doors of Bert's Cantina, but visions of lobster with all the trimmings danced in my head and kept me on the straight and narrow. After letting Rocket tank up at another of the unique pet-and-human water fountains that had been stationed outside of the grocer, I hooked his lead to posts that had been erected for just such a purpose, then went into the small shop. Grabbing a rather tired-looking hand basket with faded red paint, I began to work my way up and down the cramped aisles, searching for vittles to accompany my main course. Fortunately, fresh ears of corn from a farm in Windeport had arrived on the overnight supply boat; putting several into my basket, I shifted my attention to the new potatoes stacked in a nearly perfect pile beside them and instantly decided to have potato salad as a side dish. Mentally trying to recall my mother's recipe, I snagged some scallions and a clove of garlic; I had leftover bacon I could cook and crumble into the mix but needed Miracle Whip and some vinegar for the sauce, two items not normally found in the produce section.

Looking up, I scanned the hand-lettered signs that were hovering over the handful of aisles and realized they were no help at all. Sighing, I hefted my now-heavy basket and rounded the corner where the produce department intersected with the smallest pharmacy counter I had ever seen — and then came up short, for Suzanne was standing there conversing with the gray-haired pharmacist. I didn't realize I'd let out a sight gasp of surprise until her beautiful blue eyes turned in my direction; the gentle smile she'd been wearing shifted into something less welcoming when she recognized me. Despite suddenly wishing for an island-wide emergency that would have given me cover to drop my basket and flee the premises, I steadied my nerves and took a step toward her, trying to smile but knowing it probably looked less than tentative at best.

"Suzanne," I said when I felt I was close enough (and had regained my vocal abilities). "I didn't know you were on the island."

Those expressive eyebrows of hers twitched. "Nor I, you," she replied. "How long have you been here?"

The reproachful tone of voice was hard to ignore; while I hadn't been secretive about my escape from Windeport, neither had I thought she'd be interested in knowing where I had gone. I'd deduced from the uncomfortable conversation we'd had the night she'd returned from Portland Suzanne wanted time and distance to figure out where we stood with each other. From the look on her face, it was clear she was more than a little annoyed at my sudden disappearance from the mainland; waves of confusion washed over me, for I was rarely wrong when reading people.

Then again, I thought morosely, *I'm oh-for-three when it comes to people I love.*

"I came over Sunday," I answered. "I'm babysitting a dog for a friend."

Suzanne eyed me for a moment, appraising me with the same coolness I knew she used when reviewing a patient chart. "I'd heard you had some time to kill before you started your new position with the State. Interesting way to spend it."

"The solitude has been refreshing," I said, allowing my irritation over her view of which of us was failing at communication to add a little bite to my response.

The way her eyes widened for a moment told me the message had been received. "There are times when everyone needs to be alone," she added after a moment. "I imagine Carpenter's Island has fit the bill quite nicely for you."

"It has."

She glanced at my basket. "Stay away from the blueberries," Suzanne said as she turned her eyes back to mine. "That's the reason I'm here."

I felt an eyebrow go up. "You're here because of *blueberries*?"

"I'm not completely certain yet, but a batch used in a fruit dish at the hotel last night appears to have taken out half the guests with symptoms akin to food poisoning. I was lucky enough to be the doctor on call when the County Sheriff came knocking on my door this morning."

My other eyebrow went up. "Suze, you're the *only* doctor for miles in any direction."

"Also true," she chuckled. I felt my heart skip a beat at the welcome sound. "The Harbormaster ran me over at dawn."

"How bad is it?"

"Bad," she sighed. "I'm halfway through checking the patients, but the symptoms are consistent — and only afflicting those who had the fruit dish." Suzanne nodded to the pharmacist who had tactfully stepped away from the counter to give us some privacy. "I wanted to cross check with Madge to see what she had in stock that I can use to treat the victims before I go any further."

I glanced at the single set of shelves showing the prescription drugs on offer. "I am going to go out on a limb here and say she doesn't have what you need."

"Not hardly," Suzanne frowned. "She's calling the Rite Aid on the mainland to see what they might be able to spare; the Harbormaster has already agreed to bring anything over that I might need — or take anyone back to be treated at my clinic or the hospital."

"Could it get that serious?"

"Not usually, but you never know," she said, but her grim expression spoke volumes. "I'll be here for a bit treating them."

No small part of me wanted to offer up the cottage for her, but I managed to squelch the offer. "Staying at the hotel?" I asked diplomatically.

"Yes," she nodded. "For a few days, at least."

"I hope it's not longer than that," I said before realizing how it might sound. Something crossed her face, telling me I'd inadvertently scored a direct hit.

Suzanne's expression hardened. "Well, I'd better get back to it."

"Good luck," I replied lamely.

We looked at each other for an uncomfortable moment; I made the first move and gracefully withdrew. Fortunately, the particular aisle I had chosen contained my final two ingredients which I quickly dumped into my basket before hurrying to the single checkout lane. Escaping into the daylight, I tried to set aside the roiling emotions in my stomach as I placed my bags on the sidewalk so I could untie Rocket from the post. For a couple whose lives had been so closely intertwined for more than a year, the abrupt halt to our relationship had left me with a gaping hole in my soul and a heart that felt like it had been torn to shreds. I'd thought I could repair everything that night in my bungalow — the night Suzanne had courageously revealed the horror that was her ex-husband. As time had passed, though, I'd become less and less confident there was any chance to return to the love I had once known.

Wrapping the leash around a hand, I rebalanced the bags and then started for the edge of the village with the assumption I'd meet Corinne just as she arrived. My timing appeared to be off, however, so I was forced to retreat to a small bench below a grizzled looking oak tree to wait for my friend's arrival. The temperature had remained pleasant despite the pending arrival of the noon hour; a gentle breeze from the ocean behind me carried the unique scent of the sea, and I closed my eyes for a moment so I could consider just what kind of an idiot I had been. Rocket stirring at my feet had me blinking them back open to see Corinne standing just above me, a slight smile on her lips.

"You look exhausted," she said as she moved to sit next to me. I scooted over to give her room. "I didn't think shopping would take that much out of you."

"The storm kept me awake last night," I replied. "Rocket slept more than I did, I think."

"I heard some thunder, but the time difference between here and the West coast finally caught up with me. I was dead to the world until breakfast."

"Nice." I was suddenly struck by a thought. "Wasn't the bachelorette party last night?"

Corinne rolled her eyes. "Such as it was, yes," she sighed. "We pretty much sat around eating canapés and staring at each other. I left the first chance I could get."

"And you feel okay this morning?"

Her smile widened. "I can hold my liquor," she said. "As you well know."

I waved at her response. "No, it's not that. I heard through the grapevine that a bout of food poisoning hit guests at the hotel."

"That would explain why they only had cold cereal and toast at the restaurant this morning," Corinne replied. "But no, I feel fine. I munched mostly on the nuts the bar put out, honestly. I'm not one for those fancy desserts or heavy hors d'oeuvres."

"Unless it's jalapeño poppers, if I recall correctly."

"Well, yes, *except* for those," she chuckled. "I *am* surprised you remembered that."

"I still have the scars at the back of my throat, so yes, I still recall the day you introduced me to them."

"They aren't supposed to be made out of ghost peppers," she replied, her face shading slightly.

"So they tell me," I laughed. "Shall we get our victims from the fish monger?"

"Sure," she nodded as we both stood. "I've been looking forward to this, actually. The lobster out in Southern California just isn't the same."

"There are firms that ship lobsters nationally," I said as we retraced my steps.

"At a pretty penny," she laughed. "I'm just a poorly paid municipal employee."

"Aren't we all. And we're going to pay tourist—"

My sentence died when I saw Suzanne standing on the sidewalk in front of us, arms crossed. For a moment, I thought she was still pissed at my parting shot in the grocery store; it quickly dawned on me what it might look like as I walked toward the wharf with another woman by my side. Irritated that — despite how well she knew me — Suzanne seemed to have immediately thought the worst, I decided to try and short circuit whatever was going on in her head before it went too far. The frown was hard to hide when I came to a stop where she was waiting.

"Suzanne. Twice in the same day."

"Indeed," she replied icily, her eyes flicking to Corinne.

Picking up on the uncomfortable undercurrent, Corinne surprised me by smiling and holding out her hand. "Corinne Wallace," she said as they shook. "Chief Colbeth and I worked a case in Southern California a number of years ago."

"*Doctor* Suzanne Kellerman," Suzanne replied, weirdly emphasizing the honorific. Her eyes narrowed as she continued. "What brings you to Carpenter's Island?"

"Wedding," Corinne replied. "My college roommate is tying the knot."

"Up to the hotel?" Suzanne asked.

"Yes."

Something shifted in Suzanne's face. "Were you there last night?"

"Yes," Corinne continued, shooting a glance at me.

"And you feel all right?"

"I do," she replied. "Sean was telling me something about guests having food poisoning...?"

"About half of the guests, yes," Suzanne replied thoughtfully. "Look, would you allow me to examine you? I'm relatively certain I know what the cause was, but your movements last night — where you ate and drank in particular — could help confirm my theory."

Corinne looked at me again. "Of course."

"All right," Suzanne said. "The hotel loaned me a golf cart that I parked around the corner; I've got a temporary exam room up at their facility—"

"You want to do it *now*?" I asked, feeling my jaw drop open.

Suzanne's head snapped in my direction. "You of all people know how critical time is to any investigation, *Commander*," she replied before turning to Corinne. "If you'd come this way...?"

Corinne looked at me somewhat helplessly. "Raincheck?"

I nodded. "Absolutely."

Shooting one final look in my direction, Suzanne took Corinne by the arm and hurried her down a small alley between two of the buildings; in moments, I was left standing on the sidewalk with Rocket and a bag of groceries I really didn't need any longer. Staring at the ear of corn just peeking over the top of the paper bag, I decided I could easily drown my sorrows in a big bowl of potato salad and turned to head back toward my temporary home.

FIVE

The tentative knock at the screen door for the cottage interrupted my perusal of the initial budget numbers Captain Roberts had provided for my new department; looking up over the lid of my laptop, I smiled slightly to see Reggie standing on the front porch. While I'd not entirely forgotten about my curiosity over his wood-fired oven, my encounter with Suzanne in the village had left me in an introspective mood, one that was better served by being alone. Setting my laptop aside on the couch, I stood and walked over to the door with the intent of rescheduling; as I pushed the door open, though, I realized with a pang of guilt that he'd likely rearranged his day in anticipation of my visit — one I had rather forced upon him. Resetting a bit, I nodded at Reggie as I joined him on the porch.

"Good afternoon," I said pleasantly before looking at my Apple Watch. "I had no idea it had gotten so late."

"It's easy to get lost in your work," he replied with a boyish smile before nodding toward the couch where I'd been sitting. "I'm surprised you have any sort of internet here. One of the first things I discovered when I moved to the island was that the populace had overwhelmingly decided to remain disconnected from the universe when the broadband companies came calling."

"I've found it to be rather intermittent," I nodded. "My iPhone normally makes for a good hotspot, but it seems wireless coverage is also bad, much as it is in Windeport."

"The only tower for the entire island is by the hotel," Reggie said. His latent French accent was apparent in how he dropped the *h* in hotel. "Not surprisingly, it's also got the best internet."

"Shocker," I smiled. "Let me top off Rocket's water and then we can go."

"He's welcome to join us," Reggie said, a tiny note of hope in his voice. "I lost my German Shepherd back in April and haven't had the heart to replace him. I'd appreciate having a dog around for a bit."

"Then I'll get his leash," I replied amiably. "Give me a second."

Rocket happened to be slumbering in his bed beside the fireplace and wasn't all that excited at being woken up from his afternoon nap; however, once he saw Reggie outside on the porch, he perked up immediately. It was clear Rocket knew Reggie from the way his tail happily wagged as he bounded through the screen door ahead of me; I wasn't surprised that I had to wait for him to receive a few affectionate scratches under the chin before I was able to snap the lead to his collar. Reggie held the white picket fence door open for us and soon we were headed up the cart path toward the denseness of the woods.

In the afternoon sunshine, I was able to get a better look at my walking companion. He was just slightly shorter than me, though not by much, and had wavy brown hair worn in a longish style that had become quite popular. One ear was pierced with a single hoop earring; the short-sleeve t-shirt he was wearing did little to hide that he had some sort of aggressive workout routine (or that kneading dough counted as high-intensity cardio). A sharp nose sat between eyes of the strangest shade of gray I had ever seen; a sheen of stubble accentuated a very masculine square jaw, offset slightly by a dimple in his chin. The t-shirt appeared to hold a logo for a band I'd never heard of and seemed entirely appropriate to the drab olive-green cargo shorts that rounded out his attire. As we walked, I couldn't shake the sense I had seen him somewhere before, despite knowing I'd only just met him the day before yesterday.

"I thought you had to pick up supplies," I said when I suddenly realized the wheeled cart was missing.

"With all of the baking I'm doing for the wedding, I had to make a run this morning instead," he replied as we entered a shady part of the forest.

As he reached up to brush his hair behind an ear, I caught sight of a bandage around the palm of his left hand. "On-the-job injury?" I asked good naturedly. Rocket took that moment to sniff around a juniper bush.

Reggie's eyes went wide and then shifted to the bandage. "Yeah," he said after a moment. "Stupid, actually. You'd think I'd know how to slice bread by now."

"Happens to the best of us," I said. "Though the size of that bandage makes it look kind of serious."

Somewhat self-consciously, Reggie turned his hand over as he smiled ruefully. My eyebrows went up at the line of crimson that had stained the fabric. "It looks worse than it is. A few days of antibiotic gel and I'll be as good as new."

"Are you sure?" I asked, my eyes returning to the dark stain. "I ran into Dr. Kellerman earlier. I'm sure she wouldn't mind taking a quick look—"

"No, it's fine," Reggie said, cutting me off. "I've cut myself hundreds of times. This is nothing."

"All right," I nodded, chiding myself internally for letting my curiosity get the better of me. *Professional hazard* I thought before nodding toward the pathway and changing the subject. "Do you live off this section of the trail?"

"Just beyond the clearing," Reggie nodded as we continued. Rocket, as always, took point. "There's a fork in the cart path that heads to my place."

I nodded again, wondering how I had missed such a fork in the road; the answer became evident when we arrived at the designated spot a few minutes later, for Reggie's definition of a *fork* and mine were quite different. While the walking path did indeed continue to curve around the perimeter of the island, my companion had to push back a few branches from the undergrowth to reveal a far less travelled trail. *Trail* was as loose an appellation as I was willing to apply to what we transitioned too, for other than the hint of where the wheels of Reggie's cart *might* have created a slight rut in the path, the heavy layer of pine needles and molding leaves more or less obliterated any clear signs we were going in the right direction. While I wasn't all that worried about getting lost — I was on an island, after all, so in theory I could walk in one direction long enough and come out *somewhere* — the sense I was getting that Reggie didn't want his home to be easily found was nearly overwhelming. It hadn't helped that Vasily had "treated" me to a series of horror movies during my weeks recuperating from my injuries in February. More than a few of them seemed to start out with the first victim stumbling upon something in the deep, dark woods and not surviving the encounter.

Rocket, on the other hand, seemed quite comfortable; I wasn't sure if it meant my canine companion had sold me out for a few scratches beneath the chin, or if he'd been to this spot on more than one occasion himself. Deciding to test my theory, I broke the uncomfortable silence that had descended upon us after turning off the main path. "Rocket seems to know where he's going."

Reggie looked over his shoulder at me and smiled, revealing that mouth full of perfect teeth. That sense I'd seen him before was nearly overwhelming. "Julie makes a point of buying bread directly from me each week," he said. "Rocket is usually with her."

"Is the markup at the grocer that high?"

"Oh yes," he laughed.

The forest had begun to thin out at that point, then suddenly revealed a small glade similar to others I'd encountered on my wanderings around Carpenter's Island. This particular glade had a smart looking one-story cottage off to one corner, built entirely from brick. Two quaint multipaned windows sat to either side of a white screen door; parts of a third window were obscured by some sort of creeping vine that was dotted with late summer blooms in subtle shades of purple and white. A tall chimney rose up from the center of the sloped and shingled roof; a classic television aerial antenna had been bolted to the top and was aimed in the general direction of the mainland. The path below my feet became far more defined and ran between two sizable vegetable gardens, both of which were well tended to as evidenced by abundant verdant leaves. Reggie guided me toward the house and then turned to the left, taking me toward a smallish outbuilding; as we neared it, I saw a squat, beehive-shaped item constructed out of a yellow tile that had to be the wood-fired oven. An iron door with a small window faced us, and a wisp of smoke curled away from the chimney above it.

There was a sizable wooden table beside the oven just beneath the canvas of one of those portable shade structures; unfamiliar implements in all shapes and sizes littered the surface, making me wish I'd tried to do an internet search on bread production before making my visit (despite how bad access was). The doors to the outbuilding were open, and just inside I could see massive bags of flour stacked one on top of the other; other necessary ingredients were arranged on shelves beyond that receded into darkness. Taking what appeared to my eye like a large wooden cutting board that had been bolted to a broom handle from the table, Reggie looked at me before nodding to the oven.

"I've got to take a quick peek at what's baking, and then I can give you the tour."

"Of course," I said. "Can I let Rocket off the leash here?"

Reggie nodded again. "He knows the boundaries."

As I bent to take the led from the canine's collar, I caught Reggie wince as he gripped the handle with his injured hand. Frowning, I couldn't help myself from saying: "You really should have that hand looked at."

Pulling the iron door open with his other hand, Reggie glanced at me with a resigned expression. "You're not going to let this go, are you?"

"Job hazard, I suppose," I shrugged. "Or more likely it's not in my nature."

Shaking his head, Reggie smiled ruefully again. "Where is this doctor you mentioned?"

"Up at the hotel," I replied. "They called her in from the mainland — apparently there is some sort of outbreak of food poisoning."

If I'd not been watching Reggie, I'd have missed the slight shift in his face. "I heard about that when I dropped off their morning order," he replied. "Sounds really bad, especially since the big rehearsal dinner for that wedding is tonight." Reggie sighed. "I hope that doesn't mean they cancel my delivery for this afternoon."

Catching a whiff of baking bread for the first time, I shook my head. "With something that smells so good? I highly doubt that."

I saw Reggie smile. "That is one of my favorite parts of the job," he said as he used the gizmo to shuffle small rectangular items inside the oven. Stepping a bit closer, I could see the glowing embers of the wood in the far corner of the oven, presumably the heat source baking the bread. "These are actually just about done," he continued with a frown. "I was afraid the wood I'd used burned warmer than normal. I'm glad we didn't dally on the walk back."

"Is anything burned?" I asked, concerned.

"No," Reggie replied as he began to use the flat part of the wooden device to shovel loaves of bread out of the oven and onto a wire rack that ran the length of the table. "At least, not yet."

"Thank God," I smiled. "What wood do you normally use?"

"Anything I can get my hands on," he smiled as he continued to get loaves out of the oven. My eyebrows went up at just how much the petite-looking oven appeared to be able to hold. "Honestly, the hardwoods here on the island burn hotter, letting me get the space up to temperature faster. But I'll use whatever I can find. Deadfalls, branches, pretty much anything."

"No wonder the trails are so clear," I chuckled.

"Exactly," he nodded.

I looked at the small loaves. "Is this a family recipe?"

"Actually, yes," he replied. Reggie's face took on a slight look of nostalgia. "My grandfather had a bakery in Paris, and this is his unique take on a baguette. I can't quite get the texture the way I remember it as a child; I think the water on this island is too hard."

My eyebrows went up. "I read an article years ago about a specific pizza dough from New York City; it needed whatever is floating in the Hudson River to give it a particular taste and feel. I thought the reporter was being specious."

"That is a very real thing," Reggie said as he closed the door on the oven. "Some of the most famous dishes in the world can only be made where they are famous for that very reason."

I smiled slightly. "I am totally going to use that as my excuse the next time my baked beans don't come out as good as my cousin's."

"There you go."

"Did you make this oven?" I asked, nodding to the beehive.

Reggie nodded his head. "It took most of my first summer. The plans are based on the one in my grandfather's bakery, though his was indoors. I had to make some modifications in order for it to withstand the winters here."

"I'm sure," I said. "How many loaves can you make?"

"Two dozen," he replied easily. "Or half as many loaves and four dozen small rolls."

My eyes widened. "You must bake all day."

"I do," he nodded with a smile. "The work is tough, but I love the peace it brings."

I glanced at the table. "I don't see any sort of mixing equipment...?"

Reggie held up his hands. "All I need is right here," he smiled.

"Do you do *everything* by hand?"

"Yes. Though I do have a stand mixer in the house; I use that for boutique items like cakes or macaroons on an as-needed basis."

Having watched my cousin, Charlie O'Conner, try to make the notoriously finicky cookie at her farmhouse, my eyes widened again. "How on earth do you bake macaroons in that thing?"

"Very carefully," he laughed.

"How long have you lived on the island?"

Reggie's eyes shifted away from mine. Had I been interviewing him, it would have been a classic tell that he was uncomfortable answering the question. "A few years now," he replied before smiling. "It's so timeless here, I think I've honestly lost track."

"Are you from New York?"

"France," he reminded me.

"Oh, right," I replied, feigning sheepishness. "You mentioned that already. Did you grow up in New York, then?"

"Why do you ask?" he replied. It wasn't lost on me he'd answered my question with a question.

I smiled. "I'm trying to place the rest of that accent of yours. There's a touch of Boston in there somewhere, but also a bit of New York City if I'm not mistaken."

"I grew up in Manhattan, actually," Reggie said after a long moment. "I... I worked in Boston for a few years after high school."

"That must be it," I smiled. "What did you do in Boston? Is that where you honed your baking skills?"

Reggie shrugged. "Baking was part of growing up for me. No, I was in... promotions."

The undercurrent of reluctance had grown stronger; though I had no reason to, I found myself pressing him. "Promotions? Of what?"

"Clothing, mostly," he replied, again with a slight pause. Reggie made a show of tapping a loaf with a knuckle. "I've got to get these wrapped up so I can take them up to the hotel," he said as he looked at me. "Can you find your way back to the village?"

Recognizing my little tour had come to an abrupt end — and

wondering why my curiosity about his background had made him anxious again — I decided it might be best to withdraw. "I think so, yes. Thank you for the tour." *Such as it was,* I added mentally.

"My pleasure." Reggie looked at the table for a moment, then reached down and grabbed a loaf. "Here," he said. "Take this. It's cooled enough to handle."

"Thanks," I said as I accepted the gift. The ambient heat in my hands was pleasant, the smell of fresh bread nearly divine. "I will enjoy this immensely this evening."

Reggie's eyes widened. "You're not going to eat that *whole* loaf tonight, are you?"

"Swimmers love their carbs," I reminded him with a smile.

"Then enjoy," he replied somewhat incredulously.

"Thanks again for the tour," I said again.

Reggie simply nodded before turning back to his task at hand.

Thus dismissed, I wandered over to where Rocket was lounging in the long grass and snapped the lead back onto his collar. His eyes went to the loaf in my hand and seemed to recognize it for what it was; standing, he immediately started toward the pathway, making it very clear he'd made the round trip on more than a few occasions. I made a note to ask Julie about that when she returned, for it seemed like a learned behavior — especially at how Rocket unerringly returned us to the master walking path for the island. The day had warmed pleasantly, though as we skirted the coastline on our way back to the cottage, the onshore breeze brought the temperature down a degree or two; not enough to be unpleasant, just a reminder once more of the unique weather along that part of the coast.

The walk back to my temporary home seemed to go faster than I expected, helped along perhaps by my having been deep in thought. My visit with Reggie had only made me *more* curious at how the young man had wound up living deep in the woods on an out-of-the-way island making baked goods in a wood-fired oven. It was such an unusual story, it nearly felt like the beginning of a fairy tale — or, perhaps, the opening paragraphs of a story where the lead character was in some sort of witness protection program. As I exited the forest and saw the row of cottages appear in the distance, I slowed my pace and wondered if I had, in fact, accidentally stumbled upon someone trying to live discreetly for just that reason; asking the deputy managing the satellite office felt like the wrong direction in a way that calling in an early favor from Captain Roberts wouldn't.

No, I thought as I shook my head. *Knowing the truth about Reggie's situation only satiates my curiosity — nothing more. Not everyone that has a secret is worth investigating; I think this might be a time to let sleeping dogs lie.*

Glancing at Rocket, I smiled before adding aloud: "No offense."

My companion didn't seem offended, so we continued onward; to my surprise, as I neared the A-frame where I was staying, I saw Suzanne pacing back and forth on the small front porch. The *clunk* noise from my opening up the front gate caught her attention, and she looked up; her wild expression was a mixture of cold fury and, oddly, deep concern bordering on fear. Kneeling to remove the lead from Rocket's collar netted me a few seconds to consider how to proceed; as I slowly stood, I felt all of my investigator instincts go onto high alert.

"What happened?" I asked simply as I stood there on the stone pavers. Rocket decided to sit down beside me, somehow intuiting that I needed some moral support.

"Where the *fuck* have you been?" Suzanne demanded.

My eyebrows went up. "I was walking Rocket," I replied. "And visiting with a neighbor."

She folded her arms across her chest, tightly. "I tried to call you on your cell, but coverage is for shit out here. So, I drove down from the hotel only to find your cottage empty and your damn phone on the counter."

"As you say, wireless coverage is for shit," I said, smiling slightly. "There was no point in bringing my phone with me. How long have you been waiting?"

"About an hour," she replied, the exasperation evident in her voice. "I need you."

Part of me was tempted to spin that into a joke, but the deadly serious way she'd spoken set off more investigator alarms. "Suze, tell me what's going on."

"Sean," she said calmly, "there has been a murder at the hotel."

Six

As I'd never known Suzanne to be hyperbolic, I immediately shifted into full-on law enforcement mode. "Is there room on your golf cart for Rocket?" I asked.

"I have no idea," she replied. "I wasn't exactly paying attention when I borrowed it."

"All right," I said. "Let me get Rocket settled in and then you can take me up."

Suzanne nodded and then took a seat on one of the Adirondack chairs beside the door to wait; I pulled open the screen door and quickly set about preparing an early dinner for my canine companion, one that Rocket made short work of once I put the bowl down on the floor. Sneaking him a few extra treats, I whispered assurances in his ear that I would return at a not unreasonable hour before grabbing my offending iPhone and heading back out to the front porch. Suzanne immediately stood and hurried down the steps to the front yard; I was forced to adjust my stride to catch up to her despite usually being the one *she* had to keep up with. As we exited the yard and turned toward the village, I wondered a bit at the effort it had cost her to seek my council given where things stood between us. Seemingly sensing where my thoughts were at the moment (which was not unusual for the love of my life), Suzanne glanced at me as the cart path widened into a full road.

"I know you're not officially on duty, but Deputy Williamson is part of those who've gone down with a case of food poisoning; I honestly had no one else to turn to. Not without trying to get someone here from the mainland."

I stopped and gently put my hand on her arm. "You can always come to me, Suzanne," I said softly. "No matter what."

She looked at me and for a moment her expression softened into one I'd seen many times before. "I suppose I intrinsically know that," she replied quietly. "We didn't leave things in a good place the last time we spoke, so you could forgive me for thinking the situation might have changed."

"It hasn't," I assured her. "Tell me what you know."

Looking relieved for the first time, Suzanne nodded and then started walking again. "The cart is just over here," she said as we approached a small parking area.

Several gas-powered carts were present, including one bearing the logo for the golf course at the hotel. My eyebrows went up when I saw two bags of clubs hooked to the rear, which in turn prompted a mental image of Suzanne yanking an overweight duffer from the seat as though she were in some sort of action movie. I had to work hard to stifle a smile considering the gravity of the situation.

"Like I told you this morning, I've been treating a number of victims suffering from acute food poisoning," Suzanne continued as she came around the front and took up position behind the wheel. "Most are members of the wedding party or the extended family attending, though quite a number are island residents who had the unfortunate timing of eating at the hotel sometime in the last twenty-four hours."

As I slid into the passenger seat of her cart, I frowned. "I ate there myself yesterday."

"If you didn't have the fruit compote or the blueberry cheesecake, you're probably going to be fine," she said as she twisted the key and then spun the tires slightly in the gravel as she backed out of the slot. "Near as I can figure, it seems to be the blueberries that were the vector; I've already called the Maine Department of Public Health to get an inspector here — and have a sample tested for *E. coli*."

"It will be a bit before they arrive."

"Yeah, Monday if we are lucky." She stepped on the accelerator which caused the small gas engine to choke before we shuddered forward slightly faster. "Both of those dishes were on special, and neither required the berries to be cooked; I suspect they were not washed appropriately but haven't had time to look at the kitchen."

"I can do that," I said. "Though it's just as likely whatever evidence you need to prove the bacteria was present has been long since been washed away."

"Agreed," she nodded, "but we may still be able to see what sort of preparation practices the kitchen staff adhered to. Obviously, that's not our primary concern at the moment."

"I'm reading between the lines here, but it sounds as though you must have come across a body while doing your rounds?"

"Essentially," Suzanne nodded. "I won't say more until we get to the scene. I don't want to bias your perception of what you'll see any further."

My eyes widened. "I appreciate that."

We rode on in silence for the next few minutes; at length, Suzanne piloted the cart up the oval driveway to the hotel, then parked just beyond the ornate front door. "This way," she said as she slid out of the cart.

I followed her through the front door and found the sudden quiet of the lobby unsettling. Save for a single person behind the reception desk, the space was completely devoid of people. "How bad is this outbreak?" I asked as we turned and went down one of the wide corridors leading away from the lobby and toward the northern wing of rooms.

"Bad enough," Suzanne acknowledged. "I've enlisted the aid of the only two EMTs on the island and have a call in to my colleague the next county over to join us as soon as she can hitch a ride with the Harbormaster, but I could probably use more help."

"I'll make some calls," I said as we arrived at a small elevator alcove.

Suzanne pressed the button and then turned to me. "I know you're not quite on duty yet—"

"It's not a problem," I assured her. "Honestly. This is what I do."

For the first time, I thought I saw cracks in Suzanne's professional façade. "Shit, Sean. Just... *shit*. I'm sorry to drag you into this. And I'm sorry I've been an asshole. This whole thing between us... it's on me."

I put a hand to her arm. "You've been there for me more times than I care to admit," I said quietly. "Let me return the favor. Then, once we get through this crisis, we can take stock of where we stand." I leaned in. "If you'll allow me to remind you just how much you mean to me, that is."

Suzanne's eyes danced merrily for a moment. "Yeah," she nodded slowly. "I... I think I might be so inclined, kitty."

My heart skipped a beat at the use of her affectionate moniker for me. *I'll take my wins where I get them,* I thought as the elevator doors sighed open for us.

The ride to the top floor took longer than I expected, exacerbated by both my impatience to visit what was certainly now a crime scene and the aging mechanics of the device. Vowing to take the stairs the next time, I exited the carriage on the heels of my girlfriend and paced her down the long hallway to a door at the very end. I didn't need to see the sign beside the room number to know the room in question had to have been one of the premium suites; given the hotel's layout, I guessed the windows had an amazing view of the ocean and wasn't disappointed when Suzanne unlocked and then pushed the door open for me. The slight stench of death was in the space; it was a unique mixture of scents I had never gotten used to that generally presaged the discovery of someone who, in my line of work especially, had met an untimely demise. Suzanne didn't spare a moment in the main living space of the suite and instead turned smartly to walk through a second, open door to the adjoining bedroom; following her through, the smell became nearly acute, the source of which appeared to be a body-shaped lump atop the queen-sized bed covered by a crimson-stained sheet. My eyes went up a bit at the pattern of blood on the white fabric, almost as if a toddler had been using watercolors and had randomly shaken out a brush full of red paint against the bed.

"Shit," I breathed.

"Yeah," Suzanne replied. She dug into the pockets of her jeans and retrieved two pairs of latex exam gloves; she smiled slightly as she handed me one set. "I assumed you didn't have any with you, seeing as though you're in between jobs at the moment."

Pulling them on with the requisite snap, I returned the smile. "Prescient as always, Milady."

Her mouth quirked at the reflexive use of my affectionate moniker for her. "I try."

Reaching for the sheet, Suzanne carefully folded it back to expose the pale face and clouded, sightless eyes of a young woman. Her head was against a pile of pillows, framed by a mass of blond hair that looked as though it had originally been tied up for the night. Sliding the sheet down to a point that just exposed pallid breasts confirmed the young woman didn't appear to be wearing pajamas of any kind; a small pendant on a gold chain hung just off center, holding a gemstone that looked rather expensive. I could see an earring shaped like a humming-bird in the ear facing me; while I was far from an expert in such matters, I'd seen something similar that had been handmade at the jeweler where I'd purchased my engagement ring for Suzanne — with an appropriately extravagant price. Leaning down, I took a closer look at the jagged wound along the right side of the woman's neck; it appeared deep and had clearly opened the jugular. The sheet below the head and pillow was a deep, deep red, telling me where most of the blood had gone; based on how little lividity there was in the face and torso, it was more than likely the poor woman had bled out nearly completely. Squinting at the cut, I thought I saw something reflecting in the light from the bedroom's window, but my near vision was bad enough whatever it was wouldn't resolve.

"Is there something in the wound?" I asked as I looked to Suzanne.

She nodded. "Glass," she said as she produced her iPhone and brought up a photo. Tapping to expand an image of the wound, she pointed to the irregularly shaped piece of crystal. "Clear, too, telling me it wasn't a mirror. I'd have to get it under a microscope to tell you more, but then again—"

"Yeah, I know," I sighed. "The coroner is our best bet. I think they just jumped up the list of priorities."

"I figured."

"What else can you tell me?"

"Victim appears to be in her mid-to-late twenties," she began in the clinical voice I'd often heard her use with patients at her practice. "Based on the blood pooling and rigor, I'd said she died sometime overnight. The coroner will have to tell us more beyond that, assuming we can get them to the island."

"I don't think that will be a problem," I said as I slid my iPhone out of my pocket and started to take notes on it. I paused long enough to take a photo or two of the body, then nodded toward the jagged gash along the woman's neck. "Just between to the two of us, do you think that's the cause of death?"

"It does seem obvious," Suzanne said with a slight sigh. Pointing to the deep red stain on the sheet below the head, she sighed again. "Not the best way to go. In cases like this, there can be three or four minutes of awareness as life begins to slip away." She looked at me. "This one would have been markedly faster than that Davies fellow who died back in February."

I nodded as I flashed back to the body we'd found together in a cottage owned by a popular radio host a few months earlier. The body had been tied to a recliner before their wrists had been slit, an attempt to make a murder look like suicide. I tried not to think about how the ending of that case had landed me in the intensive care unit at UCLA Medical, not to mention also on Suzanne's shit list for nearly getting myself killed. Digging out of that hole with her had been difficult enough; with time and distance, it now felt like it had been infinitely easier when compared to our current situation.

"It doesn't look like the body was moved in any way," Suzanne was saying, pulling my attention back to the scene. "There is also staining to suggest she'd been sexually active fairly close to the time of death."

My eyes narrowed. "Killed by her lover?"

"That's where this gets complicated," Suzanne said.

Drawing the sheet back over the head of the victim, she moved to the closet that ran along the far wall of the room. Grasping the handle, Suzanne slid one of the doors open to reveal an extravagantly beautiful wedding dress straight out of a fairytale hanging to one side; a few everyday items — blouses, slacks, and even a hoodie — were hanging an appropriate distance away, making it look for all the world as though a no-fly zone had been created between two halves of reality. On the shelf above was a small shoebox of a sort found in high end department stores like Nordstrom's, and if the small icon on the side was any indicator, contained a pair of white high heels designed to match the dress. I felt myself frowning as I turned to Suzanne.

"Tell me this isn't the bride-to-be."

"I wish I could, but there's a purse over there on the dresser. I'm afraid I went through it earlier; I know I should have waited for someone in authority, but I had to know myself."

I frowned deeper, for Suzanne had knowingly altered a possible crime scene. It felt better to not call her out on it, especially since I wasn't entirely on duty myself. Moving over to the dresser, I opened the clasp on the medium-sized leather purse and poked around the interior, ultimately locating a small leather wallet that had a driver's license in the outside pocket. My head shook with disappointment as I read the name printed on the plastic card.

"Dorothy Fernyhough," I said, looking back at Suzanne. "I presume 'Dot' is a shortened version of Dorothy."

"It can be."

My eyes flicked to the vital details on a life that had been halted just twenty-nine years in. "Walk me through how and when you found her," I said as I put the wallet down on the dresser and then tapped the voice memo function on my phone. "And just so you know, I'm recording this for the record."

"Understood," she nodded. "As I told you earlier, I've been working the food poisoning outbreak at this hotel. Given how many people are affected, I triaged who I could in the ballroom downstairs and then went room-to-room for anyone unable to get to me. The hotel staff provided me with a list of guests, which was cross-referenced with those who had called the reception desk for medical assistance; I used that to know who needed a visit."

Suzanne paused with a glance at the bed. "Dot was the last person I checked, for she had never called for help. Once I realized most of the afflicted had either been at the bachelorette party or had eaten the special at the restaurant, I immediately realized it would have been a tremendous stroke of luck that she'd escaped harm. I knocked on her door about three; when she didn't answer, I called down for the manager who let me in. I went for you about twenty minutes later."

"What did you touch, exactly?"

"The sheet," she replied, nodding to the bed. "I already had gloves on, so I doubt my prints will appear anywhere," she added.

"Okay."

Looking around the room, she continued. "The light switch, the closet door and the purse on the dresser. That's as far as I went before I knew I needed professional help."

I started to ask a follow-up question before something else occurred to me. "Who was the manager who let you in?"

"The owner," Suzanne replied. "Tessa Polanski."

"Thank God it wasn't Tim," I said. "If what Corinne told me is accurate, he's the co-owner and, unfortunately, the groom."

Something quirked at the edge of Suzanne's mouth. "How do you know Corinne?"

I looked at her. "Jealousy doesn't become you, Milady," I said, correctly reading her expression. "And for the record, my heart has been spoken for."

"Oh?"

"Yes," I said as I turned off the recording. "By a beautiful woman with raven-black hair who beguiled me quite some time ago." I paused, then searched her eyes before continuing quietly. "You know better than most that once my heart has been given, it's done so completely and unequivocally."

Her face softened a bit. "I suppose I do," she replied softly. "Though you would be well within your rights to have reclaimed it and moved on."

Taking a step closer to Suzanne — and trying to ignore the dead body a few feet from us — I put my hands on her shoulders. "That's not in my nature."

"No," she replied after a moment. "No, it's not," she added with a genuine smile, the first I'd seen since our discussion in my bungalow. "I've messed things up pretty badly."

"You said that earlier," I replied. "Maybe? Maybe not. The important thing here is for you to remember I am nothing like your ex-husband. And never will be."

Eyes glistening, Suzanne nodded. "Yeah. I think I've known that, deep down, for a while, too."

"Good," I smiled as I squeezed her shoulders. "I've got to make some phone calls, but maybe — assuming we can get away — we can talk about this further over a nice glass of Pinot later this evening."

"I'd like that," Suzanne said before smiling a bit wider. "I've missed you. *Us.*"

"Same," I replied. "Though, honestly, I didn't think it would take a dead body for us to have a breakthrough."

"Miracles come in all forms, kitty," Suzanne replied.

"That they do."

SEVEN

My first phone call was to Captain James Roberts of the Maine State Police, my decades-long friend and about-to-be new boss. The conversation was short and resulted in my start date being set retroactively to the prior weekend, unlocking all of the resources of my new department. Unfortunately, the same didn't apply to the two-dozen people I had re-hired from the Windeport Police Department; since they were scheduled to start in September, just about all of them were enjoying an extended vacation and were unavailable — including my number two, Norm Thomas. While I was comfortable working a case solo, I'd done the job long enough to know it never hurt having someone else to bounce theories against; Suzanne had often been a sounding board for me, and would likely be willing to do so again, assuming the thawing out between us was real and not just the temporary byproduct of the stress from having found a dead body. There was one other person on the island likely to want to sink her teeth into a case, too; I'd known Corinne long enough to expect she'd appear on my doorstep before too long and planned accordingly.

My second phone call was to a number I had long ago memorized. Rather fortuitously, Heather Graham happened to be just south of

Windeport finishing another case and was willing to immediately head for Carpenter's Island; somewhere close to seven that evening, Suzanne and I met her and the rest of her ace crime scene team as they disembarked from the Windeport Harbormasters' boat, and then shuttled them to the hotel in golf carts we'd commandeered from the facility. Knowing it could be a few hours before Heather summoned me back to the crime scene, I took the opportunity to return to my borrowed cottage to check in on Rocket; as I suspected, he'd been snoozing on the couch, but perked up immediately when I made my appearance. Already feeling guilty for shirking my caretaking duties, I decided to bring him with me to the satellite office for the State Police; now that I was a fully deputized member of the force, Jimmy had thoughtfully texted my new credentials for the State's private network, allowing me to make use of what he'd assured me was the best high speed broadband access point on the small island. I figured I could give proof to what I assumed was a beneficent lie by getting a head start on some of the routine paperwork while I waited. Grabbing my laptop, I stuffed it into my backpack and then added a bag of treats for Rocket; pondering just how long we might be out, I filled a second bag full of his normal morning kibbles and stuffed that into the bag as well. Rocket happily followed me down the stone walkway to the waiting cart just outside the gate, then easily hopped into the passenger seat to patiently wait for me to buckle him in for our quick trip to the village. Based on how he sat proudly in the seat, it was easy to infer he'd done something like that in the past; still, I got a kick out of how my canine copilot seemed to carefully observe every yard of our route along the way.

The satellite office was little more than a renovated shack at the edge of the main drag that was the commercial center for the island. By the time I pulled into the single open slot in front of the building, the sun had long since set, forcing the carriage lamps along the paved road into service as the sole source of illumination. Somehow, the way the soft amber light hit the ramshackle clapboard structure made it seem quainter than it had in the daylight. Shutting down the cart, I slid from the front seat and went up the two wooden steps to the elegant wood paneled front door; I smiled slightly at the classic shingle posted beside the door bearing the logo for the State Police, a total New England affectation I'd seen in other small coastal towns. I wasn't entirely surprised to find the office unlocked when I tried the handle to the door, nor was it a shocker to discover the interior housed but a single desk in front of the window facing the ocean. Just visible through an open door on the rear wall was a small kitchenette; beside that, an even smaller holding cell barely large enough for the cot it was holding, protected with bars that looked like they had come directly from the Old West. The entire facility was hardly larger than my old office at the Windeport Police station, and that was being generous in my estimates.

Rocket seemed to know his way around the space, though, for as soon as we entered, he immediately dashed into the kitchenette; a moment later, I heard the telltale sounds of him lapping up water, telling me he was a frequent guest. Smiling, I moved over to the desk and jiggled the mouse for the desktop computer; the PC lethargically beeped and then chugged into life as though it were an old-fashioned steam engine attempting to build up to the proper operating pressure. Deciding I didn't want to begin drawing on my pension while I waited for the computer to finish calculating whether it was a good day to function, I pulled my trusty MacBook out of the backpack and set it atop the desk; by the time the logo for the operating system appeared on the flatscreen monitor, I'd already connected to the wireless and had quite nearly finished logging into the State's case management software. Rocket rejoined me and settled in beside the ancient chair I was sitting in; as I created a new file in the system, he yawned, and then a few moments later, began to snore. I hoped it wasn't his commentary on how intrigued he was with my profession.

I was just finishing up getting my notes from the scene into the file when the door opened, and Corinne poked her head around it. "I thought I'd find you here," she said with a smile.

"I figured you'd turn up sooner or later," I replied with my own smile. "Though for the record, there aren't very many places to hide on this island."

"You'd better hope that is true, if what I'm hearing through the grapevine is accurate," Corinne continued as she closed the door. Standing in front of it, she eyed me. "Is it a murder?"

"That grapevine seems particularly well informed," I said, arching an eyebrow.

"I may or may not have caught your girlfriend in the elevator," Corinne continued. "She might have also suggested you could use a hand."

I stretched my arms out to encompass the empty space of the satellite office. "As I do appear to be understaffed at the moment," I said, "I'll gratefully accept the help. I should warn you that, unlike consulting in California, the pay here's for shit."

"Cook me those lobsters at some point and I'll call it even," she laughed.

I watched her for a moment. "Are you sure?" I asked. "This involves someone you know. People you've interacted with in a non-official capacity."

"Yeah," she nodded. "Suzanne told me who it was. So yes, I'm sure."

"She's usually more discrete," I said, frowning.

"She also knows I'm a cop," Corinne reminded me. "We had quite a chat when she did her once-over on me for the food poisoning."

In more ways than one, I thought. "Okay then," I said as I stood and offered my hand. "Welcome to the Maine State Police."

"Thank you," she chuckled as we shook. "So formal."

"I have an image to maintain," I deadpanned.

"Ah," she rolled her eyes. "Catch me up to speed, then."

I took a few moments to sketch in the events of the afternoon, including my very quick review of the hotel room; I ended by describing my flurry of phone calls and the arrival of Heather and her team. "I didn't want to get too involved before the techs arrived," I said as I tapped my finger on the surface of the desk, my only visible sign of impatience. "But I have to admit to wanting to get back up to the hotel."

Corinne looked thoughtful as she digested what I'd told her. "I can imagine."

"Did Dot have any of the blueberry treats at the bachelorette party?"

"Suzanne asked me the same thing earlier," Corinne replied. "Maybe? Like I said earlier, it wasn't all that much fun. In fact, now that I've had time to think about it, Dot seemed kind of off her game."

I raised my eyebrows. "In what way?"

Corinne shrugged. "She seemed distracted. Like she wanted to be somewhere else but had no way to leave."

"It *was* her party," I observed.

"Exactly."

"Who else was there?"

"Oh, Lord, I think there were a half-dozen of us," Corinne answered. "I only knew one other person from our days together at school — Helena Scott — and even that is on the vaguest terms possible. We lost touch after graduation, so this is the first time I've seen her since. The rest were people Dot knew from her life in Boston."

"I don't suppose you kept track of their names?"

"Hardly," she smiled. "Once it became apparent the party was more like a wake, I began looking for ways to escape. Which I did; that might be why I'm not sick, as I don't think anything with blueberries was served until after I left."

"That seems to have been quite lucky," I nodded, then paused. "Look, you know as well as I do that I have to ask: when, exactly, did you leave the party?"

Corinne smiled slightly. "You wouldn't be the investigator you are if you didn't," she replied after correctly intuiting my line of thought. "With the time difference between here and California, my internal clock is a still a bit scrambled." Corinne paused. "Maybe eleven? I flipped the television on when I got back to my room and the local late news was running."

"You didn't leave your room afterward?"

"No," Corinne replied after a moment of hesitation. It was slight, but enough to attract my investigative attention. "I took a shower and then went to bed; I got up around seven and went down for breakfast only to find the restaurant was closed. I found out later it was due to the outbreak. I had to make do with some muffins from the coffee shop."

My eyes widened. "I didn't realize they had one at the hotel."

"It's just the lobby bar redecorated with pastries and silver vats of coffee," she laughed. "They switch back to spirits at lunchtime."

"Ah."

"And before you ask, I went back to my room, ate my erstwhile breakfast and then took another shower before walking down to meet you in the village."

I nodded. "Anything odd stand out to you?"

"On my walk?"

I shrugged. "Or anytime between the bachelorette party and meeting me for lunch."

"That's a pretty big window."

I shrugged again. "I don't have enough information to filter it down yet."

"I figured. No, not really. But I've only been here a day or two; I wouldn't know what looks *normal* versus *not*."

"Point taken," I said.

"I'll think about it, though," she mused. "I may have seen something that I didn't recognize as being important. It might come out as we dig into this case."

"Agreed," I said, then looked down as my iPhone began to ring. "Good thing we have that out of the way," I smiled as I picked it up to answer. "It looks like Heather is ready for us."

"Good."

Much like my call with Captain Roberts, the one with Heather was brief; unwilling to leave Rocket to his own devices at the satellite office, Corinne and I drove him back to the cottage so he could sleep in his own bed before continuing to the hotel. For whatever reason, despite having visited the resort a number of times since my arrival on the island, it wasn't until I drove past the lighted monument at the base of the long, circular driveway that the actual name of the hotel finally stuck in my consciousness. While *Inn By The Sea* wasn't exactly the most creative moniker possible, it certainly described the property in a succinct phrase — assuming your idea of an "inn" was something that looked nearly as large as the Marriott back in Windeport. Parking my purloined cart on a small patch of grass just beyond the main entrance, Corinne and I got out and hurried through the lobby toward the elevators for the wing where the crime scene was located; when the doors to the carriage opened for us on the top floor, it was easy to see a beehive of activity was still going on at the end of the hallway.

Heather appeared in the doorway to the suite as we neared; she was unusually attired in a Margaritaville t-shirt and cutoff jeans wholly at odds with the purple latex gloves and paper slip-ons over her sandals. "Hey," she smiled tiredly. "You'll want these."

I felt myself frowning as I took the gloves and footies she handed me. "I didn't know the Crime Lab did dress-down days."

"We don't," she replied. "I'm supposed to be off today; Jimmy Buffett is playing Fenway tonight." Heather looked at her watch and groaned. "*Played*, rather."

"Oh, *shit*," Corinne breathed. "I caught him in Anaheim last year. It's one helluva show."

Heather brightened somewhat. "You're a Parrothead?"

"From the womb," Corinne laughed. "Mom played everything he had on a loop during her pregnancy. I've loved him ever since."

I felt myself looking between them. "Using context clues, I am going to assume he's some kind of singer?"

"More like a lifestyle," Corinne chuckled. "How have you not heard of him?"

"Sean lives in a bubble," Heather replied.

"I do not—"

"I'm Heather Graham," she continued, her attention directed to Corinne. "You are...?"

"Corinne Wallace," Corinne replied. "Deputy Chief of Police for Riverside, California."

Heather's eyebrows went up. "Is that close to Rancho Linda?"

"Two towns over," she nodded. "Vasily speaks highly of his time here in Windeport," Corinne added with a glance at me.

"Corinne and I go way back," I said, picking up the thread. "I've consulted for her department on a number of occasions over the years."

"Small world," Heather observed wryly.

"Isn't it?" I laughed. "Since I'm insanely shorthanded at the moment, Corinne has thoughtfully volunteered to return the favor and help out on this one for a bit."

"Of course," Heather replied before looking at Corinne. "Are you here on vacation?"

"No," Corinne replied. "Full disclosure: I'm part of the wedding party and know the alleged victim personally. She was my roommate in college."

Heather shot a look at me. "I'm fine with it," I replied to her unspoken question.

Oddly, Heather pursed her lips. "Sean, you're not running your own independent department any longer; there's an unusual amount of oversight at this level. Given how things went in Windeport..."

"Nothing can be as bad as the Village Council," I replied.

"Says the guy who *already* went a round with Professional Standards."

Corrine's head snapped in my direction. "That sounds like quite the story."

"I'll tell you over drinks later," I said before turning to Heather. "What have you got?"

Considering me once more, Heather finally nodded and stepped away from the door to allow us inside. "We're wrapping up now," she pointed out rather needlessly, for it was obvious her techs were breaking down the light stands and packing up other equipment. "I'll start in the living room, but before I begin, the body has already been sent back to the mainland. I spoke with Lou directly and she's agreed to do it over a video conference connection so you don't have to leave the island."

I nodded. "Our Chief Medical Examiner is quite considerate."

"Indeed," Heather nodded then took us over to the small couch and coffee table that comprised what she was referring to as the *living room*; just beyond was a sliding glass door that led to a balcony overlooking the shoreline. "We found circular stains on the surface of this table," she said, pointing to polished dark wood surface. "To my eye, they look like two tumblers sitting side by side, which would be about right for a couple having cocktails on the couch."

I made the leap. "You didn't find any glasses?"

"No. And the mini bar appears to be fully stocked. Before you ask, the stains had dried, so it's conceivable they've been there a while, but given the nature of the wound on the victim, I have my doubts." Heather paused. "That, and this appears to be a marquee suite. I doubt the hotel would allow stains like that to linger between guests."

I nodded after looking at the twin circles again. "Those do stand out."

"Yes. We've bagged all of the trash in the suite, but there isn't much there. Kleenex, some random Boston newspapers, gum wrappers and foil that could be from the back of the antihistamine packet we found in the bathroom."

"We can check with Room Service and see if something was brought up," Corinne suggested. "Or, more importantly, if anything was picked up."

"I was on the same wavelength," I said as I glanced at Corinne with a smile. "Any prints?" I asked Heather.

"Multiple throughout the suite," Heather nodded. "We'll get a more definitive answer back at the lab, but our portable reader thinks just two distinct sets."

"Makes sense, if the cleaning staff wears gloves," I mused.

"Now, on to the bedroom," Heather said as she led us through to the adjoining room.

The bed had been stripped to the mattress, exposing the crimson stain of blood on the fabric. I suspected a new bed would be required before the suite could be rented out again. Heather paused at the foot of the bed, then consulted the tablet I didn't realize she'd been holding before speaking again.

"We took a liver temp before they carted off the body; my rough math puts time of death somewhere between midnight and three this morning. The lab can be more precise, but that seems pretty close."

I nodded at the bed. "COD seems pretty straightforward, but I'll wait for Lou to make her conclusion."

"Always wise," Heather smiled. "I confirmed Suzanne's report that the victim had been sexually active; I swabbed semen from the sheets, which seems to support that it was unprotected."

My eyebrows went up as I turned to Corinne. "Do you know if Dot's fiancé was staying with her?"

"I don't," Corinne replied.

"I doubt it," Heather added. "We only found one set of clothing."

"Maybe he visited?" I asked. "His family owns the hotel, perhaps he had a sleepover then went home in the morning."

Heather looked thoughtful. "Lou will be more definitive, but based on what I'm seeing, the sex happened fairly close to when the victim died. That theory might work if he was here for a brief tryst."

I frowned. "I might be the wrong authority on this, but it seems odd he would have an intimate moment and then scurry off, considering they're getting married in two days' time."

Corinne nodded. "You think it was someone else?"

"I'm not sure. What I *do* know is we'll need to collect DNA from everyone."

"Oh, joy," Corinne said.

I glanced at heather. "Any chance you have some spare test kits with you? I'm not hopeful what kind of inventory I'm going to find on hand at the satellite office."

"No," Heather shook her head. "We didn't restock before coming over, and I used everything I had when we processed the room. I can put in an emergency request to send some out to you, though it might be a bit."

"I'll take any help I can get," I sighed before looking at the bed.

"High-end toiletries were in the bathroom," Heather continued after scanning the iPad. "Also, a massive amount of makeup and hair product." Heather looked up. "Honestly, I don't want to tell you how much money was tied up between those and the designer wedding dress that was in the closet."

"I'm afraid to ask, then," I said.

"Probably wise. One other thing, there was a small dental appliance sitting in cleaning solution beside the sink. I've seen it before; I think it's of a type for those who grind their teeth at night."

I blinked. "Something she would have been wearing had she actually been sleeping?"

"Exactly."

"Interesting," I said, turning it over in my head.

Corinne looked like she wanted to ask something but decided against it.

"And before you ask, we didn't find blood anywhere else in the suite beyond what is around the bed. I am reasonably confident telling you she was killed right there."

I glanced at the bed. "Killed after having sex with her killer?" I asked. "That would be rather cold."

"Or would represent an escalation — maybe the killer was triggered by something during or just after they made love," Corinne said. "That would explain the timeline slightly."

"Yeah," I said, though deep down I wasn't truly convinced. I looked at Heather. "You really didn't find any blood anywhere else?" I asked.

"No," she replied as she eyed me. "You think that's significant?"

"I do," I nodded after a moment. "I mean, given all of that blood, wouldn't the killer have been covered in it? Getting back out of here without leaving so much as a trace is quite a feat." I glanced out at the main room. "And they had to have cleaned up the glass — and yet, still didn't leave a trace?"

"If it was post-coital, maybe your killer was naked," Heather offered. "A quick shower would have made short work of any evidence. Except," she added with a slight smile, "there was no evidence of a recent shower."

"There goes that theory," I sighed.

"It was worth a shot," Corinne chuckled.

I looked at the bed again, then started at something Heather had said. Turning back to her, I felt myself frowning. "Wait — what do you mean, 'reasonably confident?'"

The lead tech frowned slightly, then went to the side of the bed. Pointing to the crimson stain on the bed I'd noted earlier, she frowned deeper. "This seems wrong to me, but I can't tell you why."

"What exactly feels wrong?"

"You saw the sheets," she said as she came back to me. "There was a ton of blood on them. And yet, the staining on the mattress looks nearly incidental."

My eyebrows went up. "You know, there *would* be more blood in the mattress, wouldn't there?"

"I can't say for certain without doing some estimates, but yeah." She looked to the bed. "I guess I can't rule out that the sheets and body came from somewhere else."

I nodded slowly. "We'll keep that in mind, then," I said. "But for now, we'll operate under the assumption this is our primary scene."

"Until we find something that points us elsewhere?" Corinne asked.

"Exactly." I glanced at the mattress again. "Which I think we ultimately will."

"How did this get so complicated so fast?" Corinne sighed.

"Vasily tells me things *are* far simpler in California," I teased.

"Hardly," she sighed again.

"That's about it," Heather said as she held the tablet to her chest. "Everything is off to the lab for further analysis; I'll update the case file as soon as we have anything."

"I appreciate it," I said. "Thanks, as always."

"Of course," Heather nodded. "We'll be done here within the hour."

"Then we'll get out of your way," I said with a slight smile at the dismissal.

Corinne followed me out of the suite and made it halfway down the hallway before putting a hand to my arm. "What did you mean back there?" she asked. "I feel like I missed something."

"I'm not sure there's anything *to* miss, yet," I smiled. "It's just a feeling I got when Heather mentioned the dental appliances."

Corinne rolled her eyes. "Vas told me about those 'feelings' or yours," she said.

"Did he?" I laughed quietly. "Spilling all of my secrets now, is he?"

"I had to ply him with vast quantities of wine at the last conference we attended together, but yes, he waxed rather poetic about your instincts."

"He's pretty damn good himself."

"That he is. So what is your gut telling you?"

"I'm not sure yet," I hedged, "other than I feel like we have something of a timeline. I mean, you wouldn't wear one of those night guard things while having sex, right?"

"It wouldn't be my first choice," Corinne replied.

"I guess what I'm thinking is it's not a stretch to presume she had an intimate moment with someone, maybe followed or preceded by a nightcap; that visitor — presumably her fiancé, Tim — left soon afterward. Before she could get fully ready for bed, she was interrupted by the person who ultimately killed her."

"Heather said there were only two sets of prints in the suite," Corinne reminded me.

"There are all sorts of explanations for that," I smiled wryly, "but I admit it does make my theory a bit weak. For now."

"It's solid enough to start with," Corinne assured me as we resumed our walk to the elevator. "What do you want to do next?"

"'Round up the usual suspects,'" I said with a laugh.

Corinne looked at me. "For someone who lives in a bubble, you know your classic films."

"I blame my girlfriend," I said with a smile before getting wistful for a moment. "Let's start with members of your bachelorette party, and then follow that with the wider wedding party. We'll need to borrow some space for the interviews."

"I'll speak with the front desk," Corinne replied, then glanced at her watch. "Unless you want to wake everyone up at this point, should we set the first round for nine?"

"That works," I said. "That will also give me time to search the satellite office for DNA testing kits. If there aren't any, I'll need to contact the mainland for that and any other supplies."

"Sounds good." Corinne paused. "Sean, I think this is the start of a beautiful friendship."

I laughed as the doors to the elevator opened. "I'll get you recruited to Windeport yet, Corinne."

EIGHT

True to form, it felt like I had barely slid beneath the sheets before I found myself watching the first rays of dawn streaming across the skylight above my bed. The dark slash of deep burgundy against the otherwise golden sky worried me, though; as someone who had lived most of his life along the shore, I had long ago learned to heed that old sailor's adage:

> Red sky at night, sailor's delight.
> Red sky in the morning, sailor's warning.[1]

Uncertain when the coming storm would hit, it seemed prudent to try and get a run in before the weather turned; yawning, I reluctantly pulled myself out of the bed so I could sort through my workout gear for something clean enough to wear. Rocket's ears perked up from

---

1. *Author's Note: yes, this is really a thing! If you want to know more, the Library of Congress has a wonderful article describing the actual science behind the adage. Check out the details on their website at https://www.loc.gov/everyday-mysteries/meteorology-climatology/item/is-the-old-adage-red-sky-at-night-sailors-delight-red-sky-in-morning-sailors-warning-true-or-is-it-just-an-old-wives-tale/.*

where he was casually lounging on his dog bed; by the time I was kneeling to tie the laces on my sneakers, he was sitting beside me, tail wagging in anticipation of an outing.

As tempted as I had originally been to use the pool at the hotel, now that I was up to my curly hair in a possible murder there it felt slightly unethical to do so. So off the two of us went, slowly jogging around the island on the perimeter trail I had truly begun to love. Normally when I worked out, I pondered aspects of the case that were troubling me; that morning, while I had plenty to chew on, most of it was unrelated bits of information that were far from being anything concrete. I had a body and unusual evidence without context in the room where we found it; mix in a hotel full of guests, most of whom knew the victim, and I had an interesting stew that had barely begun cooking. The interviews planned for later that morning might add some additional spice to the dish, but I couldn't help the feeling I was working from a half-completed recipe card, or one that had all of the measurements listed as "to taste."

That nagging sense I was missing the larger picture was something I always felt at the beginning of a case; I'd done the job long enough to know that I'd begin to paint in details, but it nevertheless was always frustrating right out of the gate. Running past the hotel seemed to exacerbate the feeling, so I relegated it to the back of my brain and instead focused on my breathing, trying to center myself for the slog to come. The final portion of the route had me running directly into the freshening wind; by the time I was ending the workout on my watch, the strong breeze was slicing rather efficiently through my compression gear. Rubbing my hands together as though I'd done a workout in the depths of February, visions of hot coffee danced in my head as I walked back to the cottage. Rocket, for his part, didn't seem phased in the least by the yin-yang temperature extremes Carpenter's Island seemed to experience; the same couldn't be said when he saw the elegant form of Suzanne sitting in one of the Adirondack chairs on the front porch. Bounding through the gate as soon as I swung it open, he dashed to her feet and then patiently sat so she could reach over and scratch between his ears.

Pausing at the steps to the porch, I leaned on the railing and smiled. "I had no idea you were stepping out on me, Milady," I said. "I thought you only liked cats."

"I'm equal opportunity," Suzanne chuckled as she leaned down and kissed Rocket on the head. "Though I have no idea what I did to get such adoration from your dog."

"I think he's picking up on my sympathetic vibrations," I replied. "And channeling them, maybe."

"Maybe," she smiled again then looked up at me. "Sorry to drop in on you unannounced."

"Don't apologize," I said. "You are always welcome on my doorstep. Even if it's not technically *my* doorstep."

She smiled. "Good to know."

"Have you eaten breakfast?" I asked. "I'm just about to feed Rocket, and then was going to make an omelet. I picked up some fresh produce the other day — onions, peppers, tomatoes."

"Add in some cheese and I'll join you."

"As long as Swiss is all right?"

"Perfect."

"Come on in, then."

Suzanne took up position on the couch, and Rocket joined her on the other cushion. It was hard not to smile when he gently placed his muzzle in her lap, then dozed off contentedly while she stroked his ears; despite knowing he was unlikely to eat at that point, I still rustled up his breakfast and set it beside his water dish before moving on to my own meal. Pulling the ingredients out of the fridge, I washed the produce and then began to carefully chop up the vegetables; looking over my shoulder, I frowned at how tired Suzanne looked.

"Coffee?" I asked as I wiped off my hands and went to the coffeemaker. I'd loaded it up with water and grounds before going to bed, and simply flipped the switch to begin brewing.

"God, yes," she sighed.

"This will take just a moment," I said as I leaned against the counter. "I've decided my Keurig has ruined me. I'm too impatient to wait for one of these old-fashioned devices."

"I can buy that."

I smiled slightly. "Having said that, I'm not sure I should admit that I think the coffee tastes better brewed this way."

"That seems to be the price of modern living." She smiled slightly. "Though I can't argue with how much slower your uptake of caffeine is with such a device. It might do you good to trade in your K-cups for a bag of ground."

"I don't think I would survive," I said, horrified at the very thought of giving up my beloved Keurig.

"I've weaned addicts off worse," Suzanne laughed. "I can get you through this. Trust me."

My heart did a little pitter-pat at what that sentence implied. "Don't take this the wrong way, Milady, but you look exhausted. Were you up all night?"

Suzanne nodded. "Pretty much. I snagged about an hour of shuteye in there somewhere, but it's been like my days as a resident." She yawned. "The extra help you asked for arrived this morning; it was almost blissful handing it off to someone else, even if just for a few hours."

"What's the prognosis?"

"Everyone will recover," she said. "The biggest challenge in these situations is staying hydrated, and that will continue to be true for a few more days. Only three are still bedridden — the parents of the bride and an aunt. They seemed to have been disproportionally affected, possibly due to their age."

"Is that normal?" I asked, something teasing at the back of my brain.

"I don't know. Maybe? Age often can be a contributing factor in how one deals with health issues, but I'm too tired to recall any journal articles about it."

The coffeemaker chugged to completion behind me, so I turned and pulled down two mugs from the cabinet. Filling one with the steaming concoction, I carried it over to Suzanne and handed it to her. "I need to interview people today," I said, trying not to smile as my girlfriend clearly savored her first sip. "Would that be a problem?"

"I'd say they would be up to it," she replied as she took a second sip. "Save for those three."

"I can come back to them." I returned to the counter and started to chop the onion. "Are you still certain about the blueberries?"

"Yes," Suzanne replied. "Every single person I've treated had one or both of those dishes I mentioned. I asked that the kitchen stay closed until we've had a chance to review it."

"That better be my first stop, then," I said. "Otherwise, there will be a lot of unhappy guests." I glanced at Suzanne. "I've already requested an inspector, but they can't get here before the beginning of the week; I'm not sure we can keep it closed that long."

"Probably not," Suzanne agreed. "And like you said earlier, whatever might have been wrong with the blueberries was likely washed away the same day everyone was affected."

"Yeah," I sighed. Cracking some eggs into a bowl, I added some salt and pepper and then quickly whipped them with a fork before pouring the mixture into a hot frypan. As the egg began to cook, I put two pieces of sourdough into the toaster. "What I do need to confirm is whether the blueberries came from the grocer down in the village, or if they were shipped in independently."

"Probably the latter," Suzanne said. "I've only been dealing with people at the hotel; so far, no one living on the island proper has come to my attention, save for those who happened to eat at the restaurant that day."

"I'll try to verify that this morning. I've got to go down to the satellite office before I head to the hotel, so I can poke my head in at the grocer."

"I'll go with you," Suzanne offered.

"I'd appreciate the company," I said. Deftly sliding the finished omelet onto a plate, I grabbed a fork and carried the dish to Suzanne. "This feels a bit like old times," I said softly, carefully risking destroying the moment in an attempt to gauge what was truly going on.

Taking the plate with a smile, Suzanne replied the way I'd hoped. "I have come to realize just how much I've missed this," she said as she gently slid Rocket's sleeping form from her lap so she could eat. "I've been a bit of an idiot."

I crouched down to be at eye level with her. "You were hurt by someone," I reminded her. "I can't blame you for trying to protect your heart; I also can't help but continue to remind you every chance I get that I am not your ex-husband."

"No," she said softly as she reached a hand to my face. "You most certainly are not."

I took her hand into mine, then kissed it. "I screwed up, too," I continued. "I ignored the little signs you were giving me, which in turn only made the situation worse. I won't make that mistake again."

"I know," she replied. "I mean, I know that *now*. I guess it took a bit for the concept to sink in."

"I get it."

Her eyes glistened slightly. "Can you forgive me?" she asked quietly.

"Suze," I said, "There's nothing to forgive. But if it helps, yes, I wholeheartedly do."

She leaned over the plate she'd carefully balanced on her lap and pressed her lips to mine, softly at first, then with the barely restrained passion the weeks apart had likely augmented. As tempted as I was to allow what she so clearly wanted, I also knew I had a bit of a schedule to keep to; sadly, I pulled away, though not without making it clear to Suzanne I was completely on board.

"Maybe you could stay over tonight," I said, my voice husky.

"I'd like that," she replied, her eyes dancing merrily. "If you wouldn't mind the company."

"I wouldn't."

As much as I wanted to linger in the moment, I instead returned to the kitchen and hurried through making my own omelet, which I downed as fast as was practicable. Running through the shower equally as quickly, less than twenty minutes later I was driving back to the village in my borrowed golf cart with Suzanne in the passenger seat. Rocket had been somewhat put out that he couldn't come this time around but seemed placated — slightly — when I promised to be home for lunch and another long walk.

The wind had continued to increase, forcing me to pull out the one and only windbreaker I'd brought with me; Suzanne for her part had already been wearing a light jacket, but neither of us seemed to be properly prepared for the dipping temperatures presaging another storm. A quick glance at the now fully overcast sky told me an umbrella might be warranted in as little as an hour, though it did also make the day seem unusually dramatic. I parked once more in the spot directly in front of the satellite office, marveling at just how ramshackle the small structure appeared in daylight.

"I've got to try and locate some DNA collection kits," I said as we exited the cart in tandem. "There should be a few in the supplies here, but I doubt it will be enough to test everyone I want to test."

"I imagine the state never considered a situation such as this," Suzanne said as I pushed open the door.

"Likely not," I agreed. "Assuming as much, I put through a requisition for more last night before I hit the sack, to be delivered as soon as possible."

Suzanne looked at me. "Someone else didn't get much sleep, either."

"Par for the course," I said. "Look over in that cabinet, will you? I'll check out back."

"Okay."

It took longer than I wanted, but between the two of us we ultimately located what amounted to a supply *drawer* in the desk. There wasn't much in it beyond two DNA kits, a small cache of plastic evidence bags, a half-full box of exam gloves and a spare set of breathing masks for a type of CPR we no longer practiced. I wasn't terribly impressed and made a mental note to put a bug in Captain Roberts' ear about the lack of preparedness on the island. While it was statistically unlikely another murder would occur, there were all sorts of reasons to have the proper equipment on hand for any sort of investigation; we all hoped the stuff would never be used, but the reality was often far different.

After loading up the rear of the golf cart with what little supplies we did find, Suzanne and I walked the short distance to the grocery store and went inside. Since it was barely seven, there were more staff stocking the shelves than customers making it fairly easy to track down the produce manager, Oneida White. Dressed in a green smock stained with use, she looked at me through glasses that made her eyes seem larger than normal as I explained what I was hoping to learn. I'd barely mentioned the word *blueberries* before she began to frown.

"We don't supply the hotel," she said firmly. Her slightly stooped figure belied years of bending over boxes of produce, hard labor at any age. "Haven't ever since Tim took over the hospitality portion of the business."

My eyebrows went up. "When was that?"

"About three years ago," Oneida replied. "Before that, they purchased *everything* from the stores here in town. It was a nice virtuous cycle, keeping all of the businesses afloat during the periods when tourism was light."

"And now?"

"Boat comes up from Searsport," Oneida said with such distaste I thought she wanted to spit. "Two, three times a month. Not just with produce and other food for the kitchen, but also things like cleaning supplies and toilet paper."

"Ouch," Suzanne said.

Oneida nodded, then glanced at the front of the store before lowering her voice. "The owner would hate me to say it, but we're on the verge of going under. There aren't enough year-round residents to keep us going; I mean, the writing's been on the wall for years, but the hotel cutting us off accelerated things."

"Damn." I looked around the cramped space anew and felt my heart sink; there had been a rumor back in Windeport that our little IGA was also on the verge of going under, victim to the super-sized Walmart that had opened twenty miles outside of the Village nearly a decade ago. That same store had been the trigger for my father to sell his pharmacy and retire a few years earlier than planned. It hadn't helped that his son had steadfastly refused to follow in the footsteps of a few generations of Colbeths and run the family business after college.

"Can I help you with anything else?" Oneida was asking, pulling me back from my thoughts.

"Just one more thing," I said. "Do you get your bread from Reggie?"

A wide smile broke out on Oneida's face, wiping away many of the craggy age lines. "Heavens, yes. That man knows how to bake; it's one of the few items we have trouble keeping in stock."

"I had a chance to see his oven the other day," I said. "I was amazed at how manual his operation is."

"Then you have been truly blessed," Oneida said, her face betraying surprise. "Reggie is quite private."

Thinking back to how hidden his cottage was, I nodded. "I could see that. How long has he been on the island?"

That seemed to give Oneida pause. "You know, I don't honestly recall when he arrived."

I smiled slightly. "Almost like he's been here forever?" I asked.

"Yes," Oneida nodded. "Exactly."

Suzanne was eyeing me, but I ignored her. "Thanks for your help, Oneida."

"See you around," she smiled, then returned to sorting small potatoes.

As we exited the store, Suzanne lowered her voice. "Who's Reggie?"

"An oddity," I said simply as we crossed the street. "A round peg on an island of square holes."

Suzanne frowned. "I think you have that metaphor backwards."

"Not in this case," I said to her face full of puzzlement. "Come on, let's get to the hotel."

NINE

I wasn't all that surprised to find a welcoming committee waiting as Suzanne and I pulled beneath the entrance portico for the *Inn By The Sea*; while the mother-son duo running the resort had been on my list to speak to for a variety of reasons, gathering up the early threads of the investigation had pushed meeting with them toward the middle third of my burgeoning to-do list. It was rather clear from the crossed arms and deep frowns they were more than annoyed not to have been given a higher priority; Suzanne heard my sigh as I applied the parking brake and gently squeezed my bicep in quiet solidarity. Hopping out of the cart, the first wave of rain began to splatter against the asphalt shingles of the portico, echoing unusually due to the acoustics driven by the architecture of the building. Suzanne and I grabbed what we needed from the back of the cart before walking over to where our chilly reception was awaiting.

If I'd not known in advance that the two individuals were related, I would have been hard pressed to place them in even *adjoining* family trees; the mother — Tessa Polanski, if I was remembering what I'd seen in the incorporation paperwork I'd reviewed the prior evening — was short and exceptionally overweight. She'd tried to hide that fact using an

"

oversized muumuu bearing a colorful floral print far more appropriate to resorts from the Hawaiian Islands. A necklace containing several small, hand-carved giraffes rested atop her bosom and mirrored earrings featuring the same animal. Wide-rimmed glasses were nestled on the very edge of her nose and were connected to a glittering gold chain that clashed horribly with the muumuu.

In contrast, the son — Timothy — stood nearly six feet tall and was rail thin, almost in an unhealthy way and was wearing a rumpled button down untucked over jeans that were fashionably threadbare. He also seemed to have inherited the gene for premature baldness, which made him look far older than his actual twenty-something age. A dense haze of dark stubble across his cheeks and along his neck seemed to be making up for the lack of hair on his pate, though it didn't seem to be a good look for the young man. If anything, it appeared as though he'd slept in his clothes and rolled out of bed and into the day without so much as a shower. Considering he'd lost his fiancé overnight, I wondered if that actually had been the case. As I drew to a stop on the step below the pair, I was tempted to draw conclusions about the dynamic of their relationship based on their posture, but decided to let the scene play out instead.

The mother was the first to speak. "Chief Colbeth?"

"It's Commander now, Ms. Polanski," I smiled.

"Ah, that's right," Polanksi said, frowning deeper. "You were fired."

"Yes," I said simply. "And then promptly re-hired by the State of Maine."

Tessa thought about this for a moment. "And you're the one assigned to this... situation?"

"Yes," I replied.

"Would you care to explain to me, then, why our kitchen remains closed?"

My smile thinned at the tone. "Not until I've had a chance to look it over, Ms. Polanski," I replied. It wasn't lost on me that we hadn't yet gotten to first names. "I'm headed there now with Dr. Kellerman; I'd like to speak with you and your son afterward, if you can spare the time."

"I'd prefer we talk about it now," she replied, crossing her arms tighter across her generous girth.

Based on the anger I could see in Polanski's eyes, I thought perhaps we'd hash out our differences right then and there on the steps of the hotel, but sanity in the form of her son interviewed. He leaned down and spoke softly to her. "Our office would be a more suitable location, Ma."

Polanski glanced at him and then nodded tightly. "Fine. How long do you think you'll be?"

"I have no idea," I answered. "How about I check in at the front desk when I'm ready to meet?"

"We can do that," the son said, cutting off what looked to be a less affirmative answer on the lips of his mother.

"I appreciate your patience," I said. "We have a number of balls in the air right now and too few people to manage them."

"Of course," he said as he grabbed at his mother's arm and tugged her up the steps. She glared at me for a moment before reluctantly trudging after him.

Suzanne and I watched them disappear into the lobby. "Tessa seemed a bit territorial," she observed.

"Not surprising," I said as we waited another beat and then followed the duo into the lobby ourselves. "Though it's probably just covering her shock over what's happened."

Suzanne snorted. "She doesn't strike me as someone particularly cut up over losing her future daughter-in-law. In fact, she seems more upset that you've thrown her well-oiled machine off kilter."

I glanced at Suzanne. "Maybe. No two people react to death — to murder — quite the same way; focusing on keeping this hotel functional may also be a coping mechanism."

"That sounds suspiciously like something I told you," Suzanne said as she led me down a side corridor I'd missed earlier. The first few feet matched the theme from the lobby, but after that became quite utilitarian; I'd seen my share of back-office hospitality operations over the years and remained intrigued at where the industry cut costs.

"I try to pay attention," I reminded her. "I've learned quite a bit from my girlfriend."

Suzanne paused in front of a metal door. "Have you now?"

"Yes," I nodded sagely. "And not just about the medical profession."

Her eyes danced with merriment. "Maybe you can show me the... depth and breadth of that knowledge later tonight."

"Maybe," I allowed with a slight smile. "Though I *am* a bit rusty."

"Are you now?" Suzanne smiled. "We'll have to see what we can do about that. Welcome to the kitchen," she added as she pushed through the metal door.

The facility was not as large as I was expecting, but at first blush appeared very modern. It felt like stainless steel covered nearly every surface, from the counters to the appliances to the walls behind the dish-washing area; the banks of bright LEDs nestled into the ceiling banished any sort of shadows, providing a surprisingly even light that didn't feel as harsh as traditional florescent bulbs. My nose immediately wrinkled at the overwhelming smell of cleaning chemicals, confirming my suspicion that we'd be unlikely to find anything egregious in the kitchen; the eye-watering scent underscored just how personally the kitchen staff had taken the outbreak.

That there was no activity at all was a reminder that pickings were rather slim for the guests in the hotel at the moment; while I'd not expected to see any, I had assumed we'd find the head chef present, or at the very least some poor underling taking inventory. Wondering if the latter was happening, I strode over to the walk-in fridge and yanked the door open; the blast of cold air from inside was the only thing that greeted me. Poking my head just inside, I could see a wide variety of fresh produce stacked on several shelves to one side; packages of other items like meats, cheeses and translucent plastic containers with various liquids were on the wire shelves opposite. Closing the door, I looked at Suzanne.

"I'm not a food inspector," I said. "I have no idea what we are looking for."

"Same," she said. "What I do have is my own kitchen common sense," she continued as she pointed to a small stainless-steel counter with an embedded sink. "For example, there are three sinks in the food preparation area, not counting the one that's part of the dishwashing station. This one seems small enough to be the one where produce would be prepped."

I started to remark on her observation when a doorbell rang out in the space. It took a moment for me to locate the source, which turned out to be a massive double door at the rear that looked appropriate for receiving deliveries. The deadbolt to the door was surprisingly tough to open, but once I did, the door swung outward easily. My eyebrows went up at the sight of Reggie standing on the other side, his wheeled cart behind him; he was wearing a brilliant yellow raincoat which was glistening. His cart had a blue tarp protecting the baked goods from the downpour.

"Sean?" he asked, his eyes widening. "What are you doing in the kitchen?"

"Investigating," I deadpanned. "Is that today's delivery?"

He nodded. "I'm quite late today. I accidentally overslept, and then all of this rain has made the trail nearly impassable. I had to come through town." Reggie tried to look around me. "Where's Chef?"

"I have no idea," I replied. "The kitchen is closed due to the outbreak."

"She mentioned that yesterday," he said. "I thought it would be open by now."

"I'm not sure we're going to find anything," I replied honestly, though I also avoided answering his unspoken question. "This place seems spotless, but until the inspector gets here it will probably stay closed." I turned to look at the gleaming stainless steel again. "All over blueberries."

Reggie was shaking his head. "I told Chef not to use those."

My eyebrows went up. "Really? When? And why?"

"A day or two ago," he said. "I was doing my morning run and Chef was unpacking the produce from the latest boat. She had the pints stacked up over there," he added, pointing to the very spot Suzanne had identified. "She was in quite the mood, too, as Tim had overseen the delivery. That never goes well."

I frowned. "Pints?" I asked. "That seems smaller than what a kitchen of this size would use."

Reggie nodded. "I said as much, even told her it must have cost a fortune to get them — especially since they were from out of state." That last part was added with an appropriately indignant tone, given how Maine blueberries typically held their own against the competition.

My frown deepened. "That seems at odds with Tim's push to cut costs by not using the local grocer."

"You'd think," Reggie replied. "I know it's hurt the market. I'm afraid they might not survive with just the residents using them. What's left of us, I guess."

I decided not to add my personal observation that I agreed with his assessment. "Seems like bad timing on his part, too; the grocery store had blueberries on special this week," I said. "I wasn't paying attention, but I think they were regional."

"Rockport area, actually," Reggie said. "I've used a pint or two in my blueberry bread. They are larger than normal and hold up well to baking."

"Where were those other blueberries from?" Suzanne asked.

"I didn't recognize the logo," Reggie hedged. "I just knew it was from out of state."

"Does Chef do the ordering?"

Something washed across Reggie's face. "These days, she just sets menus and then gives Tim the list of ingredients; he does the actual ordering. Has for a few years now." Reggie paused. "I'm not part of the kitchen staff, of course, but they chat with me when I'm making my delivery; I gathered this week was a bit unusual in that both Dot and Tim had a hand in arranging the menu, too." Reggie smiled wryly. "That didn't seem to go over well, especially Dot's emphasis on blueberries — Chef absolutely *hates* the fruit."

"Why force them on her, then?" Suzanne asked. "I'm sure Chef would have been capable of whipping up nearly anything in a kitchen like this."

Reggie looked wistful for a brief moment. "I think it was a favorite of the bride."

"Ah, that makes sense," I said before circling back to something Reggie had said earlier. "Tim does *all* of the ordering? Even the bread?"

This time, the look of distaste was more pronounced. "Yeah, even that."

"How much longer does your contract run?" I asked. Suzanne shot me a look of surprise, but I ignored it.

"Labor Day," he said after looking away.

"The unofficial end of tourist season," I sighed.

"I'm too expensive, so he's shifting to an out of state bakery."

And yet he orders blueberries from out of state at twice the cost? I thought. *How is that economical?*

"How on earth can that compete with what you bake fresh and deliver daily?" Suzanne asked, putting words to my undercurrent of disbelief.

"I can't compete on price," Reggie shrugged. "It's been a good run. Supplying the grocer will get me through the winter, but I'll have to decide what my path is come Memorial Day next year."

"That sucks," I said. "I'm truly sorry."

Reggie shrugged again. "Do you mind if I unload? I need to get back to the oven."

"Sure," I said, stepping aside so he could enter.

"I'm glad you were here," Reggie said as he walked over to a small cupboard and opened it. His boots squeaked as he crossed the linoleum. "I'd forgotten my key."

That frisson of excitement I get when a clue materializes hit me. "You normally let yourself in?"

"Yeah," he said as he moved back outside and slid part of the tarp away from his load. Grabbing a crate of fresh bread that itself was covered in a trash bag, he returned to the cupboard and started to pack the shelves. "Like I said, I'm normally earlier — like pre-dawn — so they have pastries for breakfast."

"Does every supplier have a key to this door?" I asked.

"Maybe," Reggie said. "You'd have to ask."

"Indeed," I said, then looked at Suzanne. "Well, we'll leave you to your work."

"See you around."

I took one last look at the gleaming kitchen before Suzanne and I exited; once we were in the hallway, she stopped me. "You barely poked into anything back there. That seems out of character for you; is everything all right?"

"Yes," I nodded. "Honestly, I just wanted to walk the space and get sense of it. Without an epidemiologist, I'm not sure I'd have even known what to do if I'd stumbled across the bacteria that had caused the outbreak anyway."

Suzanne arched an eyebrow. "Epidemiologist? This wasn't the start of some sort of pandemic, kitty."

"I have a hotel full of victims that might disagree," I smiled slightly. "I'm off to talk to management. I presume you'd prefer to check on your patients?"

"Yes," she said. "I can join you later if you're still planning on doing that group interview."

"I am," I nodded. "I'll see you then."

I parted ways with Suzanne when we reached the lobby — but not without a smoldering kiss that was a reminder of what was to come; pausing long enough to get my heart rate back under control, I then wandered over to the registration desk and waited for the clerk to look up. As they appeared engrossed in their computer terminal, I turned and idly scanned the lobby; compared to the day I'd been there with Corinne, it was extremely quiet save for a custodian energetically vacuuming a portion of the carpet close to the restrooms. The giant windows looking out onto the front of the property showcased the dark clouds that were currently emptying their contents against the glass; what trees were visible appeared to be leaning significantly, a clear indicator the wind had come up quite a bit. I wasn't looking forward to going back out into the storm.

"May I help you?" I heard from behind me.

Turning, I saw the young man who'd been on the computer now smiling at me.

"Yes, I'm Commander Sean Colbeth. I believe Ms. Polanksi is waiting to see me."

"Of course, Commander," he smiled and then held his hand to the left. "If you'd follow me...?

I nodded and then followed him to the end of the counter, then around a corner to another utilitarian corridor that ran behind the counter. This one was unusually dark, though, save for the spill of light coming from an open door at the end of the hallway; my guide paused at the threshold, then knocked. After seeing some sort of high sign from inside the room, he turned and smiled at me.

"Come on through, she's waiting."

"Thank you," I said.

Stepping through the open door, I found myself in a rather elegant office from another era. Wainscoting in a dark wood complimented a light wallpaper with some sort of elegant pattern in light blue; one wall housed floor-to-ceiling bookcases in the same wood and were tastefully full of books in varying sizes and shapes. A small Shaker-style round table sat in front of tall windows that looked out into the bay; a smattering of glossy magazines were arrayed on top, with more than a few open to specific articles as though I'd interrupted someone's coffee break. The table was surrounded by, conservatively, several thousand dollars' worth of Thomas Moser chairs and gave me pause; the desk behind which Tessa Polanski was sitting was of a similar style and vintage, making me realize the entire space could easily have been featured as a catalog photo for the furniture manufacturer. I'd worked a case a few years back in Portland, looking into the suspicious death of a wealthy widow; her home had been full of the furniture, which the killer — the son — had been planning on liquidating to pay off some business debts. The price tags for what I'd seen back then had been eye-popping and rather unforgettable; I could only imagine what the hand crafted and nearly artistic pieces went for currently.

Two more Moser chairs were facing the massive desk; Tim was sitting in one, balancing a MacBook on his lap. Polanski waved me into the other. "Coffee?" she asked as I took the proffered spot.

"I wouldn't say no," I smiled.

Polanski glared at her son, who set his laptop on the edge of the desk and stood. "How do you take it?" he asked as he moved to a banquet housing an impressive looking coffee maker.

"Black, thanks."

Something shifted in Polanski's face. "A traditionalist?"

"Of a sort," I replied. "Or I'm in the minority of those who favor the flavor of coffee, not the crap that gets mixed into it."

I was slightly amazed at the smile that appeared. "Hear, hear," she said. "This particular blend is from my family's land in Kona."

My eyebrows went up. "You have Kona coffee? *Real* Kona coffee?"

"It's one of the signatures of our hotel," Tim said as he handed me a steaming mug. "My uncle is our supplier."

I took a sip of the hot brew and savored the flavor. "This is a fine cup of coffee," I said appreciatively. "Thank you, Ms. Polanski."

"Our pleasure," Polanski said. "And please, call me Tess."

"So long as you call me Sean," I smiled. "If you don't mind my asking, how did a nice girl from Kona like you wind up here in Maine?"

Tess smiled. "Love," she said simply. "I met my late husband when we attended the University of Hawaii in Honolulu."

"He convinced you to trade palm trees for pine?" I asked as I sipped again.

"It was an easy sell," she replied. "I'd never left the islands; *anything* seemed exotic — and better than where I was."

"Do you miss any of it?"

Tess thought for a moment. "Fresh papaya," she replied. "And, believe it or not, poi."

"Poi?" I asked. "I don't think I know what that is."

"Be thankful of that," Tim said with a shudder. "The stuff is horrific."

"My own offspring, turning his back on tradition," Tess laughed.

"With good reason," he said, shuddering again.

I savored another sip of the coffee. "Again, my apologies that I've not connected with you sooner; this situation has been rather unique and extremely fluid."

Tess sighed. "I should be apologizing to you," she said. "Having a hotel full of guests is never easy; doing so when more than two-thirds are sick *and* the kitchen is closed is a challenge of an entirely different order. I think the stress is getting to me." She shot a glance at Tim. "To us."

Tim looked away. "Yeah."

There was an undercurrent to her comment that I couldn't quite place. "Not to mention a wedding."

Tim turned back to me. "That certainly upped the level of difficulty," he smiled slightly. "Not that it matters now."

I was about to say my usual caveat about having not yet confirmed the identity of the victim, but realized it was likely irrelevant; Tess had probably seen the body when she'd helped Suzanne gain access to the room. Shifting tactics slightly, I leaned into the opening Tim had given me. "I'm sorry for your loss."

He just nodded.

"You met your fiancé at a conference?" I asked.

"In Boston, yes," he nodded again. "We hit it off in the vendor room; I gave her my cell and we met for drinks that evening. Dot was just getting out of a difficult relationship and, frankly, had needed to bend someone's ear; I was a little worried about being a rebound boyfriend, so I politely listened and then forgot about her after the conference."

My eyebrows went up. "Not an auspicious beginning."

"No," he smiled, "but the way she described the jerk she'd been dating, I felt it was best to steer clear so her heart could heal. The guy was some sort of supermodel and had dragged her into a life of paparazzi and tabloid drama. Getting out had cost her quite a lot, emotionally."

"I take it you must have met again?" I asked. "Considering you were engaged."

Tim smiled, this time a warm, genuine affair. "She tracked me down here at the hotel," he said. "Ostensibly, she was on a sales visit, but when I saw her at the reception desk, I knew she'd taken the next step. We started dating at that point."

"When was that?"

"Four years ago," Tess spoke up. "Their love apparently had to mature."

"Ma!" Tim said, clearly irritated. "Love takes time."

"I want grandchildren," she said to me. "I'm not getting any younger; can you blame me for wanting to speed things up?"

"I suppose not," I smiled. "If you don't mind me asking, was Dot planning on working here after the marriage?"

"Yes," Tim said. "She'd put in her notice at Spranger's before driving up for the wedding. They weren't happy to lose her — she's their top salesperson."

"Until she had my grandchildren," Tess amended.

Tim looked away again. "We'd not talked about that phase," he said softly. The tinge of sadness in his voice spoke to the greater loss he was suffering.

As fresh as the wounds appeared to be, I decided to shift the conversation slightly. "Dr. Kellerman and I just finished looking over the kitchen," I said. "I think it's safe to open with the understanding that a State inspector is on the way and might likely close it down again."

"We can work with that," Tess said.

"Good." I looked to Tim. "I understand the blueberries that caused this problem in the first place were from out of state."

"Were they?" he replied. "I order through a wholesaler; they source everything."

"Could you provide me their name?"

"Sure," he nodded. "Why?"

"We'll need to notify them if there is something wrong in the batch you received," I said, somewhat amazed I'd need to explain that to him. "I need to ensure anyone else who received fruit from that same batch is aware of the issue."

"You don't know it's the blueberries for sure," Tim countered.

"True," I said. "Your kitchen staff seems to have disposed of what was left and sanitized the kitchen before we knew there was an issue."

"Then why notify the wholesaler?"

"There are public health protocols in play here," I said. "Those mandate our actions in situations such as these."

"But—"

"Tim will dig out the packing slips and provide the contact information to you later this morning," Tess said, her tone brooking no argument. "Is there anything else we can provide to you?"

"A list of people who have key access to the hotel after hours, beside the guests," I said. "As well as any security logs or video for the property from the last few days."

Tim glanced at Tess. "It will take an hour or two, but I can do that."

"Then that's it for now," I said as I stood. Tim stood as well and took my mug. "Thank you for the coffee; I appreciate the shot of caffeine."

"My pleasure," Tess said. "We've also made one of the smaller ballrooms available to you for interviews," she continued. "The other detective you are working with made arrangements earlier. If you need anything else, please reach out."

I nodded. "We hope to get those out of the way as quickly as possible so your guests can get on with their lives," I said.

"If only it were that easy," Tim said quietly.

"Yeah," I said as I turned to go. "I hear you."

Passing the small huddle table on my way out, I glanced down at the smattering of magazines spread out on the table; I'd seen them on my way in, of course, and hadn't thought much about them at the time. On the way out, though, the light from the small lamp beside the table had been at a different angle and happened to highlight the smiling face of a tall model walking along the pathway between the hotel and beach wearing what looked like a classically cut business suit. The bolt of recognition that hit me was nearly physical, but I managed to mask it with a smile as I half turned back to Tess and Tim.

"Checking out the fall fashions?" I asked, nodding to the magazines.

Tim's eyes shot to the table; that undercurrent suddenly was back in the room. "More like research," he said amiably. "We host photo shoots for the major brands each year; one of them is booking for October and wanted to re-create something we'd done for a competitor. I couldn't remember what it was and had to pull the magazines from our files."

"Ah," I nodded. "And now I know why this hotel seemed so memorable."

"It's been the backdrop for lots of things, including a movie or two," Tess said. Her smile suddenly seemed strained.

"Very cool," I said. "Well, thanks again for both your time and the coffee."

"Of course."

I felt the eyes of Tess and Tim on my back as I exited; I was less concerned with that than the fact that the model in question on the page Tim had left the magazine open to was my baker-in-the-woods, Reggie.

TEN

Suzanne discovered fairly early in our relationship that I'd had zero exposure to pop culture growing up; it wasn't entirely my fault, for when you're spending every waking hour in or around the pool prepping for the Olympics, there tended not to be a lot of spare time for anything not germane to the pursuit of a gold medal. Vasily had tried to buff out the worst aspects of my ignorance during our years living together in the apartment over the pharmacy, but by that point, my swimming obsession had been joined by an even deeper one focused on becoming the best investigator in the business; his final shot had been dragging me to Bangor to see the first movie in a new *Star Wars* trilogy in the hopes it would kickstart a love of science fiction. When I didn't immediately run out and purchase a lightsaber (let alone understand what the damn thing was in the first place), Vas had thrown his hands into the air and given up.

This was the sorry state of affairs that the love of my life found me in that night at the Windeport *Not So Scary Halloween Party* — the same one where I'd barely understood the backstory to the animated superhero whose costume I'd happened to be wearing at the time. Suzanne had taken up the challenge I'd presented, and, true to form, had carefully been helping me to explore what amounted to a three-decade gap in my experience as a human. I'd surprised myself by taking to the subject matter, eagerly absorbing her curated list of television shows, classic movies and concerts in the short year we'd been together. Her private tutoring nearly always entailed being curled up together on my couch or her loveseat (depending on which house we were using at the time), discussing whatever it was we'd just experienced late into the evening; her nonjudgmental kindness had slowly begun to open doors I'd never known existed.

Of the many classic movies we'd shared, Suzanne had revealed an annoying penchant for big screen murder mysteries; I wasn't entirely certain if it was a ploy to see if I could deduce the whodunnit long before the leading man (or woman) had, or if she just genuinely enjoyed the rather frothy depiction of what I did in real life. For many reasons, I wasn't a fan of the genre, but I also had to admit that a few of her selections were, on the whole, quite good. One of the best was based on an Agatha Christie novel I'd actually read in college, *Evil Under the Sun*. Made in 1982 and starring the remarkable Peter Ustinov as Christie's Belgian detective, Hercule Poirot, I'd long felt the story — with its creatively complicated underlying murder plot — had withstood the test of time, besting some of the more modern detective movies that had been made since. I always figured it was high on my list due to its exotic location, or the equally colorful cast of characters Poirot was forced to investigate; I'd had many a thorny mystery, to be sure, but nothing had yet come close to what Dame Christie had pulled from her own creative mind back in the early 1940s.

Evil Under the Sun was very much on my mind as I walked into one of the larger meeting rooms the hotel had provided for my interviews. Toward the end of the movie, Poirot gathers up all of the suspects and then weaves his tale of how he thinks the crime has been committed; while I didn't feel as though I was at that particular stage of the investigation — how could I be, given what little I knew at that point? — seeing the semicircle of chairs the hotel staff had arranged around the perimeter of the space somehow gave me comfort that I might actually have my own moment at some point. Putting my hands on the back of one of the chairs, I considered how I wanted to handle this first round of interviews; while it wasn't normally my style to speak to suspects in a large group setting, expediency seemed to dictate the necessity of doing so. There was a very real concern that hearing stories out in the open in such a forum might shade people's recollections in a way that would come back to haunt me, but I was also betting on my own abilities to weed out just such an occurrence.

Or at least, that was the working theory.

There was a gentle knock at the door behind me, and I turned to see Corinne standing in the frame; Suzanne was just beside her. "Ready?" she asked.

"Yes," I replied.

She nodded, then looked away to speak to someone on the other side. "This way, please."

I watched as she led an eclectic group of people into the room; some I recognized from my brief time at the lobby bar with Corinne, but the rest were not familiar in the least. All, though, looked like they had gone ten rounds in some sort of prize fight — and had lost; the drawn faces and pale complexions were a reminder that nearly the entire group was still recovering from a serious bout of food poisoning. Much like teenagers entering a high school classroom for the first time, there was a serious undercurrent of discomfort as chairs were selected and people took up their chosen position; Suzanne was the last one into the room and carefully closed the door behind her before she quietly pressed herself into the shadows behind me. Corinne, on the other hand, had staked out a spot beside me and had a pleasant expression on her face that helped mask how she, too, was scoping out those now assembled before us. The silence in the room was pierced only by the distant mechanical hum of the air conditioning; I let it linger long enough that more than a few people began to fidget in their uncomfortable banquet seats. Taking that as my cue, I smiled, folded my hands behind my back and then began.

"I'm Commander Sean Colbeth of the Maine State Police," I said pleasantly. "I appreciate the effort it took to join me here this morning; I'll try to keep this brief so everyone can return their focus to their recovery."

There were a few murmurs of assent, but nothing more.

"By now you are probably aware that there was a death in the hotel last night," I continued, carefully watching faces so I could gauge reaction to my statement. "While I'm still piecing together the details, I have enough so far to treat this as a murder investigation."

I heard several sharp intakes of breath and saw more than one already pale face turn paler. Knowing how ill most everyone one in the room was, I really couldn't read into those who didn't react; then again, it was just as likely I had a killer hiding in plain sight.

"The victim appears to have been Dot Fernyhough," I continued, "the young woman who was planning on getting married this weekend."

I let the concept sink in for a long moment, carefully observing the group without actually appearing to do so. Nothing out of the ordinary presented itself; to a person, they all seemed genuinely shocked. Mixed in with the already strong undercurrent of fear from having to meet with me, the level of discomfort in the room was nearly palpable. Oddly, at that moment I realized the wall sconces were shaped like tall pine trees, a strange affection for a hotel on an island.

"I believe most of you knew her personally?" I added, pausing when I saw nodding. "You have my sincerest condolences on your loss." Waiting a beat, I continued. "I rarely do these sorts of group interviews, but the unusual circumstances we find ourselves in demands expediency. So, I am going to beg your indulgence in answering a few questions, mostly to help me get a better picture of the events leading up to last night." I paused and scanned the crowd again. "If anyone feels uncomfortable talking to me in this venue, I'll be available afterward to speak one on one. I've also arranged to have the hotel operator put you through to me directly if you call the front desk from your room."

I saw a few nods, and no small amount of terror; I'd found hearing the word *murder* tended to have that effect on people. Glancing at my chair, I decided sitting down would give the session something of a survivor's recovery group feel; coming around, I took my seat and casually crossed my legs as though I were leading the group through some sort of meditative exercise.

"I'd like to talk a bit about the bachelorette party two nights ago, which I believe all of you attended?"

First three heads nodded, then one more in a tentative, please-don't-call-on-me manner. Making a note of that person in particular, I glanced at Corinne; she also nodded, oblique confirmation everyone she'd seen herself that evening (save for the bride-to-be) had been accounted for. Turning back to the women who had volunteered their attendance, I considered my next question carefully.

"I can appreciate that such events are usually private, intimate affairs, so I'll do my best not to steer clear of adding anything embarrassing to the official record," I said, electing a few wan smiles. "Let's start with the easy stuff. Please tell me your name, where you are from and how you know Dot — I'll start with you on the end."

The older woman in the chair closest to me was startled to have been selected first; it didn't help that she'd also been one of those who had very reluctantly raised their hand initially. "Marilyn Hartley," she said after a moment of what looked like absolute terror.

I smiled my warmest Maine smile. "Good morning, Marilyn. It's nice to meet you."

"Hi," she said. "Uh... what else did you want to know?"

"Where are you from, Marilyn?"

"Washington, D.C.," she replied. "I'm a senior aide to Senator Robert Meade."

"The Senator from Massachusetts?" I asked.

"Yes," Marilyn nodded. "I've been with Mr. Meade since he was speaker of the Massachusetts House."

My eyebrows went up. "If memory serves, that is a rather significant amount of time."

"Twenty-two years," she smiled slightly.

It was painfully obvious that Marilyn was skewing the demographic of those who had attended the party; I sorted through my options and settled on a question that wouldn't throw the focus onto that fact. "How do you know Dot?"

"I... my daughter grew up with Dot," Marilyn said, essentially going there anyway. "The two of them were inseparable from kindergarten until they went their separate ways for college. They remained close after that; Dot was in Lisa's wedding last year." Marilyn looked away. "I lost Lisa to breast cancer in April; she was supposed to be here. Dot asked me to attend instead."

"I am... so very sorry for your loss," I said, seeing the emotion on the woman's face. "Were you also close to Dot?"

"Heavens yes. I think of her as my daughter." Marilyn's eyes watered. "*Thought* of her," she corrected.

I nodded; there wasn't much more to say, so I moved to the next woman. She was nearer to Corrine's demographic. "And you are?"

"Janet Cornflower," she replied. "From Boston. I work with Dot — *worked* — at Sprangers and Sons."

"They're in the hospitality business?" I asked, thinking back to my conversation with Corinne at the bar.

"Yes," Janet replied. "We sell hotel supplies wholesale to the industry. Several of the major worldwide chains are our clients, but we also work with smaller independent resorts."

"Like this one?" I asked, waving at the ballroom with my hands.

"Yes," Janet nodded.

"Thank you," I said, then moved to the next woman. She was sitting with her arms wrapped around her midsection, tight enough I thought it might be difficult to breathe. "Good morning."

"Hi," she replied tightly.

I looked at her for a moment.

"I'm Helena Scott," she finally replied when the silence seemed nearly overwhelming. "I'm sorry, this is a bit overwhelming. I had drinks with Dot last night and now you're telling me she's dead? It's all so unbelievable."

"I can understand that," I said easily. "Please feel free to take as much time as you need to answer."

Helena looked at me. "What was the question again?"

"Where are you from?" I reminded her. "And how do you know Dot?"

"Oh, right," she said, then looked away. Dabbing at her nose with a wadded-up Kleenex, she seemed to consider her response as though it were a Calculus problem she'd forgotten the formula for. At length, she turned back to me. "UCLA," she finally replied. "I first met Dot there when we were undergrads; I live on the South Shore now, but I'm originally from Cambridge."

"Cambridge is a beautiful city," I smiled.

Helena lit up. "You've been there?"

"Several times," I nodded. "Usually for a regional swim meet, but once or twice on business."

"Business—?" she started to ask before the answer came to her. "Oh," she said. The level of disbelief that someone with my professional talents would be needed in Cambridge seemed anathema to her.

"And how do you know Dot?" I gently prodded.

"Sales," she replied. "I mean, I *sell* bathroom supplies to her company as a wholesaler."

I felt an eyebrow arch. "You sell stuff to Dot, who in turn sells it to hotels?"

"Yes," she nodded.

That explains where the markup must come from, I thought. "All right," I nodded. Thinking I'd gotten as much out of this particular turnip as I could, I turned to the next person who had raised their hand. "And you are...?"

"Samantha Cooke," she replied. "I also went to high school with Dot."

"Are you still in Boston?"

"No," she shook her head. "I live in Raleigh-Durham; I flew up for the wedding."

"Portland?" I asked. "Or Bangor?"

Samantha looked at me with a blank expression. "I'm sorry?"

"I was just wondering which airport you came into," I replied. "Both are quite a drive from here."

"Ah," she smiled slightly. "Sorry, I thought you were asking something else entirely. It was Boston, actually; the schedule was better and, honestly, the flight was cheaper."

"Not the first time I've heard that," I replied. "We don't have a lot of options this far North."

"Clearly," she said. "Which makes it all the more amazing Maine is considered such a tourist destination."

"When you want to get away from everything, we fit the bill rather nicely," I smiled, wondering if my home had just been insulted. I turned to Corinne. "In the interests of completeness, you were at the party as well, right?"

"Yes," Corinne replied. "Dot and I were roommates in college; it had been a while since we'd spoken, so I was a little surprised that she'd invited me to the wedding."

"Friendships have their quirks," I said, then turned back to the crowd. "Aside from what appears to be a tainted batch of blueberries served during the party, did anything else seem unusual last night?"

"In what way?" Helena asked.

"Something out of the ordinary," I explained.

"That's hard to say," Samantha said. "We're not from around here, so how would we know if something was odd?"

I nodded. "Good point. Let's try something different then; walk me through how the evening went. Who arrived first?"

"I did," Samantha said. "About six, I think. Marilyn was literally right behind me."

Corinne nodded. "The two of you were at the table when I got there. I think Janet was next?"

"I was held up in waiting for the elevator," Janet explained. "I think we were all seated when Helena arrived."

"And Dot was right behind me," Helena said. "Once we sat down, the first course came out along with the wine."

"What was the first course?"

"A charcuterie board, selections of rolls and a blueberry compote."

"Ah," I nodded. "The blueberries make their appearance."

"We all tried them," Helena said, "save for Corinne over there."

I turned to my fellow detective. "Not a fan of blueberries in general," she said.

"And yet you'll eat avocado," I teased.

"It might be a California thing," she offered with a shrug.

"That seems to have worked to your benefit," I observed. "What happened next?"

"I think we had a round of drinks," Janet said.

"Yes," Helena nodded. "Dot ordered a bottle of pink champaign which we used for a toast, then we thought it would be fun for all of us to have a Cosmo."

"Oh God," Corinne groaned. "I forgot about the Cosmos. We didn't stop at one, did we?"

"No," Marilyn smiled slightly. The memory of the event had clearly chased away the more somber aspects of what happened later. "If the blueberries hadn't gotten to me first, I think I would've had a hell of a hangover."

"Wasn't there a second bottle of champaign?" Samantha said. "I feel like we toasted again. And again."

"And again," Corinne groaned again. "How much did we have?"

"Enough that the bartender came over and cut us off," Janet said. "Dot had words with him."

I felt an eyebrow arch. "What did she say, exactly?"

"Something along the lines of 'I'll be married to your boss, so be good to me,'" Samantha said. "That didn't go over well."

"No, it didn't," Janet said. "Tim showed up after that."

"And he was *pissed*," Helena continued.

"Over what?" I asked.

Samantha frowned. "You know, I thought it was because Dot had drunk her way through half of the bar's inventory, but now, I'm not so sure. He wasn't there very long — just enough to whisper something to her. Whatever he said, though, her mood shifted instantly."

"When did he appear?"

Corinne answered. "I think the dessert dishes had just arrived, so close to the end of our meal."

"Yeah," Janet continued. "He really was upset, wasn't he? I didn't know him all that well, but the party was pretty much over at that point."

"Really?" I asked.

"Yes," Corinne nodded. "Dot excused herself before she ate her dessert. Which was criminal, for the chocolate cake was to die for."

I glared at Corinne, who clearly regretted her turn of phrase. "Did anyone happen to catch the time that she left the party?"

"I wasn't in any shape to remember such a thing," Janet said.

"Me either," Helena said. "Marilyn seemed the most put together; if anyone noticed, it would have been her."

I looked at the older woman. "Is it possible?"

She looked thoughtful for a moment. "Yes," Marilyn ultimately said. "I think I do - it was around ten. I know only because I took the opportunity of her departure to pull my phone out; this is going to sound odd, but I wanted to check the score on the Red Sox game. It had gone into extra innings and was running later than normal."

I smiled slightly. "I can actually understand that. The game didn't turn out well for the Sox."

"No," she frowned, "it certainly didn't."

Samantha shifted in her chair. "You know, now that I'm thinking about the party last night, there was something weird."

"What was that?" I asked.

"I might have the timing wrong, but I think there was a commotion at the bar," she said, screwing up her face as she tried to recall a memory. "Maybe?"

"Oh God, are you talking about that hunk who was drunk?" Janet asked.

Helena's eyebrows went up. "I'd forgotten about that," she said, smiling slightly as she looked at me. "Honestly, when he stumbled over to the table, we thought he'd been hired for the party."

"Oh man," Samantha smiled herself. "The way he draped himself across Dot, I was right there with you. And he had muscles, didn't he?"

"That shirt didn't hide much," Janet replied.

"Did Dot recognize who the guy was?" I asked. "I take it he wasn't a stripper."

"Stripper? Sadly, no," Helena sighed. "Dot did seem to know who he was, though it was hard to tell if she was happy to see him or not."

"It was the former," Marilyn said. "I got the sense they went way back."

My eyebrows went up. "Is he part of the wedding?"

"I don't think so," Janet replied, "at least, that was the first I'd seen him. I don't think he was family."

"Anyone one else recognize him?"

"No," Helena said after another long moment of thought. "I mean, not among us; the bartender seemed to know him, though. He was the one to escort him out after Dot pushed him away."

I nodded, making a mental note to check in with the bartender at the restaurant. "It's a small island," I smiled. "Someone is bound to know who this guy is."

"I hope so," Helena said. "If you find out his name, could you get me his number?"

"That's not usually how these investigations work," I laughed, glad of the brief levity.

"Damn," she sighed.

There didn't seem to be much more to glean from the group at that point, so I took down their contact information and let them gingerly file back out of the ballroom. I felt like some interesting tidbits had surfaced, but I couldn't shake the sense that something about the session felt off to me. Disabling the recording function for my iPhone, I stared at the screen without really seeing it, trying to nail down what, exactly, was bothering me. Group interviews were never satisfactory for a variety of reasons, one of the most important being a creeping group-think among the participants. Once one witness planted a seed of a memory, others often mistook it for a shared experience, crafting their own version of events that might, at best, be little more than a fictitious wrapper around a sliver of truth.

At worst, it could help mask an outright lie.

I straddled the chair I'd been using and leaned my arms against the back, nodded at Corinne, then looked over to where Suzanne was still leaning against the wall. "Thoughts?"

Suzanne frowned slightly. "I know I'm not a trained investigator, but did anyone else think it was odd how they had amazingly clear recollections despite having drunk quite a bit of alcohol?"

I felt myself nodding. "It was certainly unusual," I said. "If they drank what they said they did, I'd have been surprised at their collective ability to return to their rooms unaided."

"And yet, to a person, they each had a clear memory of the fiancé arriving," Corinne said, "as well as the appearance of a mysterious stranger that Dot also knew."

"Also exceptionally unusual," I nodded again. "Eyewitnesses are notoriously unreliable under the best of circumstances. These were certainly anything but."

"Alcohol affects people differently," Suzanne said. "I feel obligated to point out there's an outside chance that this crowd is in the top percentile for holding their liquor."

I felt one of my eyebrows arching. "Seriously?"

Suzanne smiled. "The odds are against it, naturally."

"Naturally." I looked at Corinne. "How about you?"

"I drank my supervisor under the table at her retirement party," Corinne said. "For the record."

"Good to know," I said, shaking my head. "But more to the point—"

"Yeah, I'm with Suzanne," she said. "So many people having such solid recollections — I agree with you, that's highly unusual in my experience." Corinne looked at me thoughtfully. "Do you think they were lying? As a *group*?"

"I'm not sure at this point," I allowed. "There was definitely an undercurrent to our conversation, though I'm not prepared to say the group was collectively trying to hide something."

"Or throw us off course?" Corinne asked.

I smiled. "Oh, there's no question there was a bit of that," I replied. "No one likes having a cop poking around in their personal lives." I looked at Corinne. "Not even a fellow cop."

Corinne frowned deeply. "*Especially* cops," she said. "Even I have secrets I'd prefer the world not know."

"Don't we all," I laughed, trying to lighten the mood. Still, the discomfort persisted on Corrine's face, which naturally intrigued me. I wondered what my friend had yet to tell me about her relationship to Dot, and filed that away for later. "I suspect as we dig around, we're going to uncover some uncomfortable truths about the guests at this wedding."

"One of them being the reason behind the murder of Dot?"

"Oh yes," I nodded as I stood up. "Most definitely."

"Good to know we have a plan," Corinne said. "What's next?"

"I imagine Suzanne needs to make her rounds again," I said and saw my girlfriend nod. "Once she gives me the okay, I want to talk to Dot's parents." I paused for a moment. "While I wait, I think my next stop is the bar to see if I can get more details on the drunken friend that intruded into the bachelorette party."

"All right," she nodded. "What can I do?"

I glanced at the woefully inadequate pile of DNA tests I'd brought from the station; walking over to where we'd placed them on a spare chair, I picked them up and took them back to Corinne. "We don't have enough of these, as you know, so I need to be pretty strategic about who we swab first. Take one of these and see if the fiancé will agree to us taking a sample."

One of Corrine's eyebrows arched. "You *just* spoke to him," she reminded me. "Why didn't you get the swab then?"

"Timing is everything in this business," I smiled enigmatically. "And I have a feeling Tim will consent faster if you are the one asking."

"That's rather sexist," Suzanne observed.

"Maybe," I allowed, "but when in Rome..."

Corinne took the test, but frowned. "Fine," she said. "I'll meet up with you after."

"I'll be in the bar," I said helpfully.

"I figured," she smiled slightly. "But thanks for the reminder."

"Anytime," I laughed.

Eleven

The sense I was somehow stuck inside a classic Agatha Christie period mystery became even greater as I stepped into the main restaurant for the hotel. As with much of the resort, the space felt like a throwback to the roaring twenties, with red velvet-covered booth cushions, freshly starched white linens and gossamer chandeliers hung from the ceiling draped with reflective pieces of cut crystal. A massive set of windows looked onto the outdoor dining patio just above the beach; that morning, they provided a gloomy view of an angry ocean whipped into a frothy frenzy by the storm that had finally let loose, emphasizing the overwhelming sense of noir that seemed to have permeated into everything since the body had been discovered. As I paused just inside the double glass doors, I corrected myself; maybe it wasn't Christie, but rather something out of Raymond Chandler — or some weird fusion of the two. It wasn't lost on me how clichéd it felt, investigating a murder at a hotel on an isolated island; the only thing missing was having an ominously downbeat musical soundtrack quietly filling the room from the small speakers I could see nestled in the pressed tin ceiling. That wasn't currently the case, fortunately; if music *had* been playing, it would have been nearly impossible to hear over the hubbub of the staff preparing the restaurant for lunch, the first service since it had been closed due to the food poisoning outbreak.

I'd only eaten inside the restaurant that one time I'd been with Charlie Kampert; still, that hadn't precluded my ingrained investigator from carefully committing the space's layout to memory while eating. It had appeared at the time that the main portion of the space was able to seat a significant number of guests at any one time; capacity doubled, essentially, when the outdoor patio was also in use. While I was sure it had been many decades since the entire resort had been fully booked, the restaurant seemed to take great pains to make it clear that it still *could* handle the situation, should it ever arise again. I had my doubts that it ever would, but then again, I'd been caught off guard at how our original grand hotel back in Windeport, the Colonial by Marriott, had come roaring back from obscurity when we became a cruise ship destination.

There was a sizable bar running the length of the wall nearest the entrance made entirely from a warm-colored wood, probably cherry, that appeared to have darkened with age; behind it was a tasteful set of shelves in the same material displaying the various spirits on offer. The requisite barstools lined the front of the serving space, with smallish round tables behind them that could hold two or three people. That noir flavor became more pronounced when my eyes fell on the bartender, attired in a white button down and black slacks, with a black apron tied about his waist and a matching black bowtie. He had a towel in one hand and was just reaching for a small glass tumbler to dry when our eyes met; they were dark and knowing in a way unique to bartenders who had heard more than their fair share of personal angst from patrons slowly trying to drink away the pain. With a full head of silver hair and lines around his eyes, it was easy to see how anyone would feel comfortable confiding in the amiable-looking uncle figure.

Smiling, I moved over to the bar and put my hands on the back of a chair. "You look like a man who has seen it all," I said.

"And then some," he smiled as he dried the glass. "I'm afraid we're not going to be open for another hour or so."

"Just in time for lunch?" I asked as I glanced at my watch. It was surprising how quickly the morning had drained away.

"Yes," he nodded.

"Fortunately, I'm not here for a drink," I continued. "I'm actually looking for information."

The bartender sighed and put down the glass. "Like that's the first time I've ever heard that line," he said. "Next, you'll be pulling out a wad of hundreds and waving them at me."

My eyebrows went up. "I wouldn't have expected such cynicism from a barkeep at an island hotel," I said. "That seems more apropos of someone from a big city establishment."

There was a hint of a smile on his lips when he replied. "It would, wouldn't it?"

I eyed him for a moment. "Boston?" I asked. "One of the big hotels there?"

"Not bad," he replied, the smile going full. "The Four Seasons, actually. Spent thirty years managing the lobby bar as well as the spirits for the restaurant. I retired a couple years back."

"For a retired guy, you seem rather employed," I observed.

"Turns out, I hate fishing," he laughed. "Took two years before I drove the missus nuts. We moved here last year and I split days with Phyllis — just enough to keep an old guy from getting bored."

"Good plan," I said.

"Usually, I'm the one listening," he continued. "And yet, here I am spilling my guts to a total stranger."

"Might have something to do with my personality," I smiled as I reached my hand across the polished surface. "Or my profession. I'm Sean Colbeth, Commander of the Statewide Major Crimes Unit."

"Sam," the gentleman replied as we shook. "Sam Horner. You're that kid from Windeport? The one the Council fired?"

"I'm not sure how much of a 'kid' I am these days, but the rest is true," I nodded.

"Anyone younger than *me* is a kid," Sam said.

"Ah," I replied. It seemed best not to ask the obvious follow-up question.

Sam looked at me. "I've known my fair share of cops," he said after a moment. "And I've read what was in the papers. You got a bum deal."

"I would agree," I said.

"Looks like you landed on your feet," he said, reappraising me. "What will it be?"

I cocked my head. "You said the bar was closed."

"My bar," he smiled. "My rules."

I glanced at the gleaming taps set into surface of the bar; I wasn't a morning drinker, but lunch seemed close enough that I could make an exception. "Sam Adams."

"Good choice," Sam smiled as he put down the towel and tumbler, then reached under the counter to produce a taller glass frosted by the chill of the fridge it had been in. "I just added the Oktoberfest keg this morning."

"I noticed," I smiled.

Sam made quick work out of filling the glass with a minimum of head; placing a napkin down in front of me, it was quickly joined by the amber brew. I carefully picked it up and took a swig, relishing in the seasonal flavor I looked forward to every fall. Placing it back on the napkin, I looked up and saw Sam had returned to drying his glasses.

"Were you on duty two nights back?" I asked. "During the bachelorette party?"

"I was, actually," he nodded, then pointed with the towel-covered hand toward a table that appeared able to easily sit eight. "It was seven of them, sitting there," he continued. "I did the drinks for the party — such as they were; mostly bottles of champaign, really, and few mixed cocktails."

"How long were they here?"

Sam frowned slightly. "I think the reservation was for six? Most of them arrived about then — I only know that, because I had to get the first bottle of champaign out of the bigger fridge we have in the kitchen."

"You don't keep that out here?"

"I have *some* here," he said, "but these had been ordered specifically for the wedding. It was an expensive California *cuvee* that had been shipped in."

"Not something you'd ordinarily serve, then?"

"No," he said, then smiled. "I mean, does this place strike you as where you'd go for pink champaign?"

"I'm not sure I'd know one way or the other," I replied. "I'm more of a beer guy, though my girlfriend is working me into wine."

"Probably for the best," he nodded.

"You said *most* of the party arrived at six; did anyone come later?"

"Yeah," Sam nodded as he put down the glass he'd dried and picked up another. I wondered at just how many he had left to do, hidden beneath the bar. "Some appetizers had been brought out, and I'd opened a second bottle of champaign when I think the bride-to-be arrived. She sat at the end."

"Do you have a sense of when that was?"

Sam shrugged. "Maybe twenty past? I could probably pull the bill if you want to know exactly; our inventory system forces us to key items into the POS each time we serve."

I glanced meaningfully at my glass. "Always?"

"Well," he smiled. "Almost always. Anyway, even from over here I could tell she wasn't the happy-go-lucky person I normally saw."

"You know Dot?"

"Of course," he smiled. "She's here many a weekend visiting Tim; I have to admit, though, I was a little surprised at how willing she was to give up her life in Boston."

My eyebrows went up. "Why?" I asked. "I mean, one of them would have to have moved, right?"

"It wouldn't have been Tim," Sam said darkly. "Don't get me wrong: they've treated me well, but I see the way Tessa has been guilting Tim into staying here to run the hotel." He paused, then glanced to the ceiling. "This place is dying — the entire island is dying — and she knows it; somehow, she's convinced Tim to stay on board despite the ship slowly sinking beneath the waves."

"How bad is it?" I asked as I sipped at the exceptional beer. There really wasn't anything quite like Samuel Adams on draft.

"Tim's cut as much cost as he can, but we don't get the same sort of well-heeled clients we once did." He nodded in the general direction of Windeport. "The Colonial's resurgence has put quite the dent in tourism for Carpenter's Island; why take the mail boat here when you can *drive* to them?" Sam put down the glass and picked up another. "Not that it matters, for our clientele is literally dying off. Families — extremely wealthy families from Boston and New York — who have been coming for generations; their kids want the glitz and glamor of Orlando or Paris now, not some relic to a time long past."

"The wedding must have been a welcome spike in traffic, then."

"Unquestionably," he nodded, before leaning toward me and lowering his voice conspiratorially. "That, and it was cheaper than paying for something elsewhere."

I frowned. "I might not be up on my etiquette, but I thought the bride's family paid for such things?"

"Maybe back when places like this were built," Sam chuckled. "That's more likely to be shared by the couple today."

"Dot comes from money, though?"

"Yes. Old money that dates back to the Revolution."

"But Tim was paying for the wedding?"

"*Tessa* was paying for the wedding," Sam corrected.

I nodded slowly. "To help keep Tim here."

Sam tapped his nose. "Not bad."

"Family can be complicated, can't it?" I smiled.

"Oh yes," Sam smiled. "Fortunately, talking about such complications allowed me to put my kids through college."

"I'm glad there was some positivity to take from it," I replied. "Speaking of Tim, did he make an appearance at the party?"

Sam's face shifted. "Yeah," he said carefully.

I sipped at the beer and was surprised that I'd managed to drink half of it already. "He spoke with Dot?"

"Yes," he said.

"Do you know what he said to her?" I asked.

"No," Sam said, continuing the monosyllabic responses he'd been making since I mentioned Tim's arrival.

"I see," I said. Deciding to go for broke, I took another sip and then pushed slightly. "I understand you had to cut Dot off."

"Yes, I did," he nodded. "Her little party managed to go through a third of the champaign; we needed to save some for the reception."

"She wasn't happy with you, was she?"

"Not particularly," he admitted. "I believe she reminded me that she'd be married to the boss and could therefore get what she wanted."

"Harsh," I smiled.

"Not untrue, however," he sighed. "I'm not sure I would ever choose to work for a family-owned business again; the nepotism is nauseating."

"So I hear." I twisted the half-full beer glass in my hands. "Dot left soon after Tim spoke to her?"l

"I have no idea," Sam said a little too quickly.

"Sam," I said patiently, "if you are trying to protect the *current* boss, you should know that I will get the truth sooner or later." I paused and held his eyes. "I'd rather hear it from you now, than someone else *later*."

Sam looked away. "Yeah. Maybe five minutes after he spoke with her."

"Did she look upset?"

Sam paused again. "Yeah," he said.

"Was Tim still here?"

"I don't think so," he replied, "but I truly don't know."

I nodded. "I understand you were something of a bouncer that night, too," I continued.

Sam put his hands down on the bar. "It comes with the territory."

"Who was it that you threw out?"

"He's harmless," Sam deflected. "And Dot was okay with what happened."

"Shouldn't I be the judge of that?" I asked quietly. "Who was it?"

"Shit," Sam said then looked away. "The poor kid had his heart broken once. Isn't that enough misery for one lifetime?"

"Probably," I allowed. "If we're lucky. Most aren't, though."

Sam tapped at the counter, then looked at me. "Christ. You'll find out anyway, won't you?"

I nodded. "I always do."

He sighed. "Reggie," Sam said quietly. "He's been a regular since moving to the island; Phyllis knows him better than I do, since she's been here longer." Sam picked up a glass and started to dry again. "I only know parts of the story — she knows more — but we both have a sense the poor kid landed here on Carpenter's Island to get away from a serious heartache."

"And then found a new one here?"

"That was my sense," he signed again. "I think he had a crush on Dot."

My eyebrows went up. "Talk about a doomed romance," I said. "What with her getting married and all."

"Exactly."

"Was it mutual?"

"No," Sam said, but again, it was a tad too quickly.

I decided not to press that particular point. "How regular a customer was he?" I asked. "As a baker, I'd think he'd not hang out here too late most nights."

"Just after dinner most evenings," Sam said. "Two drinks at most —

usually a French wine we keep on reserve just for him, actually. Then he'd be off."

"Save for two nights ago?" I asked, thinking I knew the answer.

Sam hung his head. "He... he might have had more than normal, yes," he replied.

I finished the last of my beer. "Does Phyllis live on the island?"

"Yes," he nodded. "She's got a cottage off the lane that runs east from the village; most of the staff live there. It was built by the hotel to house us."

"I'd like to speak with her," I said. "Which cottage?"

"It's the one with the pink flower boxes," Sam replied. "First one on the left when you enter that area. You can't miss it."

I had my doubts, but nodded as I pulled out my wallet. "What do I owe you?"

"It's on the house," Sam said.

"Then thank you for the conversation," I said as I put my wallet away.

Sam nodded and then moved to the other end of the bar. I looked at the sudsy remains of my beer and pondered what I'd heard; while it wasn't entirely the same as what the women had told me earlier that morning, it had painted in some additional detail that had been lacking. I was intrigued mightily about whatever it was that Tim had said to Dot that had prompted her to leave; it was clear from both accounts that whatever it was had made her quite upset. That Reggie seemed to be holding a flame for Dot was... odd, for reasons that were hard to define. It certainly was unexpected, for the baker had come off — to me, at least — as an introvert more interested in his baking than the world outside of his brick oven. In either event, it was clear I needed to speak with both Tim and Reggie.

I pushed up from the bar and began to work my way toward the exit; I could feel the beer sloshing around in my empty stomach and immediately regretted not having anything in there with it. I was pondering what to do about the matter when Corinne met me at the door. Her face was unusually flushed, as though she'd been running, and one hand held a small canvas bag that had been snapped closed at the top.

"There you are," I said. "I'm afraid I'm done in here — I expected you a bit ago."

"Apologies," she replied.

My eyes glanced down at the bag. "That is too large to hold a DNA sample."

"This is why I'm late," she said, and surprisingly, her face reddened more. "I... I need to tell you something."

Sensing her rising level of discomfort, I nodded, and then pulled her over to a small alcove in the main lobby that was partially protected by a tall fern-like flower. "All right."

Glancing to make sure we were out of earshot of others, she nonetheless still lowered her voice. "I... I did something awful the night of the bachelorette party."

Taking one of the two plush chairs in the alcove, I waved her into the other and patiently waited for her to continue.

"Marco and I are in a bad spot right now," she started.

"You mentioned that," I reminded her.

"I did, didn't I?" Corinne sighed and looked away for a moment, then back at me. "We had way more champaign than we should have at the party," she continued. "And contrary to what I said in the ballroom this morning, even I have a limit when comes to alcohol. Champaign has a way of creeping up on you that I always forget."

I nodded encouragingly.

"Anyway, when Dot left, I nibbled a bit and then decided to call it a night. I... I started to go to my room but found Tim waiting in the elevator lobby."

"Corinne," I breathed. "Did you really sleep with the groom-to-be?"

Impossibly, her face turned an even darker shade of red. "Yeah."

My eyes must have been as round as saucers. "Shit."

"I... I really don't know what came over me, honestly; Tim seemed pretty broken up about whatever he'd talked to Dot about and was... well, looking for solace." She paused. "He'd tried to find it in the bottle of whiskey he was carrying, but it was obvious it hadn't helped."

"Corinne—"

"I know, *I know*," she sighed. "I was lonely, and frankly heartbroken over what's going on between me and Marco. It was an amazingly bad decision. We were both drunk and not thinking clearly."

Unwillingly chasing away the gentle buzz from the beer, I shifted back into investigator mode. "Did you take him to your room?"

"Well, we didn't do it in the elevator if that's what you're asking," she replied tartly.

"When did you leave the party?"

"Maybe... ten-thirty?" she replied. "I wasn't really paying attention to the clock by that point."

"How long was he with you?"

"All night," she said. "He was... looking for some kind of release," Corinne continued uncomfortably. "The passion was undeniable, even to someone as drunk as I'd been. He even woke me up in the wee hours to go another round."

My eyebrows went up. "My God, Corinne."

"I feel like shit for doing it," she said. "And I have no idea how I'm going to handle it with Marco."

"With honesty, I hope." I paused. "That means Tim was with you when Dot was murdered, then?"

"It would seem so," she sighed. "I've become his alibi, which means I'm going to have to tell the world about his indiscretion. And mine."

"How did you leave it?"

"We agreed never to speak of it," she replied before looking at the bag. "I don't know about you, but my investigator brain still seems to be on duty even when three sheets to the wind. This bag was hanging on one of those luggage carts in the elevator lobby when I took Tim up with me two nights ago." Corinne looked up at me. "It was still there when I came down this morning, and just now when I went back."

I eyed the bag again with new interest. "Are you telling me it's been hanging there for nearly two days? And no one has missed it?"

"Yeah," she nodded. "With reason."

Only then did I notice she'd put on a pair of latex gloves. "What did you find?"

"Look for yourself," she added as she slowly unbuttoned the top.

Peering over, my eyebrows went up at the sight of a blood-stained t-shirt bearing the logo for a band I'd never heard of — a shirt I had seen myself some days earlier. My eyes snapped to Corrine's. "You seem to have stumbled upon a clue."

"I have, haven't I?" she replied.

"What wing of the hotel is your room in?" I asked.

"I'm in the south wing," she said, then looked at me with a frown. "You look like you know who this belongs to."

"I do," I nodded. "Let's get this to the evidence locker, and then we'll pay the owner a visit."

TWELVE

I n a lifetime lived along the shoreline, I'd experienced my fair share of coastal storms. I'd always felt that no two were alike, a result perhaps from the glacier driven geology that portion of the state presented to the Atlantic Ocean. There was also likely a meteorological reason as well, something to do with ocean currents and the fierceness of the upper atmosphere winds, if I recalled what a high school science class had taught many years earlier. As Corinne and I slogged along the loop trail toward Reggie's house in the woods, heads down against the driving rain that was pelting us like a thousand little daggers, I realized I'd never ridden out a storm on one of the islands that served as a barrier to Windeport Harbor. As violent as any given storm had felt back in Windeport, it was quite easy to see just how exposed and vulnerable Carpenter's Island was; I also felt like I now had a suitable explanation for why all the trees seemed perennially bent in a specific direction, not to mention just how few truly tall trees there seemed to be overall.

Rocket had taken the news that he wasn't going to come along on our little jaunt fairly well; after feeding him his lunch and then explaining my plans for the afternoon, he looked at me, then Corinne, let out a big sigh and wandered to his dog bed to settle in for a bit. I suspected privately he was no more interested in going out into the storm than we were and had instead welcomed the opportunity for an extended snooze. I'd rifled through Julie's single closet and come up with two rather substantial rain slickers; given my size, I could barely get either of them on, but Corinne was smaller than me and easily zipped herself into some better protection against the elements. By the time I located the small pathway off the main trail for Reggie's home, my windbreaker had soaked through to the UEM sweatshirt I'd tossed on against the chill; the irony that I was layering clothing in August wasn't lost on me, nor the fact that I was actually shivering when the clearing containing the unusually shaped dwelling appeared before us.

A thin trail of white smoke was snaking its way into the sky from the chimney over the brick oven; the door was closed, so it was hard to know if anything in particular was baking. The prep table beside it was similarly cleared of any activity, leading me to surmise that the rain had chased Reggie indoors. The yellow glow of interior lighting behind the windows of the bungalow corroborated this notion, a smudge of color against the otherwise gloomy darkness of the day. Stepping to the paneled front door, I knocked several times before standing back; I was surprised to hear a deadbolt slight back a moment later, not because of the sound, but rather the fact that Reggie even *had* a lock. My experience on the island so far had told me that those who lived there felt quite differently about personal security when compared to their peers on the mainland. My curiosity at what the young man had inside his home that he wanted to keep protected was understandably piqued.

I waited patiently as the door was pulled open; Reggie stood there in a muscle tank-top and microfiber shorts over compression tights. A slight sheen of sweat on his skin emphasized the fact that we had interrupted a workout of some kind; his long wavy hair had been pulled back into a ponytail to keep it off his neck. The quick way the ponytail snapped as Reggie looked at me, then Corinne, then back to me seemed to accentuate the slight flare of panic that had flashed across his face when he found me waiting on his doorstep.

"Sean," he said, his voice cracking. "You've caught me doing my cardio."

"Apologies," I smiled. "Do you mind if we come in? We need to chat."

Reggie's eyes widened, belying some level of panic. "Right now?"

"Yes," I said firmly.

"I only have a tiny sliver of time to get this workout in," Reggie said. "I've got stuff in the oven for the dinner service at the hotel that needs to get taken care of."

"This won't take long," I assured him, trying to sell the lie with a gentle smile.

Reggie was unmoved. "Can I swing by your place later?"

"If we do it later," I said, a note of seriousness entering my voice, "it will be at the station in the village."

The young man's Adam's apple bobbed slightly as he swallowed, hard. Folding his well-defined arms against his chest, he thought about it for a moment longer before stepping aside. "Coffee?" he asked. "I've got a pot going."

"I would love a cup," I said, looking to Corinne.

"Me, too," she said. "I'm Corinne, by the way."

"Reggie," he nodded succinctly as he closed the door behind us. "You can leave your coats there."

I slid out of my wind breaker and then, after a moment of consideration, stripped off my soggy sweatshirt as well. We appeared to be in a small anteroom, for there were hooks on one wall holding all manner of outwear, and small racks of footwear rising on the wall opposite. Taking the hint, I kicked out of my also soggy running sneakers and watched as Corinne followed suit; jacket hung and shoes stowed, I wandered in the direction our host had disappeared and found myself in a cozy living room with two recliners facing a large-screen television mounted on the wall above a fireplace. The television was frozen on an image of a smiling man with a shaved head holding dumbbells in either arm; three people behind him were mimicking the action, though it was hard to know whether they were on the way up with the weights, or down. Reggie had a blue workout mat unrolled in front of the recliners with a set of dumbbells carefully placed at one end. A plastic bottle with an orange-colored liquid was presumably a sports drink of some kind and had begun to sweat in the mugginess of the interior. Tugging at my t-shirt, I realized the air wasn't moving at all inside; there was also a faint scent of something herbal in the air, though I had a hard time placing it. Glancing at Corinne, I could see that she was intently examining a set of potted plants just below a multi-pane window looking into the forest; stepping closer, one look at the unique shape of the leaf she was fingering had me understanding *why* it had attracted her interest.

I caught her raised eyebrow just as Reggie reappeared from a small archway carrying two mugs. "I hope you don't mind black," he was saying as he entered, then cut himself off when he saw what we were looking at. "Oh, *shit*."

"There's nothing to worry about if this is for medical use," I said, watching him carefully. "State law allows for up to six mature plants per household." Nodding toward the door, I continued. "That's why you have a lock?"

Reggie nodded. "Yeah. Most people don't lock up around here and don't think twice of just going into someone's place for sugar. I wanted to avoid any sort of... misunderstanding."

"You're clearly not the supplier to the island with what's sitting on this shelf," Corinne said. "Unless you have more plants out there in your barn."

"I don't," he said. "Just these. I use them to ease the pain in my lower back."

"From all the kneading?" I asked.

"That doesn't help," he replied. "No, it's an injury from my life before Carpenter's Island."

I thought back to the magazine I'd seen in Tessa's office. "As a model?"

❖

Reggie blanched. "How the *hell* did you know that?"

"Just the way you carry yourself," I said somewhat honestly. It felt right not revealing what I had seen back at the hotel — yet. "It was either that or a dancer."

Reggie smiled slightly. "I was both, actually," he said, as he handed us the mugs. "I did something to a muscle in my lower back while working on a show in Boston; I switched to modeling since it was less demanding, physically — and paid far better."

"I can imagine." I looked around the cottage. "It's not much of a stretch to assume that building your place here indicates you wanted to keep a low profile after you exited that line of work."

He folded his arms against his chest again, flexing his biceps in the process. "I'd had my fill of that life," Reggie said. "No one here knows of my history, and I'd like to keep it that way if we can."

"I can't guarantee that, Reggie," I said. "Not while I'm investigating a murder."

His eyes went wide. "Murder? Did someone die from those blueberries?"

"Indirectly," I hedged before pulling out my iPhone and triggering the recording. "I'm going to ask you some questions, Reggie, and I'll need some honest answers."

"Okay," he said, his eyes going even wider.

"Before we do, I need you to understand your rights..." I began before reciting the standard Miranda warning to him. After the debacle with Shelly West, I'd redoubled my resolve to always cover my bases. "Do you understand what I've told you?" I asked.

The color had drained from Reggie's face, but he still nodded.

"I need you to verbally confirm for the record."

"Yes," he said, his voice cracking. I didn't think it was possible for him to hug himself any tighter, but he did.

"Were you at the bar in the hotel restaurant two nights ago?"

He glanced at Corinne before answering. "She saw me there," he said. "Right?"

"I did," Corinne answered.

"So, yeah, I was there. Why? I'm there just about every night."

"That was the evening of the bachelorette party," I said carefully.

"Yes," he nodded.

"I understand the bartender had to escort you from the premises," I said.

Reggie hugged himself again and walked into the living room. "Not my finest hour," he sighed as he sank down onto the mat and sat cross-legged.

"What happened?"

"It had been a long day," he said, looking away. "I had to bake extra for the party and the wedding, so my back was killing me. I'd smoked my usual allotment of cannabis and it hadn't done much, so I... I had a second joint. Then I went to the bar for my usual after dinner drink."

"I don't imagine they recommend mixing marijuana and wine," Corinne said.

"Probably not," I said, then looked at Reggie. "And to make matters worse, you had more than normal, didn't you?"

"Yeah," he nodded. "I was kind of out of it."

"Sounds like it was a hell of a day."

"It was."

"Do you know Dot?"

"Of course," he replied with an indifferent shrug. "She's Tim's fiancé. She's here most weekends."

"How well do you know her?"

Reggie shrugged again. "Well enough, I suppose."

"From the way you were draped over her, I'd say it was something more," Corinne observed wryly. "Did you meet in Boston?"

"No," Reggie replied with a practiced ease he'd not demonstrated earlier. It was clear he'd been preparing for just such a question.

I looked at him. "It's a big city, Corinne," I said. "The odds are probably against it."

"I suppose," she said, though her tone underscored how unconvinced she was.

"Then again, the odds are appreciably higher that the Fernyhoughs are patrons of the arts," I said, my eyes firmly locked with Reggie's. "It won't take much for us to dig up the donation records. I suspect we'll find that one or more of the shows you were a dancer on were ones they sponsored; it will take longer to get ticket history, but I suspect we can find they attended, too."

"That won't prove anything," Reggie said. "Just because we were in the same room together doesn't mean we had a relationship."

My eyebrows went up. "No one is saying you did," I said softly, though from the way his face reddened, it was clear Reggie knew he'd slipped.

"How long have you known Dot?" Corinne asked again.

Reggie looked away again and remained silent.

I looked at the mug in my hands and the dark liquid within. There was a coffee ground floating on the surface, and by shifting the angle of my hands slightly, I was rewarded with it slowly circling the radius. It seemed like an interesting metaphor to our conversation.

"Were you in Dot's room at the hotel two nights ago?" I asked before looking up.

Reggie's face went from red to white in a flash. "No," he said.

I waited a beat. "I want you to think about this very carefully for a moment," I said. "And also remember that cops generally don't ask a question we don't already have the answer to."

Reggie swallowed again.

"Were you in Dot's room two nights ago?" I asked.

"You obviously know I was," Reggie finally said. "So what? Did Dot accuse me of something? The only reason I was there is because she called me and *asked* me to come."

I glanced at Corinne. "You admit to being in her room, then?"

"Yes," he said.

"Why?"

Reggie's face flamed. "She wanted to apologize for having me thrown out of the restaurant," he said after a moment. "She was drunk, I was drunk — it was all a bit overblown. I accepted her apology and left."

"When was this?"

"Maybe 11," he said. "I can show you the calls on my phone if that helps."

"It will," I nodded. "But why *go* to her? The apology could have been over the phone."

His face flamed darker. "She wanted to apologize in person," he said.

"I'll bet she did," Corinne said. "I find it intriguing that someone you barely knew had your cell."

"So do I," I added.

Reggie looked at us. "It's a small island," he offered. "Someone at the hotel probably gave it to her."

"I'm sure," I said, then looked at Corinne. "I wonder, though, what we'll find when we pull the phone records for Dot."

"That will make for interesting reading," she nodded. "How far back are you going to go?"

"I think," Reggie said, "it might be time for you to leave. Both of you."

"Perhaps you're right," I smiled, then handed him my mug. "Thanks for the coffee."

"Of course," he said, though from his expression, I could tell he'd noted I'd not drunk so much as a drop.

Turning off the recording function of my iPhone, I slid the device back into my pocket and returned to the small anteroom. Corinne was right beside me, and in moments we were both back out in the rain. She had the good sense to wait until we'd entered the forest trail before she spoke.

"That was wild," Corinne said. "You didn't confront him about the clothes we found, though. Why?"

"It's never wise to show all of your cards up front," I said. "We established he was in the hotel at the proper time, so that's a positive. Now we need to understand why we found what we found *where* we found it."

Corinne came up short. "I'm in the wrong wing," she said, smacking her face with the palm of her hand. "That's why you asked — Dot's room is in the *north* wing. I assumed the killer dumped the bag as they got off the elevator, but the two wings aren't connected."

"No," I smiled. "They aren't. I still think it's possible the killer left the blood-stained clothes there in an attempt to obfuscate their identity — but we also can't disprove the bag was intended to be found by you."

Corinne frowned. "To intentionally frame Reggie? Or to make it *look* like Reggie did it? I mean, either way, I'm liking this guy for the murder. Did you see that bandage on his hand?"

"Yes," I said. "In just the right spot you would assume an injury would occur had someone been wielding a shard glass."

"Exactly," she said. "Except you don't seem convinced."

"I'm never convinced," I nodded as we resumed our walk. "Until I am."

"Is that some sort of Maine aphorism?"

"Ayuh," I said.

Corinne looked like she wanted to press the point further, but my iPhone took that opportunity to buzz in my pocket. Looking for as much cover from the rain as I could get, I huddled beneath a tall birch tree and slid the phone out to see the familiar number of the Chief Medical Examiner's office on the display. Tapping answer, I put a smile into my voice while trying to keep from shivering in the cold rain.

"Hey Lou," I said. "That was fast."

There was a garbled burst of noise, followed by a fraction of a word. "—can."

Frowning, I did what everyone does when they have a bad cell connection and raised my voice in a futile attempt to overcome the technology. "Lou? You're breaking up."

"Sean?" was all I heard before the triple beeps of a lost connection confirmed my suspicion.

"Damn," I said as I stared at my now darkened phone.

"Who was that?"

"I *think* it was Dr. Hamilton, the Chief Medical Examiner." I held my phone up into the air and was rewarded by getting a single bar added to the signal strength indicator. "The coverage on this island sucks. I'll call her back using the landline in the cottage."

"You'd think they'd put another tower up," Corinne said as we picked up the pace once more.

"You would," I said then paused. "He said she called him," I murmured.

"Sean?" Corinne asked. "Who called whom?"

I looked at Corinne. "Did you see a telephone in Reggie's house back there?"

"Not that I recall, but we didn't get out of the living room. Why?"

"Reggie said Dot called him," I replied. "Unless he has a magical cell phone, his coverage can't be any better than ours."

"He probably has a landline," Corinne said, pointing out the obvious.

"Probably," I smiled.

We closed the final distance to the cottage in companionable silence; Rocket was still snoozing when I opened the front door and barely lifted an ear in our direction as we squished our way into the great room. It took a few more moments to jettison the rain-soaked gear, then I left Corinne to make a fresh pot of coffee while I sat down on the couch and pulled the classic Trimline phone into my lap. I had to admit, there was some pleasure in the tactile sensation of pressing each numeric button as I dialed Lou's direct line; holding the handset to my ear, I mourned the loss of something that had once been hailed as our greatest achievement in communications.

Two rings in, the Medical Examine picked up. "This is Dr. Hamilton."

"Hey Lou, it's Sean. Sorry for the delay, I had to get to a landline to call you back."

"Heather had told me cell signal was sketchy out there. How's the weather?"

"Rotten," I said, glancing toward the big windows fronting the ocean. "The water has this deep black hue to it that is never good, though the frothy waves look kind of artistic. Something straight out of a Winslow Homer painting."

"I can imagine. We're getting a bit of the deluge here, too; three days of rain and the creeks around us are starting to rise. Another three and my people are going to start coming in via canoe."

"That would be the greenest transportation alternative I could think of," I chuckled. "And totally Maine."

"No kidding." She paused, and then I heard her tapping at a keyboard. "I knew you wouldn't be able to make the postmortem, so I went ahead without you."

"I'm hurt."

"You'll get over it," she replied with a laugh. "You hate it when I start removing organs anyway."

"Guilty as charged."

"I see Dr. Kellerman had an assist on this one," Lou continued. "I could use more like her in the field; her notes were crisp and efficient."

"That's my Suzanne," I replied. "Though she was hesitant to draw any conclusions from what she'd found."

"From what I'm reading — and what the exam revealed — she was right on the money," Lou said. "COD is pretty obvious, exsanguination from the wound at the neck. I pulled a sizable shard of glass out of the tissue; the lab can match it with something if you bring it to us."

I frowned. "That was a glaring MIA," I said. "There were no glasses in the suite," I said then looked over to where Corinne was working on the coffee. "Corinne, did you confirm whether room service had been ordered for the suite?"

She nodded. "Nothing went up at all; at least, nothing that went through the POS system."

"Well," I said, turning my attention back to Lou, "it might be a bit before we find something that you can test. I'll head back to the hotel later and rifle around in their supply closet. What am I looking for?"

"Our best guess is something like a wineglass," she said.

"That's not much to go on."

"No," she sighed, "but I've given you less before and you've made it work."

"The pressure is on, then," I smiled.

"TOD is close to what Heather presumed. I'd probably nudge it closer to midnight based on the enzyme test, but no later than two on the other end."

"I can work with that range. Suzanne seemed to think the victim had sex shortly before she died; Heather seemed to concur."

"She did," Lou replied. "Within an hour of expiring, if my math is correct; the semen sample I collected is currently being run by the lab; they'll cross check it with the other sample collected at the scene. If we're lucky, I'll have a profile for who was with her."

"I'll take anything you can give me," I replied.

"While we're still on the subject of procreation, your victim was also pregnant."

"Holy *shit*," I breathed, which caused Corinne to look in my direction. "How far along?"

"Around ten weeks," Lou replied. "Far enough along that your victim *may* have realized she was carrying a baby, but that's a hard one to know. You said she was about to get married?"

"This weekend, yes."

"Perhaps the fiancé can fill in some details," she said. "I was able to take a DNA sample from the fetus if you need to run a paternity screen. That's also at the lab with the semen sample."

"I'm not sure I expected that curveball, but good to know I can if it comes up," I said. "It doesn't help how seriously short of DNA testing kits I am at the moment, though. It might be a bit before we can get anything to you; I'm waiting for the Testing Kit Fairy to drop some from the sky."

"We have one of those now?" Lou chuckled. "The things you learn on this job."

"If we don't, we should. I'll speak to Jimmy about it."

"While you're at it, ask him about the new mass spectrometer for the lab. I'm waiting on his signature."

"I thought you just *got* a new one," I said, thinking back to a recent case.

"It's cute that you assume we only *have* one," she laughed. "Anyway, other than being dead, your victim was in nearly perfect health. A little bit of cholesterol in the arteries — unusual in someone so young — and a tiny bit of degradation in cartilage of the knees. I suspect she had been a serious runner, one that didn't use the proper footwear. Or overtrained, like certain former Olympians I know."

"I'm feeling called out again."

"As well you should. Have you found a pool out there on the island? Or are you melting down from not being able to work out?"

"I've been running," I said. "Not my favorite activity, but the trail that loops around the island has some nice scenery."

"I'll bet."

"Anything else?"

"Just that we'll need an official identification of the body. Will you be able to get someone out here to the morgue?"

"I'll have to get back to you on that," I replied. "The parents are still under the weather with food poisoning, so it might have to be the fiancé."

"Both options suck," Lou said. "Let me know. We'll keep your victim on ice until then."

"Sounds good. Thanks."

"Anytime."

I played the handset back into the cradle for the Trimline and looked to Corinne; she'd perched herself on the coffee table and was holding two steaming mugs. "About what you expected?" she asked as she handed me one.

"Pretty much," I nodded as I sipped at the brew.

THIRTEEN

The rain seemed to have settled into something that was halfway between a drizzle and an outright downpour; as thick as the clouds were, it felt far later than it was when Corinne and I pulled back up in front of the *Inn By The Sea* in my borrowed golf cart. There was no spot under any sort of cover to park the cart, so I slid it in between two others on the outward section of the driveway loop for the resort, and then hurried to the lobby with Corinne close by my side. An unwelcome gust of air conditioning met us as the doors parted, a reminder that less than forty-eight hours earlier, it had been rather toasty; now it seemed like a wintry broadside, one that sliced through my soggy exterior. I'd debated changing into something dry after our last escapade, but knew the drive back to the hotel would likely make it a fruitless action; as I shivered on my way over to the reception desk, I re-evaluated the wisdom of not always having a thick raincoat in my possession.

Corinne pulled me aside a few steps from the desk. "Sean," she started, her voice quiet. "Do you mind if I take off for a bit? I'd like to check in with Marco if I could."

I looked at her. "You're going to tell him, aren't you?"

She looked away. "We've been together a long time, he and I," she replied. "I owe him that much, I think. Whether it kills our relationship or not, I've got to roll the dice and see how much damage I did."

I put a hand to her arm. "It's the right call," I said. "A tough one, but the right one."

"I know," she nodded, then smiled wanly. "It's always the weak moments that get us into trouble, isn't it?"

"One reason police officers will never go out of style," I replied sadly. "I'm going to see about those glasses and maybe check in on the parents; why don't you call it a day and meet me back at the station in the morning?"

Something quirked at the edge of Corrine's mouth. "'Station' seems a bit pretentious for that shack you're using," she observed.

"Maybe," I smiled. "See you tomorrow?"

"If not sooner," she nodded.

"Hopefully not."

I watched as she turned and headed toward the wing housing her room, then continued my path toward the reception desk. A different clerk than the one I'd spoken to earlier was there and smiled at my approach. "Commander," he said. "What can I do for you?"

The way he greeted me by name made me wonder if they'd taped a photo of me beneath the counter. "I'd like to talk to Tim if I could. Is he available?"

The clerk picked up a phone. "Let me check."

"Thank you," I said, and then waited patiently.

It didn't appear to be a long phone call, for the clerk nearly immediately put the handset back down after speaking briefly with whomever had been at the other end. "Mr. Polanski is in the kitchen at the moment. He's overseeing the dinner service, if you'd like to meet him there?"

"I can do that."

"Do you know the way?"

"Unless it has moved since this morning," I smiled, "yes."

The clerk frowned slightly, unsure if I was being sarcastic or not. "Have a good evening, then, sir."

As I suspected, the kitchen was indeed right where I had left it some hours earlier, though when I pushed through the stainless-steel swinging door, there was far more activity in the space. Just about every workstation seemed to have someone working it; the bank of stoves at the far end appeared to be doing a brisk business of sautéing, boiling and otherwise cooking various items that were hard to identity from where I was standing. Overlapping smells reminded me of the joy of spending Thanksgiving Day at my cousin Charlie's home, enjoying fine dining and the conversation that went with it. The tallish form of Tim Polanski was standing next to a rotund chef wearing an oversized white hat; the two appeared to be arguing over something, though the context was lost on me despite getting near enough to hear them over the cacophony of the kitchen.

"—too late to do it," Tim was saying.

"The dish won't be right without it," the chef replied. This close, I could tell the reason for the gargantuan hat was to hold the massive amount of hair she had; to her credit, not a single strand had escaped its captivity. Score one for food safety.

"What dish would that be?" I asked pleasantly.

The duo had been so engrossed they'd not seen my approach. Tim was the first to react. "The what?"

"The dish?" I smiled. "That you're trying to make?"

"Peach cobbler," the chef replied. "It's to replace the blueberry one that had to be scrubbed from the menu at the last minute. Except I don't have enough of the liqueur I need for the sauce."

"Yes, you do," Tim replied.

"No, I *don't*," the chef countered. "There's *barely* enough to smell, let alone cook with."

"The order doesn't arrive until next week. You'll have to make do."

"Make do? With *what*?"

"Get creative," Tim said icily. His tone bordered on dismissive.

The chef started to take off her apron. "The hell with this."

"What are you doing?" Tim asked as she hung the apron on a hook by the delivery door. "Where are you going?"

"To the god*damn* grocery store," she said. "They'll have what I need."

"You can't leave *now*!" Tim yelled. "We're in the middle of prepping for dinner!"

"It's not my fault we're doing it so late in the day," the chef shot back. "If you hadn't demanded that we steam clean the *entire* kitchen again this afternoon, I wouldn't be two hours behind."

"We can't afford to be shut down by the inspectors," Tim nearly growled. "Everything has to be perfect!"

"So you keep telling me," the chef said as she pushed through the delivery door.

"I'm not going to reimburse you for anything you buy!" Tim called after her as she disappeared. Whatever response she made was lost in the slamming of the door. Folding the paper he was holding in half, Tim turned his attention to me. "What can I do for you, Commander?"

"I had no idea our food and beverage inspector had confirmed their time with you," I said. "When do you expect them?"

"They haven't," Tim replied curtly. "I just don't want to get caught with my pants down."

"I highly doubt they'd find anything at this point," I replied sagely. "Especially after the kitchen had been so thoroughly scrubbed." *Twice,* I added to myself, wondering if I should read into the actions at all.

"Better to be safe than sorry. Is that what you are here about? The kitchen inspection?"

"Actually, I'd like to look at the stemware used in the rooms," I said. "Specifically, anything that would have been sent to the suites."

"Stemware?" he asked. "Why?"

"Can I see it?" I replied, then made a show of looking around the space. "I presume you have a cupboard or closet full of the stuff here somewhere."

"Not in the kitchen," he shook his head. "That kind of thing is part of the bar inventory."

"Then show me that, please."

"I'm in the middle of supervising dinner," he objected. "Can this wait?"

My eyebrows went up at the pushback. "Not particularly, no."

Sighing, he stuffed the paper into a pocket and then angled his head toward the door I'd used. "This way, then."

I followed him back through to the lobby, then straight over to the bar that had pride of place in the center of the space. A young woman with a mountain of dark hair piled into a tiered bun was busy making cocktails when we appeared; though I wasn't an expert, she seemed to be crafting four different drinks at the same time, and efficiently, too. Topping off each with a fruit garnish, she placed them on a small tray that one of the waitstaff picked up, then turned toward us expectantly. Her face was sprinkled with freckles that made her seem even younger.

"Greta, are you missing any wineglasses?" Tim asked without preamble.

That's interesting, I thought as I glanced at Tim. *I don't recall telling him I thought any* would *be.*

"Funny you should ask, Boss," she frowned. "We're down two; I haven't filled out the requisition to replace them yet since we've been so busy."

"Get it done as soon as you can," Tim said, then turned to me. "Anything else?"

"Do you have a sense of where they went?" I asked Greta. I ignored Tim's frown.

"Probably room service," she said. "Though normally they turn up in a day or so. Which reminds me," she added, looking at Tim. "Night shift left a note saying we're also down one service trolley."

Tim looked like he was going to have a coronary on the spot. "What the fuck! How the *hell* do you lose a service trolley?"

"Boss—"

"I'd like to see what you do have in stock," I interjected, temporarily putting a metaphorical finger into the crack of the dam holding back Tim's ire. His temper certainly seemed on a hair trigger.

She glanced at Tim before nodding. "Sure, one sec."

I nodded and waited while she went to the far end of the bar and opened a cabinet door in the wall behind it; a moment later, she returned with two tall wineglasses and placed them on the counter. "Do you have any other styles?" I asked.

"No, just the one," Greta replied, then glanced at Tim before continuing. "We, uh, replaced everything before the season started with new stuff from Sprangers and Sons."

"It was time for a change," Tim interjected. "Anything else?"

His rising impatience began to grate on me. "I'd like to take these with me, if you don't mind. Do you have a bag I could put them in?"

"*Take* them? Why on Earth for?" Tim seethed.

"For comparative purposes," I said blandly.

"What if I said no?" he asked.

"I'd be back within the hour with a warrant," I replied easily. "And as much noise and commotion as I can create while I rummage through your entire operation."

Tim considered that for a moment, then nodded at Greta. She placed the two glasses into a small paper bag, then slid them across to me. "There you go."

"Thank you," I smiled, then turned to Tim. "I won't keep you any longer."

Tim looked as though he wanted to argue the point — any point — but decided against it and left. I watched him go, then found my attention distracted by a tall form with raven hair and a medical bag coming in my direction. Smiling, I made a space for Suzanne beside me at the bar and then welcomed her with a quick kiss.

"Fancy meeting you here," she said.

"I pop up when I'm needed," I replied. "I'm glad you appeared; I was hoping to talk to Dot's parents. Are they up for a visit?"

Suzanne frowned. "I thought that's why you're here," she said. "I texted you a few hours ago — didn't you get it?"

"Apparently not," I replied as I pulled out my phone. It took that moment to *ping* with a new message. "And there it is. Cell service is horrible around here."

"Good to know," she nodded. "I'll use the land line next time. Do you want to see them now? I can take you to their room."

"Yes."

"It's this way."

Suzanne deftly navigated through the lobby and toward the south wing of rooms; I found myself slightly distracted by how form fitting her yoga pants were, which was followed by other involuntary impulses underscoring just how long it had been since the two of us had last been intimate. It seemed to be a good thing that I had the small paper bag to hold as we entered the elevator, but I also knew nothing got past the eagle eyes of my doctor girlfriend. The slight smirk on her face told me I'd not been subtle enough hiding my desire, leading her to put a hand around my waist so she could pull me close enough that her fragrant perfume filled my universe.

Leaning to my ear, she whispered a single word. "Later."

"Promise?" I managed to croak.

She turned to face me, then very slowly pressed her lips to mine. "Promise."

I was torn between equal parts of frustration and relief when the doors to the elevator parted on the proper floor. Suzanne smiled devilishly before leading me out of the carriage, then down the long hallway. We'd gone about halfway before she paused in front of a room; I caught her arm before she started to knock.

"This is their spot?" I whispered.

"Yes," she replied just as quietly. "Why?"

I nodded toward the end of the hallway. "I would have expected the parents of the bride to have been in one of the end suites."

Suzanne shrugged. "Maybe they didn't want to pay for it."

"Maybe."

Stepping forward, she knocked hard, then stepped back; a moment later, the door was unlocked and pulled inward to reveal the older woman I'd seen in the lobby several days earlier. Her face was drawn, though, and a shade of pale that seemed uncomfortably close to the pallor of cadavers. Dark eyes seemed to have sunk into her sockets, making her look severely emaciated, and her thin lips were nearly colorless. Looking to Suzanne, then to me, she licked her lips before speaking in a light whisper.

"Doctor."

"Daphne," Suzanne nodded. "Just checking in again on you and Merten. May we come in?"

The woman looked at me. "Who are you?" she whispered. The effort it was taking for her to speak was nearly painful to watch.

"Commander Sean Colbeth," I replied. "Statewide Major Crimes Unit."

Daphne blinked slowly as though she were manually processing what I'd said. "You're here about Dorothy."

"Yes, ma'am."

She blinked again, then stepped back so she could open the door further. Suzanne entered first, then made a beeline for the couch where the old man I'd also seen in line at reception appeared to be dozing. Putting her medical bag on the floor, she knelt down while simultaneously picking up his wrist; pressing her fingers to the back, she began to take his pulse while scanning his face. I took up position in front of the sliding glass doors of the balcony for the room, and waited for Daphne to slowly make her way to sit down beside her husband. The space was a quarter of the size of the suite where we'd found Dot's body, though it was just as tastefully decorated; a king-sized bed was perpendicular to the couch, though both had a good line of sight on the beach beyond the glass of the slider. I'd noted a small bathroom in the short entry hallway, as well as the smaller closet inset beside it. Overall, it was cozy but not claustrophobic.

"Merten," Suzanne was saying. "Have you been keeping up on your fluids?"

The old man's eyes flickered open. "Dr. Kellerman," he said with a slight smile. He had the thick accent of one who had lived in Boston for an entire lifetime and then some. "Good to see you again."

"Same," she smiled as she put his wrist back down. "Fluids?"

"As much as I can keep down," he said.

"Which isn't much," Daphne replied quietly.

Suzanne frowned and then shifted to the woman. "How about you?"

"Two glasses of water in the last hour," she promptly replied. "So far, so good."

Suzanne sat back, frowning. "I think we're going to get you to the mainland," she said. "You're both more dehydrated than I would like; I've got some IVs that would do the trick at the clinic."

"I don't want to go anywhere," Daphne said.

Suzanne seemed torn. "All right," she replied at length. "I'll see if I can get what I need sent over here instead. I'll still need to administer the IVs to bolster your electrolytes, though. Will that be okay?"

Neither one of them seemed up for an argument, so we both took it as a win. Glancing at Suzanne, I stepped into their line of sight. "I'm sorry to intrude on your grief, but I need to ask you a few questions about your daughter."

Daphne just nodded.

"How long did Dorothy date Régis Delannoy?"

Suzanne's eyes widened, but she remained silent. Daphne's eyes narrowed, emphasizing what little anger she could muster given her condition. "That is a name I'd hoped to never hear again."

"I take it you didn't approve of their relationship," I said.

"No," she shook her head.

"Why?"

Daphne looked at me in disbelief. "He was a *dancer*," she said, as though it were self-evident.

The blatant classism struck me as out of step with contemporary norms, but it felt unwise to opine on the subject. "And a model," I helpfully added, twisting the knife slightly.

"That came later," Merten said darkly. "After his injuries from doing *42nd Street* at the Wang."

Feeling another puzzle piece fitting into place, I nodded. "When did they meet?"

"Happenstance," Daphne sighed deeply. "Régis was one of the principal dancers they used at the fundraising gala for the Boch Center. Dorothy was home from UCLA on break and attended with us; unfortunately, the two hit it off immediately."

"It would never have happened if you'd not guilted her into going," Merten said.

"That stupidity wasn't my fault," Daphne shot back, making it clear this had been a long-running argument. "You could have stopped it yourself but didn't."

"Dorothy always charted her own course, and you know it. Nothing I said would have talked her out of anything."

"She had you wrapped around her finger," Daphne snapped. "You spoiled her rotten."

"Me?" Merten replied with as much indignation as he could muster. "You denied her *nothing*."

"I did—"

"How long did the relationship last?" I interjected, trying to forestall what was shaping up to be an epic battle.

Both faces swung toward me. "Maybe six years," Daphne said at length. "They broke up just before Dorothy met Tim at the conference."

"Six years longer than it should have," Merten added. "The scandal we endured having a daughter date someone like *that*."

"Like what?" I asked, curious just how candid about their bigotry they might be.

"He sold himself," Daphne said. "Sold his looks! Was famous for *being* famous. What kind of a life is that?"

"Correct me if I'm wrong, but my sense is that Régis parlayed his dancing skills into becoming a supermodel," I said, thinking back to the magazine I'd seen in Tessa's office and making an intuitive leap. "People like that are in high demand, especially for top brands."

"He prostituted his body for money," Merten said.

"And became rather wealthy as a result, I presume," I countered. "Surely that would have vaulted him into the same social strata as yourself?"

Daphne looked as though I had slapped her . "How *dare* you suggest someone so vile could be similar to us?" she said, her ragged voice nonetheless vibrating with anger. "Someone from such a *common* background! He had no place in Dorothy's world. None!"

I pondered that for a moment and was struck by a thought. "So, Régis might have been wealthy," I said slowly, "but he wasn't wealthy by your standards?"

"Certainly not," was Daphne's crisp reply.

"You must have been far happier when she met Tim, then," I said, watching their expressions.

"Well," Daphne said haughtily, "she could certainly have done worse. I'm not happy she fell for an innkeeper, but what are you going to do? Love is love."

My eyebrows went up at the amazing hypocrisy. "Why was the wedding here?" I asked. "And why didn't you two pay for it?"

Merten and Daphne exchanged an uncomfortable glance. "Our investments haven't done well this year," Merten said. "Dorothy was aware that we didn't have as much free capital as we'd expected. Fortunately, Tessa was able to accommodate our... situation."

I looked at the small room they were in anew and suddenly understood; their financial situation was likely far worse than how they'd presented it to their daughter. "I see." Suzanne cleared her throat; I took it for the sign it was and nodded again. "Thank you for your time," I said. "Again, my sympathies on your loss."

Daphne's look told me how much she thought of my sympathies; for his part Merten nodded solemnly before settling back in on the couch. Suzanne packed up her bag and then followed me out into the hallway. "Shit," she said. "Are all of your interviews that intense?"

"No," I said as we returned to the elevator. "I don't usually say this after interviewing people, but those two... what a piece a of work."

"Remind me not to act like that when I am rich," Suzanne said as she pressed the button for the elevator.

"Ditto," I replied. "Are you still coming over for dinner?"

"Oh yes," she smiled. "Though it depends on how long it takes for the harbormaster to run my drugs over from the clinic."

"Don't take too long," I warned her as the doors opened for us. "I might be asleep when you arrive if it's too late."

"Perfect," she smiled wickedly. "Then I can have my way with you."

I felt an eyebrow arch. "Should I be worried now?"

"Oh yes," she said again. "Definitely."

FOURTEEN

Some hours later, I found myself wrapped around Suzanne's rather sensuous form atop the twin bed in the cottage; considering how long it had been since we'd found ourselves entangled in each other's arms, it had been predictably hard to hold back. I tried not to think how disastrous that last time had been; my chance observation about us merging households had led to the fracture in our relationship in the first place. As I squeezed her sweat-soaked body closer to mine, I hoped we'd finally turned a corner; kissing along her shoulder, I resolved to once and for all remove the fear the love of my life had felt about being in a long-term relationship.

Suzanne stirred beneath me, then snuggled herself further into my midsection – an act made easier by how little space there was on the small bed. In that position, it wasn't difficult for her to detect my growing desire for her, and I felt her softly chuckle; slowly, she flipped around to face me, then, with a gentle smile, carefully guided me back inside her depths. Lying side-by-side, our angle ensured that the most subtle of movements would create just *enough* friction to keep the moment going, but not too much it would end prematurely. Running her hand through my damp curls, she then pulled my face to hers and pressed her lips to mine, lips that tasted of the red wine we'd shared over a dinner of pasta I'd made. Darting my tongue through the space, I was rewarded by a sudden squeezing of her hips that pulled me deeper and nearly over the edge; she seemed to sense how close I was and gently pushed me back so she could plant a series of kisses across my exposed shoulder.

It took me a moment to realize the guttural groaning was from me and not the slumbering Rocket on the floor below; Suzanne seemed to also register that her boyfriend was about to lose control and devilishly slowed down, then ever so carefully shifted our positions again so my back was pressed up against the pillows, allowing me to lose myself in those amazing blue eyes of hers. Kissing me lightly on the lips, she ran her hand through my damp curls again before slowly settling herself down across my hips. Leaning into me, the touch of her skin against mine was nearly electric and coaxed a shudder from somewhere deep inside of me. I pressed myself closer to her, ravenously enveloping her mouth with my own in an attempt to make up for all of the lost time between us; slowly, then with increasing urgency, Suzanne and I moved together toward a mutual release that left us gasping in each other's embrace.

Suzanne placed her head against my chest, then reached her hand to mine. Running a finger along my knuckle, she sighed contentedly, then surprised me by suddenly opening up completely. "My ex-husband forced me to have sex. Whenever he wanted it. Repeatedly."

The warm afterglow of our activities immediately faded into the background, replaced by a bubbling anger for the jerk that had once been her husband. "Fuck," I said as I hugged her closer with my free arm. "Just, *fuck.*"

"I had no control over anything," she said, echoing something she had told me in the bungalow the night she'd returned from Portland. "You already know about the finance and personal freedom parts. Now you know the rest."

"Suze, I would never—"

"I know you wouldn't," she said as she propped her head on a hand. "But I also needed you to know, on a visceral level, *why* I fear losing control — of everything." Suzanne paused for a beat. "And why I ran."

"Shit, Suzanne." My anger made my voice vibrate. "What he did to you — that was borderline rape!"

"I know," she said quietly.

"Jesus *fucking* Christ," I hissed. "How long did it go on?"

"For years."

I hugged her closer, aghast at what my soulmate had been through. It took a few moments for me to find my words. "Why didn't you tell me this sooner?" I asked. "It's not a burden you needed to bear alone."

"I don't know," she said. "I honestly don't. I guess I didn't trust our relationship enough to talk about it."

"But now you do?"

"I'm getting there," she said softly. Suzanne twisted herself around so I could see her face; tears glistened over those beautiful blue eyes. "I'm sorry it took so long."

"Oh, Suze, there's nothing to apologize for," I said as I brushed back a damp bang from her forehead, then pressed a kiss to it. "You were protecting yourself — protecting your heart. It's completely understandable."

"You're not mad?"

"Of course I am," I said, which caused a flicker of fear in her eyes. "Not with you," I hastily added, "but with that S.O.B. that called himself your husband."

Suzanne leaned back. "I've only ever seen that look on your face when you're going after someone," she said slowly. "Sean, that part of my life is dead and buried. I didn't tell you all of that just so you'd run off to New Hampshire to defend my honor."

I started to tell her that wasn't my intention but came up short when I realized that was *exactly* what I'd been thinking. Grinning sheepishly, I sighed. "Denied my one moment of swashbuckling by the love of my life. What is the world coming to?"

"Its senses," Suzanne smiled. "Finally."

"Maybe."

She looked at me again. "Sean, promise me you won't do anything rash."

"I'm in law enforcement. I'm constitutionally unable to do anything rash."

The arched eyebrow — albeit sculpted — spoke volumes. "You are a horrible liar, kitty."

"I suppose I am," I sighed again. "You can't blame me for wanting to protect you."

Suzanne smiled. "You already do, kitty — and have for some time. It just took me some time to realize that."

I hugged her again. "I love you, Suzanne," I whispered into her hair.

"And I, you, Sean," she replied.

Despite our exertions, I found myself keyed up enough that sleep didn't come easily. While I did manage to doze off briefly with Suzanne still in my arms, I awoke less than an hour later with an intense urge to use the bathroom. By that point, my girlfriend was blissfully at peace on the pillow beside me and barely stirred when I slipped out from beneath the sheet to tiptoe to the water closet. Returning a few moments later, I discovered Suzanne had somehow managed to take over the *entire* bed; unwilling to wake her enough to reclaim my side of the bed, I instead pulled on a pair of sweatpants and quietly padded down to the great room below. The last embers from the fire we'd had during dinner were still glowing in the hearth; given the slight chill in the cottage, I poked at what was left before adding a small piece of kindling to the pile. It caught nearly immediately, allowing me to build up the fire just enough to create a warm ambience.

Coffee seemed like a bad idea, so I instead opted for a cup of old-fashioned hot cocoa just the way my mother used to make it. As quietly as I could, I poured out a mug's worth of milk into a saucepan, added sugar and cocoa powder from Julie's pantry, then slowly warmed the concoction up until slivers of steam appeared. Decanting it into a mug bearing the logo for L.L. Bean, I put the saucepan into the sink and then returned to the living room to sink into the deep cushions of the couch. Sipping at the hot liquid, the intense burst of chocolate across my tongue brought to mind multiple cherished memories of my mother drawn from my childhood and later adulthood. I thought of her often; her loss to cancer years ago was one that I still felt keenly given how close the two of us had been. That hole in my heart had yet to heal, a feeling I knew I shared with my father.

Contemplating the flames as they danced along the logs, my thoughts about my own family made me wonder a bit at the one that had produced Dorothy Fernyhough. While I'd dealt with my fair share of wealthy families in my time as a cop, this was actually the first time I'd run into anyone hailing from a tony Beacon Hill address. I'd often heard it said that it was a different kind of money in that area of Boston — usually old money, something Daphne had very inelegantly reminded me during her interview. And yet, what little I knew of Dot made me think she wasn't a stereotypical woman from that background; as I sipped at my cocoa, I realized I actually had no frame of reference, and with it, very little sense of who Dot had been. Corinne had perhaps sketched in the most details and would likely be able to supply more; the group of close friends who had been at the bachelorette party could be another source, but didn't strike me as the type willing to give up much more than they already had.

They were hiding something about that night, I thought. *I wonder if any of them had known about Reggie and his relationship with Dot?*

That thought intrigued me. Daphne emphasizing the scandalous nature of the relationship had made it clear it hadn't exactly been a secret the two had been an item; the real question was whether it had extended beyond the Fernyhough social circle. Corinne had also said that Dot wasn't one to keep in touch with her friends; if that were true (and Corinne wasn't an outlier), it was possible the only outside person in Dot's orbit aware of her connection to Reggie was her colleague at Sprangers, Janet Cornflower. If that were true — and it was a big if — the fact that

Janet hadn't identified Reggie as the mysterious male who had accosted Dot was troubling. Twisting the mug of cocoa in my hands, I decided I had a reasonable excuse to try out the pool at the hotel in a few hours — and if I happened to run into Janet afterward, so much the better.

I glanced at the MacBook sitting on the coffee table, annoyed that the unreliable internet at the cottage made doing even cursory background searches nearly impossible. It felt a bit like I was one of those early Pinkerton Detectives on the American Frontier, with nothing but my wits and a magnifying lens to solve the deadliest of murders; maybe that was overly dramatic, but the situation certainly drove home the point on how much I relied on the modern data systems available to me as a law enforcement professional when working a case. The landline behind me on the end table represented a partial solution to the problem, but I was feeling *just* stubborn enough to take up the challenge and do it without my usual toolkit available.

A gentle hand at my shoulder told me I'd been so focused on my thoughts, I'd not heard Suzanne coming down the steps from the loft. Turning, I was struck by how the orange glow from the flames made her already beautiful face all the more striking; it also occurred to me that she looked rather sexy in the threadbare UEM Swimming t-shirt she'd borrowed for the evening. I slid over slightly on the couch, allowing her to sneak in beside me. Resting her chin on my shoulder, she snuggled close enough that I could feel the warmth of her skin through the t-shirt.

"Cosmic thoughts?" she asked quietly.

"Nothing quite so deep," I sighed. "Just pondering the heap of a mess I have, casting about for anything that might actually be a clue."

"Any success?"

"I don't know," I sighed again.

"That's unusual," she replied. "Normally you have a pretty solid sense of these things."

"Yeah."

"I wonder if that's what's blocking you?" Suzanne mused. "The fact that you *think* you should be further ahead than you are." She kissed my exposed shoulder. "Ignoring for the moment how you've only been working the case for, what, thirty-six hours?"

"Something like that." I twisted slightly to look at her. "Are you saying I'm stuck in a negative feedback loop?"

"Of your own making," she nodded. Suzanne sniffed at the mug in my hand. "Is that hot cocoa?"

"Yes," I nodded. "Want some? It won't take long to mix up another round."

"I would, yes," she smiled. "And while you make it, you can walk me through where you're stuck."

"Deal."

I carefully disentangled myself from my girlfriend and padded over to the kitchen, then pulled out the ingredients to make a second batch of hot cocoa. Suzanne watched me from the couch; with her back to the flames, her face was in shadows, giving her a very dramatic look. "You haven't been swimming, either, have you?"

"No," I replied as I poured in a healthy amount of milk, then stirred in the sugar and cocoa powder. "I've been running, but I just can't detach myself the same way as when I'm in the pool."

"You lean on that more than you realize, I think."

"Oh," I smiled, "that's become quite clear. Enough that I was nearly ready to borrow one of the wetsuits Julie has upstairs and do a loop around the island."

"I thought you hated open water swimming?"

"With a passion," I confirmed as I put the milk back in the fridge. Grabbing a fresh wooden spoon, I started to stir my concoction. "Anyway, I think I've got an obvious crime of passion on my hands and at least two men who could have done it; mix in a batch of acquaintances who are hiding something from me, a family that doesn't seem all that forthcoming and a future mother-in-law dealing with not one but *two* events that could damage her business permanently and you've got a smoldering fuse on a massive keg of powder."

Suzanne chuckled. "That is one hell of a visual."

"I try," I smiled as I continued to stir.

"I assume the men are Tim and Reggie?"

"Yes," I nodded. "I can't prove it yet, but I think Reggie was the one Dot had sex with; the passion portion was on full display the night he was escorted from the bar. And, of course, we've both seen the bandage on his hand."

"You think he still loved her?"

"Oh, yes," I nodded. "Which makes me all the more intrigued as to the reason they split. I think the answer lies with Dot's parents, if I can get it out of them. Or Reggie." I shrugged. "More interviews on my horizon, it seems. Goody."

"You live for that."

"There are days when I'd trade it all for a handwritten confession floating down from the heavens," I said as I turned off the stove and then carefully poured the hot liquid into two mugs.

"Do you think Reggie killed her?"

"I don't know," I replied as I walked over with the two mugs. Handing one to her, I settled back in beside her before continuing. "He admitted to being in the room; I've got to get a warrant for his phone records to confirm that Dot summoned him, but I see no reason to doubt that part of his story." Sipping at the mug, I found myself shaking my head. "Killing her? I'm not there yet."

"What about Tim?"

"That's trickier," I said. "From my own interactions with him, he seems to be quick tempered; clearly, he had an issue with something Dot had done the night she was killed." I sipped at my second cup of cocoa. "I don't have enough data to understand what it was that set him off, but I have a hunch it surrounds the magazine I saw in Tessa's office earlier today. It was a number of years old, but the cover model was Reggie."

"I know you told me that Reggie is some sort of retired supermodel," Suzanne said, referring to our earlier discussion over dinner of the interview Corinne and I conducted. "It isn't all that strange that he was hiding out here in the hinterlands of the world if you assume he was trying to get away from something in his past." She sipped at her mug. "You think Tim found out who he was?"

"Or Tessa," I replied. "Or they knew that part of his life, just not the portion where he'd been dating Tim's future fiancé."

"Oh Lord," she breathed. "I wonder if Reggie and Dot rediscovered each other?"

I nodded. "That had occurred to me as well," I replied. "Dot had to have bumped into Reggie when she came up from Boston to visit with Tim. If they had been forced to end things by her parents, it's entirely possible they picked right back up where they left off — only this time, without the watchful eyes of her parents upon her. Besides, Reggie's cabin is pretty isolated."

"This is a small enough island that it wouldn't take more than a single slip-up before word would get back to Tim or Tessa."

"Yeah," I nodded, "which goes back to my theory about Tim's ire. I think he knew or found out that Dot and Reggie were still an item; maybe he even caught them together in the suite on the night of the murder."

I saw Suzanne's face frown. "I thought you said you'd found clothing — *Reggie's* clothing — with blood on it?"

"We did, but I'm still trying to nail down whether it was planted for us to find, or if he was truly stupid enough to leave incriminating evidence right where we'd find it."

The frown went to a surprised smile. "Shit. You've got two possible suspects with the added benefit of one of them possibly being framed. I think I understand why you're a bit blocked on this one."

"That's it in a nutshell."

"What can I do to help?"

I smiled slyly. "I'll be honest, I could use a bit more mad, passionate sex. It seems to have been conducive to the brain cells."

"Was it?" she smiled as she drained the last of her cocoa. "Well, we can probably accommodate your request."

"Oh good," I replied.

Suzanne nodded at the windows facing the ocean and the slight glow that was a precursor to sunrise. "We might want to hurry, though. I suspect your canine companion will begin to get antsy once the sun appears."

"He will indeed," I said as I took her mug and placed it next to mine on the end table. "It's been a while since we've had a roaring fire in the background," I added as I turned back toward her. "What do you think?"

Leaning forward, she kissed me gently on the lips before whispering: "I think we'll have to be quiet so we don't wake the children."

"Challenge accepted," I nodded as I helped her out of her t-shirt and got down to business.

Fifteen

I'd laid out the blood-stained t-shirt with care along the top of the small counter in the kitchenette for the satellite station and frowned a bit as I took a second look at the pattern. Corinne and I had done nothing more than a cursory review of the fabric as we'd placed the shirt and shorts into matching evidence bags, and then logged them into the case system; without any forensic equipment on the island, there wasn't much I could do save for sending the package back to the Crime Lab, and that would have to wait until I called shore to dispatch the harbormaster. I wondered a bit as to whether Harold Kinneset was appreciating the extra overtime or had begun to curse my very name each time he was called upon to make yet another round trip to Carpenter's Island. I hoped the former but knew him well enough it was likely the latter.

Still, I'd delayed making the call as the clothing continued to vex me. I'd come straight down to the station after whipping up a batch of pancakes for Suzanne; Rocket had made no secret of his desire to follow my girlfriend, having seemingly bonded with her during their short time together in the cottage. She graciously agreed to give him his morning constitutional on what had turned into a brilliantly sunny morning under the singular condition I retrieve the pooch from her no later than lunchtime. Glancing back at the empty forward portion of the satellite office, I felt strangely alone without my canine companion; I'd grown used to his company, enough that I was seriously not looking forward to the return of his owner. I'd never had a pet due to the odd hours of my vocation, but the short time I'd spent with Rocket had made me want to re-assess that opinion. It was a happy thought to consider after I had the case behind me.

Staring at the shirt, I tried to recall something I had read in the literature we all tried to keep up with regarding the latest in blood spatter research. Having spent a fair portion of time listening to Lou walk me through all the possible ways a person could die had given me a bit of an encyclopedic understanding of what happened when a victim was stabbed; I also had a general sense of just how messy it could get when a major artery was severed. The vibrant slash of red across the band logo simply didn't look right to my eyes, not if the wearer had been standing where they'd needed to be in order to jab Dot with a piece of glass.

Wondering if I was reading the signs correctly, I picked up my iPhone, prayed for a solid connection and then dialed Lou's direct line. She picked up on the fourth ring. "Sean? What the hell are you doing up so early?"

I glanced at my Apple Watch. "It's nearly seven, Lou," I replied. "That's *late* in my book."

"Of course it is," she sighed. "What can I do for you?"

"Are you busy?"

"When am I not?" she laughed. "But for you, I can spare five."

"Good," I said. "I'm going to switch this to a video call."

"Oh, shit," she said. "Hang on and let me get to my computer — I can never get that damn software to work on my phone. Let me call you right back."

"I'll be here."

The phone chirped the three-beep conclusion of the call and I put it down on the counter, then picked up the takeaway mug of coffee I'd brought with me from the cottage. One sip at the tepid brew was a bitter reminder of how long I'd been staring at the shirt and shorts, trying to make sense of what I was looking at. It wasn't unheard of for a suspect to ditch clothing that might be incriminating, nor was it all that unusual for evidence to be so poorly hidden; most murders in my experience weren't premeditated, which meant that burying any connections to the crime tended to be poor afterthoughts pursued while the adrenaline was still pumping. Still, if these truly belonged to Reggie — and I had no evidence they didn't — the notion that he'd stripped down to his skivvies, dumped the clothing in a luggage cart and then booked it back to his cabin in the woods seemed contrived at best. Setting the mug aside, I squinted at the blood stains in the vain hope they might say something to me of their own accord; sadly, they continued to keep their own council.

My iPhone took that opportunity to chime out the chords indicating I was receiving a FaceTime invitation; picking it up, I tapped the accept button and immediately saw the top third of Dr. Hamilton's head — the portion covered by a blue hair cap. "You need to adjust your camera," I said, trying not to smile.

"Shit," she cursed. The picture shook for a moment before stabilizing with a new view of her deeply frowning face. "I must have knocked it asunder yesterday."

"You just hate these video conferences," I said, unable to resist teasing her.

"With a passion," she sighed. "It's all the rage now; the State doesn't want to pay for travel to a meeting if we can instead play *The Brady Bunch* and stare at each other from the comfort of our desks."

I thought about that for a moment. "Are you talking about the gallery view that the software offers?" I asked. "Norm called it that, too, but I don't get the reference."

Lou rolled her eyes. "I thought Suzanne was teaching you the ways of sitcom television?"

"I guess she hasn't made it to *The Brady Bunch* yet."

"Your loss," she laughed. "What did you want to show me?"

I tapped the icon on the screen to reverse the camera, then held my iPhone over the shirt. "This was recovered at the hotel yesterday," I said. "I'm relatively certain the shirt belongs to a person of interest, and we've already established they were in the room of the victim at some point on the night of the murder."

"Meaning these clothes were being worn at the time the murder was committed?"

"I'm not saying that," I replied. "Especially because these stains just don't look right to me, given how we think the murder occurred. I know I'm not an expert in blood spatter, so I thought I would call on one who was."

Lou was quiet for a moment. "I'm going to hedge a bit and remind you that I can only do so much without having the evidence in front of me," she started.

"I understand. These will be on their way to the lab as soon as we're done speaking."

"Okay." There was another pause before she continued. "How tall is your person of interest?"

"I'm guessing, but close to six feet? Maybe a bit over?"

"Mm-hmm," she murmured. "The victim was prone, right?"

"Based on how we found her at the scene, that's our assumption, yes. Heather's photos should be part of the file if you need angles."

"I'll check them in a bit," she said. "But if I recall what I read in the report before I did the postmortem, the only blood was on and around the bed, right?"

"Yes," I nodded, even though she couldn't see it. "We're pretty confident she was killed in the location we found her; there was no blood trail to indicate she died elsewhere in the hotel suite and was moved to the bed."

"Mm-hmm," Lou murmured again.

"So, what do you think? Am I barking up the wrong tree?"

"I think your instincts are serving you well on this one, Sean," she replied after another moment of thought. "Again, I'll reserve a more formal opinion until my minions have been able to go over the garments in detail, but I agree that what I'm seeing isn't consistent with something that would have been worn by the murderer when the kill stroke was made. Blood would *definitely* be on the shirt in that situation, but in a more haphazard way; what you have there is too linear, too orderly." Lou paused. "Someone did a good job trying to make it look right, and to the untrained eye, it would."

"And to the trained eye?" I asked, thinking I knew the answer.

"I'd have to say it's been staged," she replied. "It's good and indicates some level of knowledge — but of the YouTube amateur forensic variety."

"Or bad horror movies?" I asked, thinking of the marathon Vasily had made me suffer through back in February.

"That too," she said. I turned the camera on the phone back toward me and saw her frown. "I'm not sure what this tells you about your suspect. Or suspects."

"I'm not sure either," I said. "My aim is to clarify that little issue today, I think."

"Well, good luck with that," Lou laughed. "I've got to run. You said those will be on the way to me today?"

"That's the hope."

"I'll get them processed as soon as they land," she continued. "Maybe we'll find something on them to help assist you in clarifying things."

"You usually do," I reminded her.

"No pressure, then," she laughed. "Later."

I slid my phone into the pocket of my shorts then, after a final moment of contemplation, packed the shirt and shorts back into their plastic evidence bags before wandering out to the single desk in the lobby. Not wanting to press my luck with the flaky cellular coverage — I'd been more than surprised I'd not dropped Lou at all during our video call — I used the landline to request another run by the harbormaster only to be informed that he was currently dealing with an over-turned sailboat in Windeport harbor. As the likelihood of getting the clothing to Lou that day had become statistically improbable, I stuffed everything back into what passed for an evidence locker and headed for the hotel, annoyed that my new gig didn't come with a helicopter at my disposal.

The warmth of the morning sun against my face felt wonderful as I drove the golf cart along the narrow, paved lane that connected the hotel to the village. After a few days of gloomy overcast skies and chilly temperatures, it was nice to experience the more tourist-friendly weather — especially given how quickly it could change into something far worse. From how busy the lane was with other people out and about at that early hour, it seemed I wasn't alone in wanting to make the most of such a beautiful day. Given how much rain we'd endured over the past few days, I imaged nearly everyone on the island had a bit of cabin fever.

Pulling up at an informal three-way stop on the lane, the hand-lettered sign at the intersection noted the proper direction for the East Village served as a reminder that I'd wanted to speak with the alternate bartender, Phyllis, about Reggie. Shifting my plan on the fly, I turned East and made my way down a far less manicured roadway toward what I suspected was a prime example of a company town. I wasn't disap-pointed when I emerged from the woods at the edge of a gently sloping lane that bisected a cleared section of the forest covering the island. Identical mobile homes were placed at regular intervals along the road, all clearly bought from the same manufacturer at the same time. Most looked weatherbeaten and run down, though a few here and there appeared to have been repainted fairly recently. Sam the bartender hadn't been kidding when he'd told me that Phyllis's place would be easily recognizable; the flowerpots were far closer to neon pink in my option, though in all honestly, nothing could match the eye-popping fuchsia of the plastic flamingos that had been staked within them. The white petunias overflowing the pots did little more than emphasize the jarring color juxtaposition, though not quite as badly as the set of midnight black ceramic kittens bolted to the side of the home as though they were climbing to the roof. I half expected to find a bathtub-shrouded Madonna somewhere on the property, or a small fleet of garden gnomes protecting what little lawn was exposed between that mobile home and the neighbor.

I pulled the golf cart as far off the small lane as I could in front of the mobile home, then slid out of the front seat. The neighborhood, such as it was, appeared to be relatively quiet; considering most of the residents likely worked at the hotel, it wasn't surprising, though I also wondered just how many of the downtrodden homes were actually abandoned. A general sense of despair seemed to have settled over the entire area, one so deep that not even the day's bright sunshine could dispel it. There were portions of Carpenter's Island that felt as though time had all but ignored them; this spot was most definitely not one of them.

My attention shifted from the street when the screen door closest to me opened, revealing a short, plump women in her late fifties; her hair was tied back by a colorful scarf in bright pink, though quite a bit of the silver strands were visible spilling out from behind the fabric. Wiping her hands on a checked apron that appeared covered in several layers of flour, the woman leaned against the railing of the wooden porch that had been erected next to the mobile home. The three-inch gap between the porch and the door told me one of the structures had shifted; based on the slight cant of the porch, I was inclined not to think it was the mobile home.

"You that detective?" she asked without preamble. Her voice was deep and raspy, speaking to decades of smoking – or being exposed to it, which seemed like a hazard for those in her profession.

I nodded as I walked to the lowest step of the porch. "I see my reputation precedes me yet again."

A slight quirk of a smile appeared on her lined face; reaching into a pocket of the apron, Phyllis pulled out a pack of Marlboro cigarettes and tapped one into her hand. "Hardly. Sam called as soon as you left the bar at the restaurant. Told me to expect a visitor." She paused and smiled a grin full of faded yellow but perfectly straight teeth. "He managed to leave out the fact you'd be a hunk."

I smiled my best *aw shucks* smile and held out my hands. "I appreciate the compliment," I said. "I think I'm too old to be called that now, honestly."

Phyllis chuckled, which sounded a bit like a seagull going after a sand dollar. "Old is relative," she said. "You get to be my age, and everyone looks like they're still in high school."

Is it weird I've begun to think the same thing? I asked myself. *Norm looks even younger than that. If I'm this hung up on age now, what will I feel when I turn* fifty?

Phyllis struck a match against the wood of the porch, then used it to light her cigarette; waving the small piece of wood to put the flame out, she rather carelessly flicked it over the edge of the railing and onto the small patch of grass that was her yard. "You want to know about Reggie?"

"I do." I tried not to pay attention to the small filament of smoke that was snaking up from where the match had landed. The last thing I needed was to have a portion of the island burn to the ground while I was there.

"Not much to tell," was Phyllis's predictable next statement. "He's been on the island for some time now."

"So, I heard," I said as I rested one foot on a riser for the steps. "Seems to bake some exceptional bread, too."

"That he does."

We stared at each other for a moment while she took a deep drag from the cigarette. It never ceased to amaze me just how ugly the process actually looked; that so many people had felt otherwise decades earlier was a testament to how effective glossy advertising and tactical product placement could be. Turning slightly away from me, Phyllis pursed her lips and blew out a massive cloud of white smoke that quickly dissipated into the morning; while I was appreciative of her deference to a guest, the acrid scent of the tobacco still hung in the air in a most distasteful way. I tried to ignore it, but as she took another drag from the cigarette, I resigned myself to needing to take a shower before proceeding to my next task.

"When did he arrive on the island?" I asked when it seemed like she'd finally reached a nicotine equilibrium.

"Two, maybe three years ago?" she said after expelling another cloud of smoke. "No — three years ago, if you count his purchasing of that spot in the forest as an 'arrival.'"

I nodded. "Did he live here while the cottage was built?"

"It wasn't built so much as renovated," Phyllis said. "Old man Hermon passed, oh, what was it? Five years ago? He didn't have any kids, so the place fell into probate. I think that's how Reggie found it; had to have paid just pennies on the dollar for it." She paused long enough to top off her nicotine buzz with another drag; at that rate, she'd be lighting another cigarette before too long. "Reggie was overseeing the work, so he had a room at the hotel while the construction happened. Must have been the summer? So three months, start to finish."

"Is that when you met him?"

"Ayuh," she replied, confirming along with her accent that she was a native Downeaster. "He was a regular at the bar. Always has the same thing: two glasses of an expensive French wine we order special for him. Usually stays an hour, sometimes two."

"That's a fair amount of wine for such a short amount of time."

Phyllis shrugged. "He's got a lot of Gallic in him. They can hold their liquor — far more than some of the tourists we get."

"His accent is barely visible," I said.

Phyllis smiled slightly. "It's far more pronounced after he's had a glass," she said.

"How'd you know he was from France?"

"As opposed to Quebec?" she laughed. "I've been in the business a long time, in one bar or another along the Maine Coast. You develop an ear for it, I think; there are some unusual differences in how Reggie pronounces certain words in English than those who grew up in Canada. Something regional about where he was born, I think."

I tried to sidestep a cloud of smoke that shifted in my direction on the wind. "What kind of a customer is Reggie?"

"I'm not sure I can break the bartender-client privilege," she smiled. "People tell us stuff because we give them the air of discretion."

"Or they are lonely and are looking for a friendly ear," I countered. "And there's no such privilege."

"Perhaps," she nodded. "All the same, I'm not sure I'd be comfortable telling you anything he confided in me."

"Phyllis," I said, letting my voice harden into something more formal. "Anything you can tell me about Reggie would be immensely helpful. I'm trying to fill in some blanks in order to understand what has happened here on this island." I paused for a moment. "And to help rule out anyone... not responsible for the murder of Dot."

Something shifted on Phyllis's face, confirming for me that she had a soft spot for the baker. Still, as she shook out a second cigarette from the pack and lit it, I could tell that she felt uncomfortable telling me anything that might look bad for Reggie. I waited patiently for her to take a few deep drags on the new cigarette, allowing the silence to work the magic it always did when people I was interviewing were reluctant to talk. At length, she looked at me with a resigned expression.

"Reggie is young," she started.

"Not that young," I replied.

"Not physically," Phyllis amended. "More in the way of romance. He had his heart broken during his one and only relationship and hasn't ever truly recovered."

"First love," I nodded. "I know from experience how hard that can be to move beyond."

"Exactly," she said.

"Just so we're clear, you're talking about his relationship with Dot?"

"I didn't know it was her initially," Phyllis answered. "When I first met him, she was just this girl that had captured his soul back in Boston.

I didn't even know he was one of those big-time international models until later."

"You must have wondered where the money came from for the cottage?"

"On this island?" she laughed before devolving into a coughing fit. Once she caught her breath, she continued. "This is where people come to get away from questions like that. Reggie was just another in a long line of people running from something."

"You think Reggie was trying to escape his heartache?"

"Oh yeah," she nodded sagely. "Those first few months, his emotions were so raw I could see them seeping out of every pore. I had the sense all of his dreams had suddenly gone up in smoke back in Boston; coming here was a way to gain some measure of solace, using his forced solitude to get over it."

"Did he?" I asked. "Get over it?"

"Does anyone ever get over a broken heart?" she asked rhetorically. "No. But the pain eased enough that he opened up about other parts of his life. That's how I learned about his starring roles in the theater, as well as the modeling."

"When did you discover it was Dot?"

Phyllis took a much longer moment to suck in a huge lungful of tobacco before answering. "The day Dot arrived on the island with Tim," she said.

"When was this?"

"Memorial Day last year," she said. "It was her first visit, though I think she'd been dating Tim longer than that." Phyllis smiled wryly. "Tessa wasn't pleased, if what I heard on the company grapevine was correct."

"That her son was dating someone? Or that it was Dot?"

"Both, actually," she answered. "It's no secret that Tessa wants Tim to take over when she retires. She's got no interest in anything that might distract him from that goal."

"Ouch."

"It's that kind of family," she said, continuing a theme that Sam had begun during our conversation. "I was tending bar that night; Reggie had just arrived, and I was pouring him his first glass of wine when Dot and Tim entered the restaurant."

"What happened?"

"About what you would have expected. Dot ignored Reggie completely, though the two did see each other; I only know that because Reggie made some sort of comment about her that I'd ignored. It was a few nights later that he confided in me she'd been his fiancé."

My jaw dropped. "They'd been *engaged*?"

"Yeah," she nodded. "He still had the ring," she added. "Showed it to me once. Sizable diamond on a tasteful gold band."

"Did you ever see Reggie and Dot together?"

"No, never," she replied, but the look on her face told me she was hiding something.

"Someone else did," I said softly. "What did they see?"

Phyllis looked at the now very short cigarette between her fingers, stabbed it out on the wood of the railing and then tossed it to the grass. Tapping out her third cigarette, I found myself wondering if her pay at the hotel was sufficient to cover what appeared to be a sizable invest-ment in smoking. "I... I heard something from a housekeeper that Dot took to keeping a room off-the-books when she stayed the weekend."

"The suite?"

"No," Phyllis replied. "Nothing quite so prominent. It's on the third floor in the south wing; one of the smallest rooms we have right next to the elevators. Guests hate it because of the noise, so it gets booked last."

I nodded. "Would it also be convenient to an exit?"

Phyllis looked at me with surprise. "I'd never thought about it, but yes. That elevator lobby leads directly to the pool deck and the island trail beyond."

"So anyone visiting Dot could get to her without going through the lobby?"

"They'd need a card key after hours, but yes."

I thought about Corinne giving me her spare key and realized I had *another* excuse to try the pool later that day. "Do you know if they use manager keycards in the hotel?"

"Ones that can open any door?" she asked before continuing at my nod. "Yeah, though only a handful of people have them. Mostly supervisors."

"And Tim? And Tessa?"

"Certainly. I've seen both of them unlock doors before with their cards."

"How was Reggie after Dot became a fixture on the island?"

"Initially, inconsolable. Seeing the one you love engaged to another — and I have no doubt he still loved Dot — was hard for him, but over time, he seemed to come to peace with it."

Yeah, I thought. *By starting an under-the-radar relationship with Dot.*

"He was getting a bit antsy the closer the calendar came to the wedding," Phyllis was saying. "I think he half expected Dot to call everything off and move into his cottage."

"Did that seem likely?"

"I wouldn't know," Phyllis replied as she stubbed out the third butt. Glancing at her watch, she looked at me. "I've got to get this cake out of the oven, and then head to the hotel."

"Then I won't keep you any longer," I said. "Thanks for the chat."

Phyllis looked at me. "Reggie is a good kid. I can't believe he's mixed up in murder."

"You'd be surprised," I said as I turned to go. "People can do the damndest things when they set their mind to it."

Sixteen

After making the round-trip to the cottage to change into my workout gear, it was nearly ten by the time I tapped the card key Corinne had given to me at the gate to the pool. With an electronic *clunk*, the door popped open, and I pushed through to the tile of the deck; I wasn't surprised that the majority of the chaise lounge chairs had been claimed, given how the day had turned out, but was mildly shocked that no one was in the pool itself. I made my way along one side of the pool to an empty chair in the corner, then tossed my swim bag onto the thick cushion before kicking out of my sandals and pulling my t-shirt over my head. While not one to be embarrassed wearing a Speedo in public, I'd opted to toss a pair of board shorts on over my briefs in deference to the sensibilities of the well-heeled guests staying at the hotel. Grabbing my swim cap and goggles from the bag, I moved to the side of the pool and easily slipped into one of the lap lanes, dropping all the way to the deep bottom before smoothly kicking up to the surface. The coolness of the water was more welcome than I'd expected; I'd not realized how hot and bothered I'd become running around in the golf cart that morning.

Shaking out some excess water from my now sodden curls, I pressed the goggles to my eyes before pulling the cap over my head, then ducked beneath the water to push off from the wall for the first lap. A few underwater dolphin kicks allowed me to stretch the muscles a bit before I surfaced into a slow freestyle, gently getting into a rhythm that my body had been craving for days. Twenty laps in, my body began to take on that familiar ache that told me I was in the zone; hitting the wall on lap twenty-one, I flipped over during the turn and surfaced doing backstroke, focusing on keeping my breathing deep and regular. The deep azure of the sky was made darker by the polarizing layer on my goggles, but no less stunning; as I moved across the pool, I watched a bird or two flitter by, streaks of bold color that stood out against the background.

Flipping to my stomach in preparation for another flip turn, I caught sight of legs standing at the end of the lane and instead came up for air; Tim Polanski was wearing a frown and had his arms crossed as he looked down at me. Pushing my goggles to my forehead, I smiled at him as I bobbed in the water. "Beautiful day for a swim," I said.

"For our paying guests," he replied tartly. "Get out."

"Of course," I said.

Swimming the final yard to the wall, I reached up and then pressed myself out of the water in a fluid motion, popping onto my feet in a well-practiced move. Tim followed me over to where my swim bag was waiting, then stood at the end of the chair, arms still folded tightly against his chest. Pulling the towel out of my bag, I began to dry off; though not one normally prone to irritating another, I noted that the longer I took, the more annoyed Tim seemed to become. Since that suited my purposes (for the moment), I moved more deliberately than normal, but not in a way that would make it obvious I was doing so. After all, I'd once been teenager reluctant to leave the pool after practice; no reason not to lean into those hard-earned skills.

"Who let you in?" Tim finally demanded as I sat down to towel off the soles of my feet.

"I'm glad you appeared," I deflected. "I was planning on seeking you out later. Does your security system keep track of each card swipe?"

"Of course it does," he snapped. "So if you don't tell me who gave you a card, I can still look it up in the logs."

"That's useful," I nodded. "And you have that history on any door?"

"Yes."

"I'm going to need the logs from that entrance, then," I said, nodding my head toward the double doors leading into the hotel behind him. "And for all of the other doors in this hotel for the past week."

"You—you *what?*"

Standing, I pulled my t-shirt back on, then wrapped the towel about my waist. Eyeing my goggles and cap, I frowned slightly at having to put them into the wet pocket of the bag, but taking more time to thoroughly dry them off looked like it would push Tim over the edge completely. "I'm also going to need access to a room on the third floor of that wing, too."

"That's not data I'm willing to share with you," he said after a moment.

"I'm happy to get a warrant," I smiled. "But a warrant comes with publicity, even on an island as remote as this one."

Eyeing me, Tim finally sighed. "Fine. Come with me."

I followed him back across the deck to the gate. The other guests had taken note of his appearance and our conversation, though most were taking pains to hide their interest behind a magazine or e-reader device. Pushing out of the gate, Tim walked me up the pathway to the doors, then reluctantly held one open for me; the blast of air conditioning told me it had warmed up far more than I had realized. Goosebumps immediately rippled across my exposed arms, making me wish I'd gotten more water out of my soggy curls.

We walked past the elevators, then turned toward the lobby; given how quickly he was walking, it was clear Tim wasn't impressed his day had been interrupted by me yet again. He jabbed a finger angrily at the reception desk as we approached it. "Stay here. I'll be back with the logs in a moment."

I nodded and took up position at the end of the counter. Several lines had formed at the other end; with the wedding essentially cancelled, it looked like the attendees had decided to catch the next mail boat back to the mainland and depart. I scanned the faces and didn't see anyone I'd spoken to already; the activity reminded me I'd considered shutting down access to the island in order to keep my suspects corralled, but as the investigation had deepened, it had become clear — to me, at least — that the killer wouldn't think to leave the island to avoid detection. It was an angle I was hoping to parlay into their eventual discovery, something I was thinking would happen fairly soon.

Tim appeared from the alcove behind the reception desk carrying a sheaf of paper. Tossing it down on the counter, he tapped at it with a finger. "Everything for the past ten days for that door, the pool gate, and room 315."

I nodded. "Thank you. And if I could have a key to that room, please?" I asked.

"I can open it for you," he replied.

"A key, if you please."

My look apparently convinced him not to belabor the point. He moved to a keyboard and tapped at it for a moment, then reached under the desk to retrieve a card key. "Return this when you are done?"

"Absolutely," I smiled as I took it and the paper. Unzipping the backpack, I stuffed the printouts on top of my dry clothes I brought to change into, then zipped it back up. "Will you be here in a bit? I'll want to talk to you after I've been upstairs."

"I have to see about the lunch service, but I'll be available."

"Good."

We stared at each other for a few heartbeats, and I feared for a moment he might insist again on accompanying me to the room; I was rather relieved when he didn't follow me after I turned away and started toward the hallway for the south wing. While I didn't doubt he had duties to perform that he felt he couldn't avoid, since I had never specified *which* room I needed a key for, it seemed more likely he'd realized how much of his hand he'd accidentally tipped and needed to regroup. Heading down the corridor to the elevators, I nodded to myself at the oblique confirmation Tim had known all along about Dot's supposed subterfuge, then frowned at what such knowledge might have led to. What was worse was the fact that I now had solid reasons for *both* Tim and Reggie to be the killer; I hoped whatever I found in room 315 finally tipped me in one direction or the other.

I'd barely pressed the elevator button before the doors parted, allowing a surprised Corinne to step out into the lobby. Eying my outfit, she smiled slightly. "Tried the pool, did we?"

"And got kicked out," I smiled as I unwound the towel from my waist and threw it over a shoulder.

"Seriously?" she asked. "That sounds like quite a story."

"I'll tell you on our way up," I said as I stepped into the vacant carriage.

"Up? Up *where*?"

"We're going to visit the room where the murder happened," I smiled as she followed me in.

"Say *what*—!?" she spluttered as the doors closed.

By the time the doors opened on the third floor, I'd sketched in what my theory was up to that moment and had managed to include a brief vignette of what had happened on the pool deck. "He knew where the room was," she said as we turned down the hallway.

"Yep."

The door to 315 was just where Phyllis had claimed: directly beside the elevator lobby. I wasn't surprised in the least that it had a little sign hanging over the knob waving off any housekeeping services, though it did bother me that the staff had gone days without a courtesy check to ensure everything was okay with the guest. That sort of procedure had become standard in most hotels after a shooter used a room in a high-rise Las Vegas resort a few years back to take out concertgoers across the street from the building; the gunman had literally used the *no house-keeping* sign to prevent the staff from seeing his stacks of ammunition.

Then again, if it was common knowledge what was going on in room 315, the staff may well have had reason to avoid the room.

I waved the card over the lock and was rewarded with the light turning green. "I don't think Dot was keeping her tryst with Reggie all that quiet."

"She was going to *marry* Tim," Corinne said as I pushed the door open. "That's fucked up."

"People often are forced into situations they'd rather not do," I said. It felt best not to point out her own dalliance with Tim. "Your room is on this floor?" I asked. I pulled two sets of exam gloves from the side of my swim backpack, handed her one pair and then put on the other.

Corinne blinked. "Yes," she replied. "I'm 325."

"Interesting," I nodded before stepping into the room.

The smell hit me before I made it two feet inside the doorway; from the gagging behind me, Corinne had apparently caught a whiff as well. A slight shaft of sunlight was streaming through the gap in the curtains over the balcony windows, just enough to illuminate the bed against the wall. The sheets had been stripped completely, but the stained mattress told the story by itself; reaching for the wall switch, I turned the lamps on beside the queen-sized bed, thrusting the entire scene into full relief. Blood had pooled in the lowest section of the mattress, then had seeped over the edge and trickled onto the carpet; while I couldn't see a stain against the dark fibers of the flooring, I had no doubt it was there. Unlike the suite where Dot had been found, there was no sitting room, and no couch; there was barely enough space for the bed and matching nightstands. A dresser was opposite the bed and had a small ice bucket beside a wineglass and an empty wine bottle upon the polished surface; the television mounted on the wall above the dresser was on and tuned to some sort of twenty-four-hour weather service, though the volume had been muted.

A room service trolley was wedged in the space between the bed and the wall to the bathroom; it had a trash bag covering the surface, with another full one beneath it. Adjusting my backpack, I leaned down slightly and untied the trash bag on the lower level; a blood-stained polo with the hotel's logo was on top, with what looked like a matching pair of khakis — the standard outfit all the professional employees wore. Rooting around slightly netted me two towels, also covered in blood, and a woman's sun dress in a flowery print. Corinne hovered over my shoulder, allowing me to tip the open bag toward her.

"That's the dress Dot wore to the party," she said before turning to the bed. "Shit. This is where it *actually* happened, isn't it?"

"Yes," I said. Tying the bag up again, I nodded at the cart. "I think that luggage cart you saw held more than just Reggie's outfit."

"*Shit,*" Corinne breathed. "That's how the body was moved?"

"Maybe," I said. "Check the bathroom, would you?"

"Of course."

She went around the corner, and I tacked in the opposite direction; the crunch of glass beneath my sandal made me pause and crouch. Shards large and small were embedded in the carpet; using the flashlight on my phone, I managed to scope out the semicircle where they appeared to be, then carefully moved around them to the side of the bed. Shining the light down on the nightstand got me more shards, though between that and what was on the carpet, it was hard to know if I'd found an entire glass. Peering into the wastebasket beside the bed, I leaned closer and found blood-spattered Kleenex; pushing them aside, I located major pieces of a shattered wineglass. Shifting around the bag, it was hard to tell whether I had parts for one or two and decided I'd leave that up to the lab geeks to discover. Standing, I took a second look at the mattress and frowned at sheer amount of blood present; knowing how much a standard human body held, it seemed clear that Dot had essentially bled out in this space. Moving her after the fact would quite likely have not left much of a trail save for anything that might have accidentally dripped from her body — and even that was unlikely, depending on how coagulated the blood had been by that point.

Corrine reappeared from the corner of the bathroom. "I can't be sure, but I *think* the shower has been used and not cleaned; there's a bit of a ring around the drain that should probably be tested for blood."

I nodded. "It will be, I think. Anything else?"

"Nothing other than the amenities the hotel provides. Bar of soap was opened, but the two standard water glasses by the sink are still sealed; toilet paper seems to have been used, but that's it." She nodded at the trash bag we'd looked in. "Towels are missing, I presume that's what those were."

"Yeah."

"Why wasn't this room cleaned?" Corinne asked. "It seems like a huge risk to not dispose of all of this."

"I imagine it would have been a bit obvious if the mattress had been tossed on the refuse heap this week," I replied. "But I also think that the killer expected to have more time to clean up. They never planned on having cops on the island."

"There's always a cop on the island," Corinne reminded me. "You're working out of their office."

"You mean the same one who's out of the game with food poisoning?"

Corinne looked at me, her eyes wide. "That wasn't an accident?"

"No," I said, shaking my head. "No, I don't think it was. I think Suzanne was right all along — the killer planned on using the outbreak as cover for a death. I don't quite know how they did that part, but I suspect I overlooked something in the kitchen. I'll have to get Heather's team back out here; unless I miss my mark, the killer left something behind for us to find." I looked at the bed again. "For they didn't expect *us* to also be here; I think that's forced some improvisation upon an otherwise premeditated plan."

Corinne looked at me. "You've figured this out, haven't you?"

I shrugged. "I have a hunch, yes."

"You want to share with the rest of us?" Corinne asked, putting a gloved hand on her hip.

"Not until I can confirm my hunch."

"Shit," Corinne frowned. "Vasily told me you did this."

"Did what?"

"Look at a piece of evidence and then suddenly see the whole picture." She frowned deeper. "He also said it was damn frustrating when it happened."

"Corinne," I laughed, "we've worked together before. You've seen me in action."

"Yeah, well, I must have always missed the epiphany part each time," she groused. "I think I'm glad I did. What do you want to do from here?"

Where did *I want to go from here?* I thought. *Aside from the obvious part of getting Heather back out here for another go at this hotel, I need to be pretty crafty about how I approach my leading suspect...*

And just like that, the idea popped into my head. Corinne saw my surprised smile and arched an eyebrow. "I'm going to rescue my pooch, then take a walk in the woods. Want to come along?"

"Do I ever," she replied.

Pulling out my iPhone, I snapped a dozen or so photos of the room before flipping over to my contact list to tap the speed dial for Heather Graham. I didn't have the chance to actually call her, though, for my phone took that opportunity to burst out into song; the caller ID told me it was the Chief Medical Examiner. "Hey, Lou," I said as I answered. "You seem to have caught me with decent cell coverage for once."

"That's a first, given how it's been on that island," Lou replied.

"It helps that I'm at the hotel," I added. "They seem to have the only tower on the island on their property."

"Got to keep the guests happy," she laughed. "I wonder if that's one of the excuses they use to justify the exorbitant resort fee tacked onto every bill?"

"Capitalism," I sighed. "Gotta love it."

"Why are you at the hotel?"

"Corinne and I found the actual crime scene," I said without preamble. "I was about to summon Heather and her team when you rang."

"Indeed," she replied with a slight chuckle. "I had no idea you knew the proper magical spells for that."

"It was in the thick handbook Jimmy gave me on day one," I deadpanned. "I thought all employees for the State had one?"

"Only management," Lou laughed. "I recall Heather had some notes in the file about the murder taking place elsewhere — something about the stain on the mattress where the body was found not seeming right."

My eyes went to the deep crimson stain. "She won't need to bother with the fancy math to determine if we located all of the blood," I said. "I think it's a moot point now."

"Shit."

"Yeah. Anyway, I'm sure you didn't call to find out about my new crime scene...?"

"Hardly, though it seems fortuitous given why I *am* calling. The labs came back on everything we bagged from the scene, as well as the samples I'd sent from the body."

The way she paused had me arching an eyebrow. "Something unexpected appeared, I gather."

"As always seems to be the case with you," Lou replied, though with a touch of fondness in her voice. "You want the intriguing stuff first, or the *really* intriguing stuff?"

"Might as well build up to it," I replied, resigned that my favorite medical examiner was going to tease out her findings once more. "Give me the intriguing stuff first."

"I was hoping you'd say that," she said. "There were two discrete donors in the semen samples we took, both from the sheets and the victim."

I felt myself nod. "I expected that," I replied.

Lou was nonplussed. "Seriously? Based on *what*? Before you answer that, I'll insert another little detail—"

"One of them also left some blood behind on the sheets," I interrupted.

"Why did I even bother to expedite the lab tests?" Lou huffed. "Next, you'll tell me you know who the donors are."

"Where would the fun be in that?" I asked. "Besides, the tests were *insanely* important — they not only validate my theory on this case, but I think they also clear up what my next steps will be."

"Glad I could be of *some* help."

"Don't pout," I laughed. "Tell me your *really* intriguing stuff."

"I have half a mind just to email it to you," she sighed. "Since I expect you've already figured that out, too."

"I might surprise you."

"It's kind of you to stroke my ego, however slightly," she laughed again. "One of the donors was a paternal match to the fetus. And," she added after a dramatic pause, "they are also the same donor for the blood sample tested."

It seemed prudent not to tell Lou I had expected that result as well, so I smiled slightly to myself and played along with my friend of many years a little. "So the killer was the father?"

"That's my read on the evidence," Lou replied. "I don't suppose you're sending me DNA kits from your suspects that we can run against this data...?"

"Not quite yet, no," I sighed. "I'm seriously short of kits and have yet to get my emergency package from the mainland with more." I looked at Corinne thoughtfully. "Though while that would make this academic, I think I can get what I need without them at this point."

There was a pause at the other end. "You know who it is?"

"Yes," I replied. "I believe I do."

SEVENTEEN

To my surprise, Reggie was sitting on the front porch of the cottage when Corinne and I pulled up in my borrowed golf cart. While I was by no means yet an expert on his baking schedule, it seemed unusual he wasn't attending to his oven, though I was rather happy about not having to bushwhack my way through the island's forest a third time to reach his house. What had driven him to my temporary doorstep felt obvious, especially when considering the way he was twisting a ratty Red Sox baseball cap between his hands. His mop of long hair shifted when he looked up at our approach, revealing a face that was a study in anxiety so obvious no psychological consultation would have been necessary (had such a professional even been available to me on the island in the first place). A quick glance at Corinne as I applied the parking brake for the cart told me she'd picked up the same vibe; at my nod, she pulled out her phone and immediately triggered the voice recording application.

Sliding from behind the wheel, I pulled my swim backpack from where the golf bags would normally sit on the cart and then slung it over my shoulder. Opening the gate to the small front yard, I waved at

Reggie as I carefully approached him. "I wasn't expecting you, Reggie," I said honestly.

"But I'm sure you were looking for me," he replied somewhat morosely. "I heard about the clothing you found at the hotel."

My eyebrows went up. "I had no idea word had gotten around already," I said.

"It's a small island."

"Clearly."

Reggie looked at me, his unusual gray eyes nearly round with fear. "I didn't kill her. You have to believe me."

It was clear that the strain he was under had surfaced his French accent. "Let's talk inside, then," I said, nodding to the door. "I for one could use another cup of coffee."

The uncomfortable silence that stretched beyond a few heartbeats made me feel as though we were back at the Windeport Police Station, dealing with a suspect who has suddenly understood the significance of being "invited" into an interview room with an investigator. Reggie considered me for a few more moments before seeming to come to a decision; pushing away from the steps where he was sitting, he stood and waited for me to pull the screen door open for him. Rocket was lounging in his dog bed beside the hearth and eyed us as we entered but seemed to understand that it wasn't an appropriate time to greet the unannounced guest. I waved to the couch before heading into the open kitchen to begin preparing a new pot of coffee. Once the coffeemaker had begun chugging through its cycle, I turned and leaned my back against the counter, trying to look as casual (and non-threatening) as I could.

"I want to remind you that your earlier agreement is still in effect," I said carefully. "Before you tell me anything, do you continue to waive your right to having a lawyer present?"

Reggie nodded. "*Oui,*" he said before smiling slightly. "Yes."

"You also understand that anything you say from this point forward could be used against you in a court of law?"

"Yes."

I tried to put my hands into the non-existent pockets of my board-shorts, which in turn was a reminder I'd not had a chance to change since my abbreviated swim at the hotel. Despite feeling amazingly unprofessional standing there in my workout gear, I wasn't willing to interrupt the moment to do anything about it. "Tell me how your clothing wound up at the hotel."

Reggie swallowed. "Most of what I told you the first time was true," he began. "Dot did call me and asked that I come up to the hotel after the bachelorette party."

"That wasn't the first time you'd met her like that, was it?" I asked. "That's the context you left out, isn't it?"

"Essentially," he sighed. "We've been lovers for almost a year now."

"Dating back to when Dot started coming to the island?"

"Yes," he nodded again.

"Even though she was engaged to Tim?" I asked.

Reggie looked away from me and seemed to consider something outside the massive windows facing the ocean. "They were never a good fit together," he answered obliquely. "There might have been love between them at the beginning, but that faded pretty quickly. Tim only had eyes for her money."

Suddenly the economizing I'd been hearing about began to make sense. "I didn't realize the hotel was in such bad shape."

"This is the first weekend in nearly a year that the occupancy is above forty percent," he replied. "Though it's an anomaly since the majority of the rooms are for the wedding and got the family and friends' discount. The *Inn By The Sea* caters to a specific crowd that no longer exists. Tim would have been well served to have taken a page out of the book The Colonial is using."

"And go corporate?" I asked. "Affiliate with a national chain?"

"Or at least open themselves to allowing the cruise ships to book here," he answered. "Tessa is adamant about shutting out that end of the market, and Tim is just going along with it."

"I've lived in Windeport long enough to know that we live and die by tourism," I said. "And we were on the dying side of the line before we became a port of call."

"Exactly."

"You know a lot about how the hotel operates," I observed.

He shrugged. "Dot told me everything. She was pretty worried about the outlook."

"Did she share those concerns with Tim?"

"I'm sure she did," Reggie said, but it wasn't with much conviction.

"You never stopped loving Dot, did you?" I asked.

Reggie's gray eyes snapped to mine. "No," he said softly. "It's why I'm here on island."

"Were you intentionally trying to get away from Dot?"

"Not entirely by choice," he sighed.

"You make it sound like you were forced from Boston."

"That wouldn't be far from the truth." Reggie ran a hand through his shaggy mane. "Her family made it clear I was not welcome in Boston," he said after a long moment. "They had never approved of our relationship and had tried a few times to get her to break up with me."

"I still don't see how you wound up here," I said. "Lovers have stayed together through worse."

Reggie frowned slightly. "Have you ever done something you weren't proud of, Sean?"

"No," I said. "Unless you count disqualifying during Olympic Trials."

He smiled slightly. "I would," he replied. "When I was nineteen and just starting out as a dancer, the gigs were few and far between. I... I had to augment my income for a while so I could pay the bills."

"Doing what?" I asked. "You don't strike me as a reformed drug dealer."

"I appreciate the vote of confidence," he said. "No, I was a high-end male escort."

"With all that implies?" Corinne asked.

"Yes," he nodded. Reggie looked away. "As it turns out, I wound up being a rather popular one." He looked back at us. "For both sexes."

"Dot didn't know about that part of your life?" I asked.

"It was over years before we met," he replied.

"Her parents found out, though?"

"Yeah," he nodded. "I don't know quite how, but with their kind of money, I'm sure it wasn't hard for them to do some digging into me." Reggie leaned back on the couch. "What I'll never forget is the night her mother showed up at my apartment. She had photos of nineteen-year-old me with another man and made me an offer that I couldn't refuse, one that ensured I would disappear from Dot's life."

"Why? To keep you from you dating her?"

"I was a dancer," Reggie said. "A supermodel and a former high-end escort. Not the sort of young man a doyenne from Beacon Hill is supposed to marry."

"It's the new millennium," I said, echoing something I'd often heard Vasily say. "Times change."

"Not on Beacon Hill," he replied sadly.

I nodded slightly. "They paid you to leave."

"Yes."

"How much?"

Reggie's face flamed slightly. "Three million up front, plus a monthly stipend for five years."

My eyebrows went up. "Don't take this the wrong way, Reggie, but they must have truly hated you."

"They did."

"Did Dot know about your... arrangement with her parents?"

"Not initially," he replied. His face flamed deeper. "Not until the first night we got back together. She'd never understood why I'd left her in Boston, and I felt like I needed to explain myself at that point."

"What did she think?"

"She was pissed, to put it mildly."

The coffeemaker chimed the completion of the cycle, so I paused to dump the grounds into the trash. "How do you like your coffee?"

"Black," Reggie said.

I poured out three mugs, then ferried two of them over to Corinne and Reggie before returning to the counter and my own steaming concoction. Taking a sip of the brew, I looked at my suspect over the brim of the mug. "Why were your clothes still at the hotel?"

Reggie blew across the surface of his coffee. "I didn't have a chance to put them back on," he replied simply.

My eyebrows went up. "Tim surprised you and Dot?"

"Yeah," he replied, closing his eyes. His face flamed again. "We'd just finished making love when Tim began to pound at the door."

"Pound?" Corinne asked. "He must have had a key to the room; he could have let himself in."

Reggie shrugged. "Dot always engaged the door lock when we were together just in case."

"What happened?" I asked.

"Dot had me hide on the balcony," Reggie answered. "With the door closed and the drapes drawn, there was no way for him to know I was out there. The plan was that she'd let me back into the room once he'd left."

I nodded again. "Except she never did, did she?"

Reggie shook his head. "I waited until close to three," he said softly. "You have no idea how cold it was being out there in nothing during the storm that night. I didn't think it was possible to get as drenched as I did; when I couldn't bear it any longer, I slid the door back open and snuck back into the room."

"What did you see?"

"There was so much blood," he said softly, his gray eyes going wide. "It was everywhere. On the bed. On the carpet. On the wall." Reggie's eyes began to glisten. "But she was gone."

I pointed to his wrapped hand with my mug. "You cut yourself on the glass."

He nodded. "I was rather panicked and was desperately searching for my clothes so I could get out of there. I put my palm down on a shard I hadn't seen in the carpet when I was looking under the bed."

"What broke?" Corinne asked.

"I assumed it was a water glass from the bathroom," Reggie replied. "Dot often filled one and left it on the nightstand."

"Was there one there that night when you arrived?" I asked, thinking Corinne had mentioned seeing sealed glasses in the bathroom during our search earlier.

Reggie thought for a moment. "I'm not sure. Things, uh, heated up fast once she let me into the room."

"But you managed to avoid stepping on anything?" I asked pointedly. "Despite how much was in the carpet?"

"I did."

"Where were your clothes?"

"I'd left them on the floor beside the bed," he said, face flaming again. "I was... motivated... to disrobe as quickly as possible, so I more or less left them in a pile on the carpet."

"They were gone, though?"

"Yes. I searched the entire room and didn't find them. I wound up grabbing a bath towel and sneaking out through the door by the pool."

"No one saw you leaving?" Corinne replied.

"Not at that hour."

"Why didn't you alert us about the murder?" I asked. "Why wait until now to tell us about *any* of this?"

"I didn't know she was dead," Reggie replied defensively.

"At the very least, you must have understood Dot was critically injured," Corinne said. "And likely needed help."

"I had no proof of anything other than having been in a room that was full of blood," Reggie said. "I've seen enough movies to know how that would look."

"So you remained silent," I said.

"Yes."

"You didn't hear anything while you were out on the balcony?" I asked.

"No," he replied. "The ocean is pretty loud under the best of circumstances. With the storm howling, it was like being in the middle of a hurricane."

I drained the last of my coffee from the mug and turned to pour myself another cup. "Dot's blood is on your shirt," I said casually as I put the pot back onto the burner. "And your shorts." I caught Corrine's momentary frown when I turned back, for she knew nothing had been confirmed on that front as yet. "How do you explain that?"

"I have no idea," Reggie replied. His exasperation seemed genuine. "All I know is that Dot was *not* in the room when I returned, and neither were my clothes."

"Was there anything else in the room?" I asked.

Reggie frowned. "Like what? Besides the bed?"

"Yes."

He shrugged. "It was a pretty small space," he replied. "There was hardly enough room for the furniture crammed into it. Nothing like the wedding suite Dot had booked."

"Did Dot use that same room each time you connected?"

Reggie smiled slightly. "Interesting turn of phrase. And yes. I got the sense that it was the least desirable booking on property, so Dot generally had ready access to it."

"And there wasn't anything different about it that final time you were there?"

"I don't know what you're trying to get at," Reggie replied, "but no, it was what was normally there. A bed, a dresser and the nightstand."

"Did Dot order room service with you?"

"Room service — are you kidding? I barely had time to get my clothes off before Dot pulled me into the bed."

"You must have had time to put on a condom," I said.

Reggie looked uncomfortable. "Dot was on the pill," he said. "I've never used one when I've been with her."

That explains the semen we found on the sheets and within the victim — or at least one *sample,* I thought to myself. *I wonder how long Dot had been off the pill, though? Then again, it's not exactly foolproof technology...*

"...that's all I know," Reggie was saying. "You have to believe me — I didn't kill her."

"We're still evaluating the evidence," I said as evenly as I could. "Until then, I'm afraid you're still a bona fide suspect."

"Shit," Reggie breathed as he put his face into his hands. "What more do I have to do to convince you?"

"I don't know," I replied honestly. "Have you told me everything?"

"Yes," he answered, looking up.

"Then have faith the evidence will support your version of events. Until then, I'm going to have to ask you to come with us to the satellite station down by the wharf; you'll be our guest there until I can arrange to have you transported to a holding cell on the mainland."

Those strange gray eyes went wide again. "I didn't do anything wrong!"

"You failed to report a possible life-threatening injury," Corinne said. "Or worse. I don't know what the statutes are here in Maine, but in California citizens have a clear duty of care — something you seem to have callously disregarded."

Reggie started to say something, then thought better of it before slumping back onto the couch. "I suppose I did," he said softly. "I was scared."

"Fear can be a significant motivator," I said thoughtfully. "This is as much for your safety as anything else, Reggie. Will you come with us willingly?"

"Yes," he replied after a moment.

"Then finish your coffee and we'll take you down." Holding my mug in both hands, I looked to Corinne. "A word?" I asked.

She nodded and stood from where she'd been sitting on the edge of the coffee table. I inclined my head toward the front door and led her back out into the sunshine of the afternoon; as the door snapped closed behind us with a bang, I found myself wondering once more at just how easily humans could justify their misdeeds to each other under the banner of doing it for love. Often those actions were the very antithesis of the concept, something conveniently forgotten in the blind rage of the moment. Glancing back at the living room where Reggie waited, I thought I understood where he fell on the spectrum, but also felt like he'd not been as up front with me as he could have. I have done the job long enough to trust my gut instincts and sighed to think I might not yet be at the end of this particular slog.

Lowering her voice, Corinne also leaned into me as she spoke. "What do you think?"

"He had a role in Dot's death," I said. "How large of one still remains to be seen."

Corrine's eyes widened. "You think he murdered her?"

I smiled slightly. "When did you take Tim to your room?"

"10:30, I think."

"And he stayed until, what, two?"

"Or somewhere close to that. Why?"

"You asked if I thought Reggie did it," I replied. "There's your answer."

"I'm not sure I understand it," she frowned.

"Stick around," I smiled, "and all will be revealed. Until then, though, we'll need to keep an eye on Reggie. Do you mind camping out at the station while I wrap things up?"

Corinne looked at me. "I don't have a sidearm," she replied, "so I'll be hard pressed to prevent him from leaving."

"The cell has a lock, but you can take the golf cart," I offered. "If he escapes, use it to run him over if you need to."

She shook her head at me. "I'm having a hard time telling whether you're being facetious or deadly serious."

"It's the secret to my success," I replied dryly as I reached for the screen door.

Eighteen

The late afternoon sunshine was slanting through the massive windows of the lobby for the *Inn By The Sea*, casting long shadows across the small tables that dotted the space around the main bar. I'd chosen one that had a good view of the reception desk and had spread out the security logs Tim had provided to me earlier that day; while it took less than three sips from my Samuel Adams beer to find what I was looking for, I'd nearly finished the bottle when the man himself appeared from the doorway leading to their administrative office suite. Tim's frown appeared to deepen further when he caught sight of me sitting in his establishment; after glancing at around the lobby to gauge whether he could safely ignore me, he heaved a sigh and walked across to my table, then put his hands on the back of the chair opposite mine.

"Enjoying your beer?" he asked tersely.

"I did," I replied. "Thanks for asking."

"Why are you here?"

"If you recall, I mentioned wanting to talk to you after I reviewed these," I said. "And what was in room 315."

"I understand there are crime scene techs swarming that room as we speak. If they damage anything, I'll be contacting your superior."

"I would expect nothing less," I nodded. "Why don't you have a seat and join me for a cocktail?"

Tim looked at me askance. "I thought police officers didn't drink while on duty?"

"I'm in management now," I smiled. "The rules are a bit different."

He considered me a for a moment before pulling the chair out and sitting down. One of the many waiters immediately appeared and hovered with an order book in hand. "Whisky sour," Tim said before nodding toward my empty bottle. "And another beer for the Chief."

"Of course," the waiter said before executing a slight bow and disappearing.

"It's actually Commander now," I corrected with a smile. "If we're being all formal."

"Right," Tim said before adding acerbically: "I keep forgetting you were fired."

I shrugged, not entirely surprised he was attempting to tweak me over my recent career hurdle. "I had a good run with Windeport. I'm sure they'll be fine without me."

"That's what I've heard," he said, twisting the knife slightly.

I smiled again, then tapped at the screen of my iPhone. "I'm going to record this conversation," I said pleasantly. "If you'd prefer to have it someplace more private, I am happy to relocate."

Tim eyed the phone. "No, this will be fine."

"I'm also going to explain your rights," I continued. "And then you can formally consent to continuing our conversation."

"Are you *seriously* about to Mirandize me?"

"Yes," I replied.

Tim glared at me for a moment. "Fine."

I quoted the Miranda Warning from memory, noted the date and time for the recording and then got his assent on record. I waited a beat before starting the actual questioning. "Do you have a master key?" I asked.

Tim looked at me but took the opportunity of the drinks arriving to delay in responding. Once the waiter retreated again, he ran his finger along the rim of his tumbler a few times, then spoke. "I run this hotel," he said. "What do you think?"

I tapped at the pages in front of me. "I think you have access to every space in this building," I replied. "Would that be a fair assessment?"

"Yes."

"Who else has that level of access?"

"My mother," Tim said.

"Then just the two of you?"

"Yes. The rest of the staff hold functional cards that allow them into spaces required by their job duties," he said. "Housekeeping staff can get into rooms, but the chef can't."

"I see. That helps to explain the pattern to these transactions."

"I'm glad we cleared that up for you."

"Do all of your vendors have access to the delivery door in the kitchen?" I asked.

"Not all of them," he replied.

"Then let me be more specific — how about Reggie?"

"Yes," Tim said. "Based on how early he needs to make his delivery, it made sense to give him access to the kitchen. He's a trusted partner."

"Does his access extend beyond the kitchen?" I asked.

"Absolutely not," he replied quickly.

"Then how did he get through the door by the pool?" I asked, tapping at one of the pages of the report.

For a brief moment, I caught the look of surprise on Tim's face before he hid it. "There must be a mistake in the logs," he said after a moment. "His key only works on the kitchen's delivery door."

"Not according to this," I said, twisting the page around to show the lines I had circled. "Seems he's been coming and going rather frequently from both doors — the kitchen as well as the pool entrance. And," I added as I pulled out another page, "also room 315."

"That can't be right," Tim replied. The look of confusion on his face as he scanned the pages seemed genuine. "I never granted him access to those doors — he wouldn't need them for his deliveries."

"Who could have done that?" I asked. "Besides you?"

"My mother," he replied.

"How about the front desk staff?" I asked.

Tim looked up at me. "No, they don't have that level of clearance for the security system."

"And Dot?" I asked as I watched him carefully. "Did your fiancé have the ability to do that?"

The color drained from Tim's face. "I suppose she could have," he replied after a long moment. "She started helping out administratively a few months ago in preparation for taking some of the load from my mother once we were married."

"Would there be logs showing her making changes to a keycard?" I asked, though I knew the answer.

"Yeah," he replied darkly. "I can get them for you."

"I appreciate that."

"How much money was Dot bringing to the hotel?" I asked, again intentionally shifting the subject.

Tim frowned. "What the hell kind of question is that?"

"I've seen enough around here to know you're floundering financially," I replied. "The cost savings, the constant striving for efficiency. How bad is it?"

He stared at me for a long, long moment. "We have half a year, maybe," he finally answered. "We've never been able to crack the cruise market."

"It doesn't sound like you tried very hard."

Tim's façade cracked slightly as he sighed. "This is a high-end hotel," he said. "Very few of the clientele we used to attract book the type of cruise that docks in Windeport. We'd have to lower our prices and offer more amenities to attract the sort of price-conscious travelers that *are* coming, and that space is already dominated by the Colonial."

"Was Dot planning on investing in your hotel, then?"

Tim nodded. "It was really her family's money, but yes. She'd talked them into taking a forty percent stake in the hotel; the paperwork had already been drawn up and would have been signed after the wedding. That infusion would have allowed us to invest in updating the hotel."

"I imagine the arrangement is off, now."

"You could say that." Tim chugged a bit of his whisky sour. "Unless I find another source of capital, we're going to start winding things down in December."

"Were you marrying Dot for her money?" I asked baldly.

Anger flickered in Tim's eyes. "No."

"But you can't deny that you needed it?"

"Of course I can't," he replied, then looked at me. "That's a hell of a thing to ask."

I tapped at the logs again. "Maybe not. Considering she was having an affair with Reggie right up to the night she died, you can see how I might assume love was not a factor."

"I was unaware of that," Tim replied just a bit too quickly.

"I find that hard to believe," I said. "I saw the magazines in your mother's office; when did you discover who Reggie really was?"

Tim ran his finger along the rim of his tumbler again. This time around, it made a harsh squeaking noise. "Most people come to Carpenter's Island to escape their past," he said. "When he showed up a few years ago offering to sell us his fresh baked goods, I didn't look too far past the low cost of doing business with him."

"What changed?"

Tim took another sip of his now-rapidly diminishing drink. "I was having dinner with Dot at our restaurant a few months after we became engaged. Reggie was at the bar when we came in; it was obvious immediately that the two of them knew each other." Tim shrugged. "I hired a private investigator to do some digging, which turned up his past — and his prior relationship with Dot."

"Did you ever confront her about it?"

"No," Tim said.

I felt an eyebrow arch. "These logs show you entered room 315 the night Dot was murdered," I said. "That makes me think otherwise."

"I..." he started, then paused. "I suppose there's no benefit in denying that I did meet her in that room."

"No," I nodded. "Why were you there?"

Tim sighed and looked away. "It was an open secret that she had that room for her trysts with Reggie," he said, his voice low so it wouldn't carry. The level of embarrassment was nearly palpable. "Everyone in the hotel apparently had known for a while. I found out in the spring when I was doing an occupancy audit; 315 kept coming up as reserved whenever she was here visiting me but was always cancelled without payment." He looked back at me. "Between that and discovering who Reggie really was, it wasn't hard to paint in the rest of the picture."

"And yet you were still going to marry her?"

"Yes."

"But not for the money?"

"I *loved* Dot," he nearly whispered. "She was my entire world."

"Even though her heart was elsewhere?"

"I thought I could live with that," he said.

"Until you couldn't?"

Tim tapped at the edge of his tumbler. "I was drunk that night — or nearly. I decided to find out from her once and for all who she loved and went to her room."

"When was that?"

"Maybe ten," he said. "I swiped my card at the door and surprised her; she was setting out something from Room Service and was wearing the sexiest lingerie I'd ever seen."

From the way his face was flaming, it was easy to deduce the rest. "I take it you never had a chance to discuss what it was you were there for?"

"Yes and no," he replied. "We made the most passionate love I've ever experienced, and then she crushed my heart by telling me she was calling the wedding off." Tim smiled slightly. "I think it was her way of trying to gentle the blow, but it hit me like a live wire. Especially when she told me she was planning on returning to Boston with Reggie in the morning."

"What did you do?"

"What *could* I do?" Tim asked. "It was clear her mind was made up, so I threw my clothes back on and fled."

"And then hooked up with Corinne Wallace?"

My companion had the good sense to look uncomfortable. "I needed to soothe the ache in my heart," he replied. "It was pure happenstance I met Corinne in the elevator after I left Dot."

"You were with Corinne all night, then?"

"Yes." He tapped at the logs with a finger. "You'll probably see my movements that morning in these."

I nodded, for I had. "Did Dot tell you she was pregnant?"

That caught him off guard. "She... she was pregnant?"

"She was."

"How far along?"

"Far enough that she would have known."

"Dot never mentioned it," Tim replied.

"Do you have any reason to suspect you are the father?"

"We practiced safe sex, if that is what you're really asking," Tim answered. "Dot was on the pill."

"You didn't take any other precautions?"

"Like using a condom?" he asked. "Not always. She was on the pill — it wasn't necessary."

"Until it is," I added quietly. "And you swear she didn't tell you she was pregnant?"

"I would have remembered a conversation about fathering a child, Commander," he said churlishly.

"I suppose you would have," I nodded. "Dot was alive when you left room 315?"

"Yes," he replied.

"And you didn't visit her again that night?"

"I was with Corinne Wallace until three," he answered. "She can confirm that."

I twirled my still-full second bottle of beer. "We're already tested the DNA we collected from the scene," I said. Reading down to my backpack, I pulled out my last DNA kit and put it on the table, then slid it over to Tim. "I already know that one of the two people who had sex with Dot that night is the father of the child; there is also evidence tying that *same* person to her death. Since you've already admitted to being with her that night having unprotected sex, I'll need you to provide a comparison sample."

"Two--?" Tim's eyes went wide. "God*damn*. Reggie slept with her too?"

"I can't answer that," I replied smoothly.

The wheels were turning in Tim's head. "You're saying the kid might be his?"

I shrugged. "I look at it this way: Dot was clearly sleeping with both of you. I'd say the odds are fifty-fifty as to who the father is, but if you agree to a paternity test, I can give you a more definitive answer."

Tim looked at the test kit. "I can do that. Not that it matters at this point."

"Oh, it matters," I smiled. "It matters greatly."

It took less than a minute for me to run the cotton swab around the inside of Tim's mouth, then a few seconds more to seal it into the sample bag. Tucking it back into my bag, I looked at him once again. "Anything else?" he asked.

"Just one last thing," I said. "Why did Dot have you order blueberries from out of state?"

"She wanted them for the wedding," he replied. "I think her family loves them."

"What did Dot use on the blueberries that made everyone sick?"

Tim's eyes narrowed. "How—?"

I shrugged. "It seems clear to me she didn't want the wedding to proceed," I said. "I think you discovered what happened the night of the party and as a result ordered the kitchen steam cleaned to bury the evidence." I tapped my finger on the bottle of beer. "If everyone went down with food poisoning, that would be enough of an excuse to postpone the festivities indefinitely."

"It would," Tim nodded.

"What did she use?" I asked again.

Tim considered me for a moment. "I found two industrial-sized containers of flavorless powdered laxatives in the kitchen trash; I assumed it had been mixed into the sauce that was served with the uncooked fruit dishes. I don't know when she did it, or if she had help from someone in the kitchen, but it had to have happened during the dinner service that evening."

I nodded. "The steam cleaning was for show, then."

"Yes," he replied. "I didn't know she'd done it until I saw her in room 315 — she admitted it was part of her plan to torpedo the weekend."

"Which appears to have worked."

"Yeah."

I nodded again. "Thank you for your time. I'll let you get back to running the hotel."

"For what little time I have left to do so," Tim replied as he pushed away from the table.

Enjoy it while you can, I thought as I watched him walk away, *for you never truly know how long you have...*

Nineteen

There wasn't much to be gained by visiting room 315 a second time, but when Heather's call confirming her team had finished in the room pinged my iPhone as I was leaving the lobby bar, I decided a change of scenery wouldn't hurt and redirected toward the elevators. I found the door to the hotel room had been propped open, and the lead crime scene tech herself inside packing up the last of her tools. That the room was otherwise empty told me the rest of her team was already on the way back to the boat dock and the waiting boat from the Harbormaster; knowing Heather would also want to be on that trip, it felt right to skip directly to the main event.

"Heather."

She looked up at the sound of my voice. "I have to admit, this island is quite beautiful," she said as she stood from her small kit. "At least, the parts I've seen of it. I get why people like to vacation here."

"It's pretty quiet," I said. "And otherwise peaceful, save for this murder."

"There is that." She nodded toward the bed. "As you probably have deduced, the team is already headed back to shore with what we collected. With luck we'll be able to run lab tests of everything and get you some definitive answers."

My eyebrows went up. "I assumed you'd want to go back with them?"

Heather shrugged and then pointed to a small backpack leaning against the wall. "I knew you'd want to talk, and figured I could take a hike around the island trail while I wait for the boat to come back. I could use a bit of that peace and quiet, I think."

"You'll like it," I nodded. "What did you find?"

"Probably what you expected," she replied as she moved over to the bed. Pointing to a square patch that had been removed from the covering of the mattress, she continued. "We'll test the blood in that fabric against what we collected earlier. Eyeballing the volume in the mattress and under the bed, though, I'm confident this is your primary scene — assuming the blood matches your victim."

"I suspect it will," I said. "I've already placed her in this space close to the time of death."

"That'll narrow things down." She knelt beside the bed. "We recovered shards of glass from the carpet and bagged them for analysis. I don't have a keen enough eye for crystal to tell you if it's the same as the murder weapon; we'll know more after I get it under a microscope. I also found some slight indentations in the headboard, too," Heather added as she stood. Pointing to a spot on the wood, she looked back at me. "It's not much, but it's enough of a gouge to indicate directionality."

I nodded as I stepped closer; Heather moved away so I could lean in. "How on *earth* did you find these?" I asked, somewhat amazed. The scratches looked like a cat had run its claws along the soft wood of the frame.

"The pattern in the wood is supposed to make it look naturally distressed," she said. "When I ran my flashlight over the frame, though, I could tell that these gouges were fresh. If you look closely, you can see the underlying particle board; the other defects have been painted over."

I leaned in closer. "Without bifocal contacts, I'll have to take your word for it," I laughed. "Does this align with where the neck and shoulders of the victim would be?"

"Yeah," she replied. "Especially if the assailant straddled the victim."

Looking at the bed again, I tried to visualize Dot lying against the pillow. "That gouge had to have come from the killing stroke," I said thoughtfully. "The wineglass must have been on the nightstand."

"And was smashed against the edge," Heather added. "Based on the shards I found in the carpet, that would be the best explanation."

I frowned. "Did you find any wine in the carpet?"

"Some. I also swabbed some from the side of the nightstand. With all of this blood, though, it was hard to separate out the stains. I tagged what I could, and we'll spin down the samples back at the lab to be sure."

"Maybe the glass wasn't full at the time, then," I mused.

"That's possible."

"So the murderer is straddling Dot, reaches for a wineglass and smashes it on the table," I continued. "Then uses it like a knife along her neck." I paused. "Based on the wound, and the location of those gouges you found, the murderer was left-handed."

"Yes," Heather agreed. "It would be a near-impossible angle for a right-handed person."

"It would," I slowly nodded.

Pointing to the trolley, Heather continued. "Field test confirms the blood we found on that is the same type as what was on the mattress. The lab will run the DNA, of course., but I think it's clear the body was moved using it."

I stared at the trolley. "I'm sure that's accurate, but I'm having a hard time visualizing how the body was loaded onto it."

"Maybe not," Heather said. "A dead body isn't terribly easy to pose, but with the right amount of body strength and some patience, it's possible your suspect literally stuffed the victim into the cart and then covered everything with the tablecloth."

"That would have been a messy prospect," I said.

"Which leads me to the bathroom," Heather continued. "We found blood in the shower — two distinct samples, by the way, confirming that the whoever cut themselves on the glass was also the one washing off the victim's blood. I've also been looking at the blood pattern on the clothing you found," she added. "They *could* be consistent with someone who had held the body as it was being moved."

"Transferred, perhaps, when the victim was laid out on the bed in the suite?"

"Exactly."

"All right," I nodded. "Anything else?"

"No, nothing," she said. "At least, not until the tests come back from the lab."

"Then I will get out of your hair so you can enjoy a brief respite. My thanks, as always, for your efforts."

"Of course."

I left Heather as she completed packing up the last of her tools and returned to the lobby of the hotel; pausing, I caught the form of Tim Polanski as it slipped behind the reception desk and disappeared into the administrative offices. A slight sense of melancholy washed over me as I took in the understated space for what was likely the last time; I thought of all of the people who worked so hard to keep the *Inn By The Sea* an ongoing concern, and for a moment, felt significant heartache at what would happen to them and, in a larger sense, Carpenter's Island. The Gulf of Maine was littered with islands that had, in a prior century, been populated with a vibrant populace; the number that still boasted some sort of functioning economy could be counted on one hand. I felt like I was witnessing the end of an era, though I hoped fervently I was wrong.

Pushing aside the gloom, I shifted my backpack on my shoulder and then made my way through the front entrance; eschewing the golf cart that I'd been borrowing, I instead started down the long driveway and then set off for the small village by the wharf at a healthy clip. The sun had dropped quite low on the horizon by that point, allowing the forest that crowded the small lane to cast long shadows across the pavement. The overwhelming sense that the island itself knew that a significant chapter was coming to a close pervaded the atmosphere; it intensified further when I passed the intersection and the side lane that went off toward the small residential area for those who worked at the hotel. I wasn't one to indulge in the belief that supernatural elements existed in our reality, but I also found myself more at ease when the road opened up to reveal the village and the sparkling ocean beyond.

As the sky tinged toward the red end of the spectrum, I paused just at the edge of the street that ran down toward the wharf and watched as the sun finally sank low enough to be blocked by the distant hills of the mainland; twilight quickly descended, allowing the small carriage lamps that dotted the sidewalk to glow into life. Much like that first night I'd watched the sunset with Rocket, the small village was once more alive with activity; some sort of karaoke number was pouring out from the open doors of Bert's Cantina, intermingled with the savory smell of whatever the special was that evening. The main lights had already been turned off within the grocery store, but the shadowy figures I saw passing back and forth behind the display windows told me the overnight stockers had just begun their shift. The distant hum from the harbor told me the Harbormaster was on his way back, though despite squinting, I wasn't able to pick out the running lights for the skiff against the darkness of the ocean. Much as before, it felt like I was witnessing a slice of something from another era, though this time around, it seemed to be the final act of a town that had been unable to shake off the inevitable oblivion.

Somehow, the atmosphere seemed exactly appropriate for the first case I had undertaken as Commander of the Major Crimes unit.

Deciding I'd delayed long enough, I turned and headed for the bright lights of the Police substation, intent on wrapping things up and getting on with my own life.

TWENTY

Corinne was sitting at the desk when I entered the station. "I was beginning to wonder if you were *ever* coming," she said as she stood. "The internet here is slow enough that I think I finally understand what it must have been like trying to use those old dial-up services my parents had when they were kids."

"Apologies," I said, smiling slightly. "It took longer than I thought at the hotel."

"How did it go?" Corinne asked, lowering her voice.

"As well as expected." I glanced at the cell and could see Reggie was sitting on the small cot, his knees drawn up to his chin. "How is our guest?" I asked quietly.

She looked at Reggie. "Very quiet — almost introspective."

"That seems to be an aftereffect of being on this island," I said. "Do you have your phone handy?"

"Yes," she replied, raising an eyebrow. "Why?"

"We've reached the final act," I said. "It would be wise to record what happens next."

"Got it," she said as she pulled her phone from the pocket of her shorts.

I took a quick second to center myself and then moved toward the cell. The single overhead florescent bulb was a bit harsh, throwing the young man into stark relief; for the first time, I could see he had more than a few streaks of gray in his long hair, something that hadn't been as obvious under natural light. There were also hints of lines around the eyes, a common aftereffect of too much time spent in the sun; whether those had developed while tending to his outdoor brick oven or as a result of one too many afternoons getting a supermodel-perfect suntan was a question better suited for Suzanne to answer. Reggie's t-shirt seemed to continue his theme of favoring obscure musical acts; despite being severely faded, it nonetheless was a perfect match for the ratty pair of dark athletic shorts that bore a worn Nike swoosh. The particular way he was sitting had allowed the edge of the shorts to slip down just enough to expose the lower edge of the white compression shorts he was wearing as a base layer; it was an unusual sartorial choice, but then again, maybe not given the daily workout he went through trucking his baked goods across the island.

Pausing by the door to the cell, I waited for him to acknowledge my presence. When he rather recalcitrantly ignored me, I cleared my throat and then spoke. "Reggie."

Reggie continued to stare at the industrial tile on the floor of the cell. "When can I leave?" he asked.

Checking first that Corinne had begun to record, I answered. "Just as soon as you tell me the truth."

Reggie tilted his head up just enough that his eyes were barely visible beneath his bangs. "I've already done that."

"To a point," I replied. "You left out the fact that you killed Dot."

That caused Reggie to sit up. "I didn't kill her," he said. "I told you that."

"Yes," I nodded. "Now you're going to tell me why you *did*."

Reggie eyed me for a moment, attempting to gauge just how much I knew. I kept my expression pleasant but neutral, which caused his brow to furrow slightly. "I loved Dot. I could never hurt her."

"I don't dispute that you were in love with her," I replied. "You made it crystal clear when we spoke earlier how you felt about Dot."

Reggie's eyebrows dipped further. "Then you understand...?"

"Why you killed her?" I said, eliciting that look of shock again. "In a way, I suppose I do."

Reggie shook his head and then slumped back down on the bench before pressing the palms of his hands to his temples for a moment. "You're... you're intentionally trying to confuse me and get me to confess to something I didn't do," he said, his voice wavering as he spoke. His eyes went to mine, and for the first time there was hint of defiance in them. "That's what got you fired from Windeport, isn't it?"

"Getting people to confess?" I smiled slightly. "It's what kept me employed with them as long as it did; I'm pretty good at it." I looked at Corinne before turning back to him. "Politics, though? Not so much."

Reggie just stared at me, unsure of whether I was serious or actually making a joke at my expense. Clearly, he'd not spent much time among Mainers with a droll sense of humor. Sighing, I turned and walked the short distance to the far side of the small room to look out the window facing the street. Darkness had fallen completely, masking as it always did a variety of sins; refocusing my eyes slightly, I caught my reflection in the glass and that of Reggie as he eyed my back. Putting my hands into the pockets of my shorts, I turned away from the window as I spoke.

"Would you like me to tell you a story, then?" I asked. "It's one you already know, of course," I continued as I walked back to face him again. "I might not have all the details quite right, but you're welcome to fill them in for me as I go."

"Whatever," Reggie said as he shrugged in an almost Millennial way.

"Before I do," I said, "you earlier waived your rights to having representation. Now is the time to tell me you've changed your mind."

"I haven't," he said as he looked away.

"So noted," I replied after seeing Corinne nod. Oddly, at that moment I found myself desperate for a mug of coffee; I stifled the urge, though it was intense. "So, let's go back a few years to when you arrived on Carpenter's Island," I said. "I'm not sure I realized until now just how similar your situation was to that of my best friend nearly two decades ago."

Reggie looked at me but said nothing.

"He'd had the audacity to cross his own family and paid dearly for it; Maine was about as far away as he could get in order to bury that part of his life." I smiled slightly. "You had a similar impetus for leaving Boston, though unlike my friend, you found you'd left that which you loved the most behind."

"I didn't have a choice," Reggie said.

"I'm sure the tidy stipend the Fernyhough family was paying you made it a bit more palatable," I said charitably. "My friend didn't have the same option. Unlike you, he was forced to start over on his own."

"You act like I had options," Reggie said. "There were none. My career was over; the woman I loved, unobtainable. I had to take their money. Besides," he added after a pause, "I needed the peace and quiet this island offered."

"I'm sure you believed that at the time," I said. "Then you got here and discovered the true meaning of the 'end of the line.' It's one thing to want solitude; it's quite another to experience it."

I watched Reggie carefully for a moment before continuing. "Maybe, after a year or two, you came to think you *had* put it all behind you; life must have settled into something of a pleasant routine as you rediscovered your baking roots out there in the middle of the forest. I suspect, though, there was still a tiny ache in your heart for the one that got away, an ache that became too acute to ignore when Dot arrived on the island in her new role as fiancé to Tim."

"That part of my life was over," Reggie said. "You're right on one count, though. Those first few months — hell, the first year after I arrived was incredibly difficult. I went from being a supermodel known worldwide to a hermit working a brick oven in the middle of nowhere." He paused and then smiled slightly. "There is a certain magic to this island, though; you have to have felt it yourself. Over time, it's almost seductively easy to forget about the world beyond our shores."

"I've noticed that," I nodded. "And yet, you immediately connected with Dot when she appeared."

"*Dot* was the one that reached out to me. I didn't pursue her. I had no interest in reconnecting."

"You didn't turn her away, though," I observed.

"At first, it was just coffee at the restaurant," he said. "We were two friends reconnecting after losing touch, nothing more complicated than that."

"I doubt you met in the restaurant," I replied. "Dot wouldn't have risked anything quite so visible."

Reggie managed to look a bit chagrined. "Not after that first meeting, no. We rotated between my cottage and her hotel room."

"And you managed to stay off of Tim's radar?"

"Yes," he nodded.

"Despite knowing she was engaged."

"I told you before, she'd moved on from Tim."

I felt an eyebrow arch. "You couldn't have known that at first."

"No," he said after a moment. "I found out the first time we... well," Reggie paused, looking uncomfortable again. "When you are intimate, it's hard to hold back any secrets. Dot was pretty clear that her arrangement with Tim was going to be purely financial."

"People don't marry for money like they did back in the eighteenth century," I pointed out. "Dot could easily have invested in the hotel without having to have wed Tim."

"She didn't love him," Reggie said icily. "Not the way she loved me."

"I believe that. Dot did love Tim at one point, though." I paused. "Until she realized she'd found her original soulmate."

Reggie looked away.

"I don't quite know why she continued the charade of staying with Tim, honestly," I continued. "Other than it being a convenient excuse to come to the island and hook up with you — at Tim's expense."

There was a slight coloring to Reggie's cheeks, but he continued to keep his own council.

"For more than a year, you carried on an affair," I said. "Always at the hotel, always on her terms." I glanced at Corinne. "I'm not sure how to put it delicately, but from my perspective, it seems as though Dot was enjoying the fruits of both worlds. Are you *certain* she still loved you?"

"Yes!"

I nodded. "Then it makes perfect sense she'd planned on returning to Boston with you at the end of the weekend."

Reggie's mouth gaped in surprise. "That's the first I've heard of it."

I tried to look confused. "Really? I feel like it's the sort of thing that would have come up. Especially," I added with a slight emphasis, "with the birth of your child on the horizon."

The color drained from Reggie's face. "I don't know what you're talking about."

"Oh, I think you do," I replied. "In fact, I think that's why you killed her."

"I *didn't* kill her," Reggie said, though his voice was barely above a whisper.

"Yes, Reggie," I said, "you did. Because that last night you were with her, she told you." I stepped a bit closer to the bars of the cell and watched as Reggie tried to press himself into the wall behind him to get away from me.

"No," he said, his voice barely loud enough to be heard. "That's not what happened."

"She told you," I said with an edge to my voice, "and in that moment you realized that loving Dot would continue to be one drama after another, endlessly blending into each other until it pounded your psyche into oblivion. Moving to Boston with her wasn't an option; maybe, years ago, it might have been. But not now. Not any longer."

Reggie swallowed; his eyes had gone large, and I was somewhat concerned that the way his carotid artery was pulsing might lead to a stroke. "I..." he started.

"I think she told you as you were making love to her," I said. "Or just after you finished. Maybe she proposed a toast with the wine she'd ordered from room service; perhaps she described how your new life in Boston would unfold once you arrived. Painted you a picture of two happy parents living the good life in the Beacon Hill circle."

"I..." Reggie pressed his fingers to his temples again as though he were fending off a serious migraine. "That's... that's not what happened."

"Except you had no desire to return to that," I continued. "You said it yourself: your life here had healed all of those old wounds. You'd left that version of Reggie behind; he'd ceased to exist, despite Dot's wishes. Returning to Boston — returning to the *world* — was the last thing you wanted."

"I... I..." Reggie looked a bit frantic, his eyes darting between me and where Corinne was standing further back in the small office.

"Tell me what happened," I urged with the sort of tone you would use with a recalcitrant teenager. "Tell me *everything*."

Reggie took a long moment before seeming to come to a decision. "It wasn't my fault."

I kept my expression neutral; it wasn't the first time I'd head a murderer lead with that. "Sometimes, things happen," I replied. "Things that we don't intend."

"Exactly!" he said, latching on to the lifeline of false hope I'd just tossed him. "I had no idea what she'd wanted to tell me. It was something of a shock."

"Explain it to me," I said. "Help me understand. Tell me as much as you can recall, even if those final moments are something of a blur for you."

"I remember *all* of it," he said as his eyes focused on something only he could see. "Every second is seared into my memory. That sweet, sweet smile Dot used just with me; how her face glistened slightly with sweat from our lovemaking. Those kisses that trailed down my neck and over to my shoulder; how her nails dug into my back as she fought to keep from going over. The way she shuddered against me when we both came — and how she whispered into my ear at that same moment the words that would change everything."

I was a bit taken aback at the force of how he'd said *everything*.

"She wanted me to leave everything I'd built here on the island behind," he continued. "In a split second I realized I was nothing more than a pawn in her overarching game. My life wasn't important; what it could do for *hers*, though, was immeasurable." Reggie looked at me. "I think she loved the concept of me more than who I was."

"No question having a kid is a big deal," I replied. "But there were other options, certainly. You didn't have to move to Boston to support your child. Or Dot."

Reggie shook his head again. "Dot had me. *All* of me. My heart has belonged to her since that first night we met at the gala; I could no sooner refuse her request to leave Carpenter's Island than stop breathing the air."

"You must have felt trapped."

"There was no way out," he nodded slowly.

Reggie paused, clearly on the precipice; it almost seemed unfair to give him a nudge, but neither did I want to lose momentum. "Something shifted for you in that moment."

"She was looking up at me," he said, his eyes again seemingly unfocused. "That smile... I'd seen it before... she knew... Dot *knew* she had me. There was no way I could have refused her."

"The wineglass was on the nightstand?" I prompted.

"Yes," he said before his attention snapped back to me. "You know what she actually said? Right after revealing she was carrying our child?"

"No," I answered, though I suspected I did.

"She told me I was her personal escape hatch," he replied, his voice vibrating with anger. "I'd been that for her in Boston, too — her way to duck her parent's expectations and have a little fun. Tim had been their choice, not hers; she'd been resigned to living a lie until she found me here." Reggie stood and started to pace the small stall, his arms wrapped around his torso. "She tricked me," he added angrily. "She was *supposed* to be on the pill — she'd been on it for years — but I'd always used a condom, just in case." He paused and looked at me, the betrayal clear in his face. "Except for one night a few months ago."

"Once is all it takes."

"Yeah."

"So, you smashed the wineglass against the nightstand, and then stabbed her," I said casually.

"Yeah," he replied so matter-of-factly that it took a moment to register he'd admitted to doing it. "She'd given it to me to celebrate the news," he continued. "Instead of being happy, I was angry and incensed at how I'd been seduced into giving up everything. For a woman who really didn't care about *me*."

Reggie paused again. "I was surprised at how little effort it took to break the glass," he said. "Or how easy it was to drive it into her neck — or slice my own hand in the process. And the blood — God, there was so much blood," he added, his voice going soft. "Dot looked so scared — and then ... and then the life just went out of her eyes..."

I let the confession hang over us for a moment. "Tim never came into the room while you were there, did he?"

"No." Reggie had turned away from me and was staring at the wall. "Dot hadn't told me, but it was obvious he'd been with her before I'd arrived."

"Which meant he might have returned," I continued. "Why did you move the body?"

Reggie produced that Gallic shrug he'd done before. "I panicked," he answered. "I thought if she were found in the suite, it might give me more time to clean up the hotel room." Reggie looked over his shoulder. "It never occurred to me until I returned from moving her that there was too much blood in the mattress to hide what happened."

"You used the room service cart to move her?"

"Yes."

"I can't imagine it was easy getting her body onto the cart."

Reggie sat down and squeezed his eyes shut. "That was one of the hardest things I've ever had to do."

I decided not to give him my thoughts on that. "Once you had her back in her actual suite, you returned to the room, showered off as much blood as you could and then left the hotel," I said. "But not before you left your clothes where we could find them."

"Another mistake," Reggie replied absently. "Throwing them out was too obvious; so was carrying off a bag in the middle of the night. I couldn't risk someone seeing me or it. So I stashed them on a random luggage cart in the elevator lobby close to her room."

"And planned on getting them later?"

"Yeah." He looked at Corinne. "When I finally thought it was safe to retrieve them, someone had taken the bag."

"That they had," I replied. "Where did you get the laxative powder?"

Reggie shrugged again, though it was clear from Corrine's expression she'd not seen that particular revelation coming, as obvious as it had been. "From one of my suppliers. It arrived a week before the blueberries did," he answered.

"Was it your idea to mix that into the blueberry dishes?"

"No," Reggie answered. "Dot asked me to do it the night before the bachelorette party as some sort of practical joke; only later did I realize the dishes were also used in the main restaurant."

"How did you do it?"

"It wasn't hard coming up with an excuse," he replied. "With the added guests for the wedding, the hotel was going through baked goods faster than normal. I simply promised the extra inventory and made an unscheduled overnight delivery."

"Using your key to get into the kitchen?"

"Yes," he nodded. "Dot had browbeaten the chef into having the dishes ready early; I found everything in the fridge and simply mixed in the powders."

"You nearly killed her parents with that stunt," I observed.

Reggie looked at me. "That wouldn't have been the end of the world."

"No," I sighed, "I suppose not, given what you've told me."

"What happens now?" Reggie asked. He appeared completely deflated as he pulled his knees back up to his chin.

"Now?" I asked with a wry smile. "Now I formally charge you with two counts of murder."

"Two?" Reggie asked, eyes wide. "I only killed Dot."

"I have a feeling the prosecution will look at it a bit differently," I said. "Killing a pregnant woman also tends to not be viewed favorably by a jury, either."

I watched the color drain from his face as he realized what I was saying. "Oh... oh *shit*..."

"Exactly," I said. "Régis Delannoy, I am charging you with the murder of Dorothy Fernyhough..."

TWENTY-ONE

I decided the view from my back porch wasn't quite as spectacular as the rocky outcropping I'd frequented with Rocket while staying on Carpenter's Island; still, as the streaks of red slowly faded into the star-filled night sky, I realized just how much I enjoyed watching sunsets from my bungalow, even if the sun itself was nowhere to be found. Venus appeared to be particularly bright that evening, twinkling vibrantly against the dark tapestry of the universe. For a moment I considered an article I had read in the *Bangor Daily News* a few weeks earlier positing whether the Earth's climate crisis would result in the same sort of runaway greenhouse effect scientists were studying on our neighbor planet. I'd thought the hypothesis in question had been rather grim; it didn't help that a massive Category One hurricane had begun to churn its way up the Eastern Seaboard, a vibrant reminder that Mother Nature was truly the one in charge.

The hurricane had brought with it massive preemptive flight cancellations; that had meant saying goodbye to Corinne Wallace just a few hours after we handed Reggie to some state troopers waiting for us on the wharf in Windeport. She'd been forced to book an earlier flight out of Bangor in order to return to California sooner than she'd originally planned; if I'd not still been watching Rocket at that point, I would have happily taken her to the airport myself so as to avail myself of the informal debriefing opportunity we would have had. As it happened, that same hurricane had adjusted Julie Crabtree's plans as well, landing her back on Carpenter's Island the following morning. Leaving Rocket in the care of his owner (and after receiving a slobbery thank-you from the canine for having taking care of him), I'd done one last circuit of the island trail before calling in a favor to have the Harbormaster bring me home.

Tipping the bottle of Samuel Adams Oktoberfest up to my lips, I found I had mixed feelings about the case and how well I had handled it solo. It had been years since I'd been on my own; I had to grudgingly admit that I relied on the orchestra that had long supported me while running the Windeport Police Department and looked forward to that same infrastructure being in place as I moved into my new role with the state. Having Corinne appear on the scene had been a welcome happenstance, and I'd certainly gotten to know her better as we'd worked the case; still, I missed having Norm by my side and the shared shorthand we had developed in our short time together. Sipping again, I smiled slightly to think that I had finally allowed myself to accept my new number two as a replacement for Vasily; no, not *quite* a replacement, nor, as I considered it, an upgrade. Norm was his own kind of cop, as unique in his skillset as my best friend. I had truly missed not being able to call on him when needed.

My iPhone was sitting on the small wicker end table beside my chair, and I tapped at the screen to reveal the text message my number two had sent a few hours earlier. Norm had tested positive for HIV over the summer — a parting gift from his vindictive ex-boyfriend — and had begun dealing with his new reality almost immediately. Suzanne had started his initial course of treatment, but as a small-town doctor, was limited in what she could do; she'd referred him to a colleague in Portland who specialized in caring for members of the gay community, and they, in turn, had put Norm on a newer antiviral medication that had drastically improved his prospects. While he'd forever be HIV positive, Norm was fortunate to live in a period when that was no longer a death sentence. Glancing at the message, I smiled again at his exuberance over surmounting the first hurdle; getting his boyfriend settled into their shared home in Windeport appeared to be the item now freaking him out. Norm had asked for help getting his television mounted before Raphael arrived in a few days from Arizona; it was one task among many he'd undertaken to welcome his soulmate home, a way to burn off his nervous energy about the massive step forward he was taking in their relationship.

Turning the screen of my phone off, I found myself suddenly melancholy; thinking of Norm feathering his nest reminded me of how disastrous my initial conversation with Suzanne had been regarding merging our households. After seeing each other on Carpenter's Island, I knew we were in a better place than we had been earlier in the summer, but no small part of me was sad to think the two of us might never take the same big step as Norm and Raphael. I drained the last of my beer and then stood to go into the bungalow; watching the stars come out no longer held any appeal, and besides, I had a ton of paperwork to catch up on before rolling into the office first thing on Monday.

As I reached for my iPhone, it lit up again and displayed the smiling face of Suzanne. My heart skipped a beat as I answered the phone, that strange two-step it always did when I was about to interact with the love of my life. "Milady," I said with a smile. "Cat calling again?"

"Can you blame me when the feline is so handsome?" she asked in return.

"*Meow*," I purred, trying to channel the voice actor that played Chat Noir on *Miraculous*. I was certain he was in no jeopardy of losing his gig. "You certainly know how to get my motor humming."

"That I do."

"Are you back in town?"

"Yes," she said. "I'm just stepping off the boat now. The last of the patrons at the hotel went home this afternoon. I wish I'd known about the laxative sooner, though."

"Would you have changed your treatment?"

"Yes and no," she sighed. "There are drugs out there to counter such things, but at the end of the day, dehydration is the real worry. Keeping up on fluids would have been the prescription regardless."

"Then you did fine."

"Thanks."

I hesitated for a moment. "Are you... going back to the pharmacy?"

"It depends," she replied.

My heart did that pitter-pat again. "On what?"

"On whether you have that bottle of red I like already on ice."

I thought about the six-pack of wine I'd stuffed into the rear of my fridge earlier that day. "I might just have," I allowed.

"I suspected as much," she said with a giggle. "Then no, I am not returning to the pharmacy. I am, instead, going to see my stud of a boyfriend so I can ravish him properly."

"You did a pretty good job of that this weekend," I reminded her.

"I think there is always room for improvement in such matters," she replied. "Don't you?"

I was glad she couldn't see my goofy grin; for the first time in weeks, the world finally felt like it was spinning properly once more. "Who am I to argue with the voice of experience?"

"Good kitty," she laughed. "See you in ten."

Epilogue

"I'm not sure why you requested a background check on this guy," Norm was saying. "But the file just came through from the Feds." He paused, eyeing me as he slid the massive manilla envelope across my battleship of a desk. "Who is this dude?"

For the first time in my career as a law enforcement officer, I found myself tempted to lie; my eyes drifted to the envelope, a visible reminder that I *might* have slightly misused my new status as a member of the Maine State Police. Looking back up at Norm, I sighed and went with the truth — as far as I thought I could. "It's a cold case," I said with a wry smile. "Something I'm looking into on the side."

"Oh?" Norm said. "What's it about?"

I tapped the envelope. "Spousal abuse," I answered. "Although officially unreported."

Norm's eyebrows went up. "What kind of abuse?"

"You name it: mental, sexual, physical, financial. This guy seems to have checked more than one box over the course of a few years. The victim has only recently come forward."

He glanced at the envelope. "Are you consulting on this?" he asked.

"Yes," I said, which was technically true. Sort of. Since I had hired *myself*.

"Do you want some help?"

I smiled. "I'm good. But if it gets interesting, I'll haul you in."

"All right." Norm stood and looked at me for a moment. "It's weird seeing you back behind that desk."

"Not as weird as sitting here again," I laughed. "Still on for lunch later at Millie's?"

"Yes."

"Then I'll see you there. Close the door on your way out, would you?"

Norm looked at me again, for he was aware of how rare it was for me to close the door. "Sure."

I waited until I heard the mechanism metallically *clunk* home before I let out the breath I was holding; looking at the envelope, I couldn't stop my heart from ticking up a few beats as I reached over to pull it open. Trying to steady myself, I arrayed the thick stack of paperwork in multiple piles on my desk while simultaneously ignoring the warning bells going off in the back of my head. While heading down the path I was on wasn't *technically* illegal, it was, at best, highly unethical. Claiming I was doing it for righteous reasons would never cut it should the Board of Review ultimately catch wind of my efforts. Squeezing my eyes shut for a moment, I sent up a prayer it would never come to that.

Then, and only then, did I begin to methodically trace the recent movements of Suzanne's ex-husband.

Acknowledgments

Sean Colbeth has changed a bit over the past six books, and when I set out to write book seven, I knew I wanted to lean into that deeper understanding of him in order to deal with a few of the larger elephants in the room that had been hanging around for a while. The most obvious one was how I'd left his budding relationship with Suzanne completely up in the air at the end of *Vengeance*, an admittedly painful experience for both of us. Finding out how the two of them would react to a chance meeting after their slight rapprochement seemed like a logical place to start, especially if I set it on, say, a remote island where it would be hard to avoid each other. Throw in the baggage I'd only alluded to during Suzanne's introduction in *Blindsided* and I finally had the perfect way to share the full horror of her prior marriage while also providing some level of context to the underlying events in this book. As I like to say, I have a general sense of how my characters will react when I throw certain situations at them, but this time around, I was a bit surprised at where Sean went — and what that means for the next book in this series.

These characters never *ever* do what I want them to do!

You might have also noted that there is an unusual name on the dedication page; shortly before I started this novel, my wife and I unexpectedly lost our rescue, Rocket. He was an adorable Shar Pei who was also quite opinionated – especially when it came time to decide when and where his walks would take place. I think my most endearing memory of him will always be how he bounded from our car the day he arrived from the shelter and, without hesitation, hurried through the front door of our home as if he owned it. It was clear he had adopted us from the get-go, and our lives were improved immeasurably by having him as part of our family. We miss him dearly, which is why he has such a prominent guest appearance in this book. Thank you for indulging me.

As always, I couldn't have made it through this manuscript without the support from my wife **Paula**: while this novel wasn't nearly as bleak as the prior two Sean Colbeth stories, I did have some challenges getting the tone right in the aftermath of his ruptured relationship with Suzanne. I also appreciated the vote of confidence as I took that in an entirely different direction than the one I *thought* I was heading in when Suzanne arrived in Windeport. Thank you, thank you, thank you for being that solid rock when I begin to melt down and question every little thing about my writing. All of my love, to you, always.

—C

September 3, 2023

About the Author

Born and raised in Maine, Chris has spent nearly three decades as an IT nerd, writing just about everything other than a novel in the process. That changed in early 2019 when he was advised to find a way to wind down from his day job; sifting through his options, he recalled a child-hood ambition to become a writer and quickly found himself weaving an entirely new world from the comfort of his laptop. *Solitude* is his fourteenth book, part of the series featuring Sean Colbeth and Vasily Korsokovach.

Despite his love for the Northeast, the author escaped the cold for Arizona, where he currently resides with his beautiful wife and a Staffordshire Terrier rescue who insists on being walked as frequently as possible.

For all of the latest information, including hints about upcoming books in both series and an exclusive reader newsletter, please visit the author's website at https://chrisjansmann.com

facebook.com/christopherjansmann

instagram.com/chrisjansmann

amazon.com/author/chrisjansmann

bookbub.com/authors/christopher-h-jansmann

goodreads.com/chrisjansmann

mastodon.coffee/@chrisjansmann